Jack indicated the three doorways. "Which one's your room?"

"Back corner."

"I'll bet it has a great view."

Taking the hint, Anya led him into the room. "Ignore the mess, okay?" She'd left a pile of clean laundry on the bed to be folded.

"You consider this a mess? It's nice." Hardly high praise, but then, her plain, inexpensive furnishings didn't merit compliments.

She found Jack's nearness even more enticing in these intimate quarters. Everything about him appealed to her, from his chest-hugging T-shirt to the light in his green eyes.

Longing shimmered through Anya. As a diversion, she hurried to the window. "It's especially pretty at sunset."

"It sure is." When Jack approached, the air heated between them. His arm circled her waist, drawing her close.

Anya relaxed against him. When Jack turned her toward him, a rush of longing underscored how much she'd missed him. New Year's Eve hadn't been a tipsy aberration. She'd longed for him from the moment they'd met. And now she longed for even more....

Dear Reader,

Although each of the Safe Harbor Medical romances stands alone, I incorporate subplots that I hope will add to readers' enjoyment and build anticipation for the next book.

A Baby for the Doctor begins a three-book cycle that focuses on five hospital workers who share quarters in a large house. Three of the four women become pregnant—including one who chooses to undergo an embryo transfer—while the fifth occupant, a male nurse, provides an ironic perspective.

Nurse Anya Meeks, the heroine of this book, has a prickly relationship with handsome surgeon Jack Ryder and isn't at all thrilled to discover that their impulsive New Year's Eve encounter left her pregnant. Moving into the house surrounds her with caring friends, and the challenge falls to Jack to win her over. Sometimes this requires winning her housemates' approval, too, as he learns when he volunteers to cook for her.

Both characters were fun to write about. I hope you'll enjoy their verbal sparring and emotional journey as much as I did.

Also, please enjoy the recipe! Although we can only include one in the book, I've posted several more of Jack's favorite recipes on my website, www.jacquelinediamond.com, along with a complete list of the Safe Harbor books.

Best,

Jacqueline Diamond

A BABY FOR
THE DOCTOR

—

JACQUELINE DIAMOND

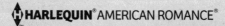
HARLEQUIN® AMERICAN ROMANCE®

For Jennifer, Steve, Jessy, Mickey and Courtney

Recycling programs
for this product may
not exist in your area.

ISBN-13: 978-0-373-75520-2

A BABY FOR THE DOCTOR

Copyright © 2014 by Jackie Hyman

Printed in U.S.A.

ABOUT THE AUTHOR

Delivered at home by her physician father, Jacqueline Diamond came by her interest in medical issues at an early age. Later, during her career as a novelist, Jackie was inspired to follow medical news after successfully undergoing fertility treatment to have her two sons, now grown. Since then, she has written numerous romances involving medicine, as well as romantic intrigues, comedies and Regency historicals, for a total of more than ninety-five books. She and her husband of thirty-five years live in Orange County, California, where she's active in Romance Writers of America. You can see an overview of the Safe Harbor Medical miniseries at www.jacquelinediamond.com and say hello to Jackie at her Facebook site, www.facebook.com/JacquelineDiamondAuthor.

Books by Jacqueline Diamond

HARLEQUIN AMERICAN ROMANCE

‡Downhome Doctors
*Harmony Circle
**Safe Harbor Medical

MYRNA'S SALMON

1–2 lbs of salmon

Marinate 2–3 hours in lime juice.

Mix together:

¼ cup apricot preserves

⅓ tsp horseradish

garlic salt

2 tsp apple cider vinegar

Spread over salmon. Bake at 375°F, uncovered, for about 20 minutes.

Chapter One

"That was unbelievable." Exhilarated, Dr. Jack Ryder stripped off his surgical gown, folded it inward to contain the soiled part and stuffed it into the specially marked laundry receptacle.

He wished his mentor, Dr. Owen Tartikoff, hadn't already left the operating suite so he could thank the man for letting him take the lead in today's microsurgery, a procedure known as pain mapping. Instead, he shared his high spirits with the anesthesiologist, Dr. Rod Vintner.

Rod quirked an eyebrow at the younger man's excitement. "Don't let it go to your head. In the Middle Ages, surgery was performed by barbers. By the way, I could use a trim." Pulling off his cap, he displayed a shock of graying brown hair.

"Getting a little thin in the middle," Jack responded. One of the techs, obviously new at Safe Harbor Medical Center, seemed startled at this exchange, so Jack explained, "Rod's my uncle."

"Barely," said the anesthesiologist, removing his glove from the edge, inside out to protect his skin from the contaminated surface. "We're the same age."

"Except that you're eight years older," Jack corrected mildly.

"Anything less than ten years is negligible." Rod slid his bare fingers inside the second glove and pulled it off, also inside out.

"In your fevered brain."

"I have much more interesting things in my fevered brain." Rod replaced his surgical cap with a fedora. The look, combined with his short beard and sharp eyes, reminded Jack of a college professor he'd once studied under, a fellow who'd also been quick to pounce on a student's vulnerability but was kind at heart.

As he washed his hands, Jack mentally replayed the surgery. The minimally invasive microlaparoscopy technique involved making an incision about the size of a needle stick. Then the patient had briefly been brought out of anesthesia, and he'd used tiny instruments to touch the organs, allowing her to react so he could identify the exact source of her pain.

After she was again under anesthesia, he'd removed the endometriosis, excess cells from the uterus lining that had spread to the abdominal cavity. The small amount might not have troubled another patient, but each individual perceives pain differently, and this patient had been in agony. Hopefully, she would now feel much better and be able to pursue her goal of having a baby.

"I can't believe I hesitated to apply for this surgical fellowship," he commented to Rod as they left the suite. "Thanks for nudging me."

"You'd been away from Southern California long enough," his uncle said. "Anyway, I needed a roommate and I like your cooking."

Jack took a quick glance around the second-floor hallway. A couple of young nurses must have been watching for him because they immediately made eye contact and flashed him warm smiles. He gave what he hoped was a friendly but distant nod in return. "Could you keep your voice down?" he murmured.

"Why is it such a big secret that you cook?" Rod strode alongside him toward the twin elevators.

"I learned a long time ago that if women find out I have domestic skills, they'll never leave me alone," Jack said. He'd unwittingly earned a reputation as a ladies' man in his younger years simply by responding to women's interest.

Whether they were attracted to him as a doctor or as a single male, he'd never been certain, but the discovery that he was a good cook acted like an accelerant on a fire.

He'd soon realized how quickly some ladies made assumptions about having a future with him and how easily feelings could get hurt. So he'd done his best to avoid involvement. Until recently…

"Women never leave you alone," his uncle commented.

"Some of them do." *Especially the one I didn't mean to drive away.*

And there she was, waiting by the elevators, freshly scrubbed after surgery. Wavy brown hair tumbled around nurse Anya Meeks's sweet face, but her full lips no longer curved when Jack appeared and her intense brown eyes avoided his even while she'd been smoothly assisting him in the operating room.

He should have followed his own rules about not hooking up with a coworker. Yet something about Anya had drawn him to her from the start—her dark, humorous gaze, her quirky energy when they joked and the anecdotes she'd shared during operations about helping raise the younger siblings in her large family. After growing up longing for a stronger family connection, Jack had found those stories especially fascinating.

Which was why when he'd run into her at a New Year's Eve party five weeks ago and learned she was ready to go home before her designated-driver roommate, he shouldn't have offered her a ride. He'd been well aware of an undercurrent of attraction between them. Still, because they lived in the same apartment complex, the suggestion had made sense. But then he really shouldn't have walked her to her door, and then walked through her door, and then noticed the leftover mistletoe and claimed a kiss and then…

The experience of being with her had been so unexpected and powerful, he'd wanted to proceed with caution. Plus, Anya had urged him to leave before her roommate came home. "Let's just keep this light, okay?" she'd said.

Jack had agreed. After all, they *were* still coworkers and neighbors, and too much closeness too soon could spell disaster. He did want to see her again, but he'd figured they'd gravitate to each other naturally and let whatever happened, happen. But she'd avoided him ever since. During the past month, he'd done his best to throw himself into her path, but that had led exactly nowhere.

Anya pushed the down button, which was already lit. Jack searched for a casual opening that might persuade her to turn around. Nothing occurred to him that wasn't unbearably clunky.

"Got any plans for the weekend?" Rod asked him.

Jack didn't want to answer such a question in Anya's presence, even though his schedule was extremely boring. "It's only Thursday."

"The lady next door mentioned baking pies with the apples her sister gave her," Rod continued. "I think she was hinting. With a little encouragement, you could..."

"She's a real-estate agent," Jack said between gritted teeth. "She thinks we're rich doctors and she can sell us a house."

Anya kept her back to them, but he saw her shoulders hunch. Didn't Rod realize she could hear every word?

Jack wasn't trying to put the moves on her. He simply regretted that, for some unknown reason, she'd taken a dislike to him after what he'd considered a thrilling encounter that had left them both deliciously sweaty and breathless. She'd moaned louder than he had, he'd be willing to testify.

Scratch that. No testifying. No public testimonials of any sort.

Anya pressed the button again. This floor didn't show the lights from all six stories, so they had no idea where the cars were.

"Must be a lunchtime holdup," Rod remarked. "There's always a chatterbox who can't stop gossiping with her coworkers."

Anya turned, finally. "Why do you assume it's a she?"

"Women usually have the best gossip," Rod replied without hesitation. "Heard anything good lately?"

Long dark lashes swept her cheeks as she glanced down. "This is ridiculous. I'm taking the stairs."

Before she could leave, Jack said, "Why don't you drop by for dinner tomorrow night? I'm broiling pork chops with an orange-rosemary dressing."

Rod stared at him, then spread his hands in a what-the-hell-gives? gesture.

"Tempting, but no," Anya replied, flicking the tiniest of glances at Jack but otherwise keeping her eyes on the ground. "See you around, doctor."

Off she went, a cute figure in that blue-flowered uniform. Even cuter without it...

Stop that, Jack reprimanded himself and started after her. He caught the heavy door to the stairs before it could close in her wake. "Hold up!"

She halted. "What?"

"I..." *Think fast.* "I want to apologize if I've offended you. I didn't call you...afterward...because, well, you gave me the impression you wanted to take things slow."

"That's right," she said.

"You're not mad?"

"No, and thanks for the African violet. Zora and I will give it a suitable burial." She began her descent.

Jack paced alongside. "You killed it already?"

"Not yet, but the light in our unit is terrible," Anya said. "Also, I know you don't usually do laundry on Sunday mornings, so don't pretend otherwise."

"I ran into you by accident." *Weak, Jack, weak.* "Spilled stuff on my clothes the night before."

"While cooking?" Beside him, she lifted a dark eyebrow. Much more effective than when Rod did it. He had no quick comeback with her.

But he'd better speak before they reached the bottom, which was coming up fast. "New recipe. Kind of exploded."

"Sorry I missed the fun."

"So everything's normal between us?"

"Why wouldn't it be?" With that nonanswer, she shouldered the exit door.

Although not completely reassured, Jack hoped that in a few days she might reconsider joining him for dinner. He wanted to be alone with her, to have her bright spirit focused solely on him.

One problem: he'd have to get his uncle out of the apartment. Jack supposed he might encourage Rod to go out with their Realtor neighbor or join an internet dating site. One lousy marriage shouldn't sour the guy on women forever.

"If you're headed for lunch, we could share a table," he said to Anya just as a muscular guy in a dark blue nurse's uniform materialized. He had dark hair, a confident swagger and a couple of tattoos extending from beneath his short sleeves.

The bar pin disclosed the stud's name as Luke Mendez, RN. Jack had never seen him in surgery or labor and delivery, so most likely he worked in the adjacent office building.

"Hey," the man said to Anya. "New developments. You won't want to miss this."

"Miss what?" Jack asked.

"Nothing important," Anya told him. "See you around." Off she went with Nurse Tattoo in the direction of the cafeteria.

Well, damn. Briefly, Jack considered buying lunch at the cafeteria, too. He wouldn't sit at the nurses' table, of course; the only doctors who did that were married to nurses, and even then they usually respected each other's separate social circles. Still, he was curious about what he might overhear.

Don't be an idiot. She'd said everything was fine between them. Furthermore, having been up since before dawn, he could use a nap. The shortage of office space at Safe Harbor forced newcomers like Jack to see their patients on evenings and weekends in shared quarters. It was after one o'clock now, and he had to return by five.

Why should he care about Anya and her chums? Whatever they were doing, he'd find out soon enough via the hospital grapevine and his uncle. So why did he feel as if he was missing something?

So JACK COOKED, Anya mused. It gave him a certain domestic appeal—as if a guy with bright green eyes, thick brown hair and a million-watt smile needed or deserved any further advantages.

As she accompanied Luke—Lucky to his friends—to the cafeteria, Anya felt propelled by her own mental kicks in the butt. Downing two drinks on New Year's Eve was no excuse for jumping into bed with her handsome neighbor. His clumsy attempts to score a second time—which is what she assumed he was doing, given his reputation—were mildly amusing, but she wasn't that big a fool.

She had a more pressing problem—her period being three weeks late. The pill was 99.9 percent effective when used properly, which she did. She ought to take a pregnancy test, but she was almost certain it would prove negative. When it did, Anya preferred to have expert advice on hand because there was definitely something wrong with her.

She doubted it was stress. She wasn't *that* upset about her stupidity in bedding Jack, nor about her roommate pressuring her to move to a cheaper place rather than renew their lease. So was this a hormonal imbalance? An autoimmune disease? At twenty-six, surely she was too young for early menopause.

She checked her phone. No text from Dr. Cavill-Hunter's nurse about working her into today's schedule.

In the cafeteria, Anya studied the posted menu. "What's the special? I don't see it."

"They're out of it," Lucky told her. "It's nearly one-thirty. Just grab a sandwich, will you?"

Anya folded her arms. "What's the rush?"

"People have to get back to work."

She hated pressure. It usually inspired her to go even slower, but she was hungry. Also, across the busy room, she spotted a halo of short ginger hair that identified her roommate, Zora Raditch, sitting across from patient financial counselor Karen Wiggins. Karen's hair color this week: strawberry blond with pink highlights.

The third woman at the table, Melissa Everhart, projected pure gorgeous class with her honey-blond hair in a French twist. Melissa worked with the hospital's recently opened egg bank as egg donor coordinator.

They weren't sharing a table by accident, nor from long-standing friendship. They had serious business to discuss, and it included her.

By now, Lucky was jogging in place. Anya chose a pastrami pita sandwich with avocados and sprouts, sweet-potato chips and iced tea. She paid the cashier and followed her impatient companion.

The three women huddled over a sheet of paper. "You could have this room in the front and Anya this one on the side," Karen was saying as they approached.

Glancing over her roommate's shoulder, Anya saw the floor plan of a two-story house. "I thought you were all set for renters, Karen."

Zora swung around, braced for action. "We're getting a second chance, Anya. Come on! We'll never find a more fun place to live than Karen's house, and it's really quiet and backs onto a park."

Here we go again. For the past year, Anya had relished both the close companionship and the comparative privacy of living with just one friend. Having grown up in a crowded household where her family's expectations, assumptions and criticisms weighed on her constantly like a heavy coat in summertime, she had no interest in sharing quarters with a group.

"That isn't a park—it's wetlands. Mosquito central," Anya responded, setting her tray on a clear spot. "What happened to the two guys who'd signed on?"

"Ned Norwalk decided he prefers living alone." Ned was a fellow nurse. "I wish he'd told me sooner." Karen scowled at Lucky.

"I had nothing to do with that." Turning a chair backward, he sat at the other open space. "I like him."

"But you hate Laird," Melissa noted.

Lucky shrugged. "Karen, I'm sorry, but you know how he is. A few drinks and he's making passes at random women." Catching Karen's eye roll, he added, "*Unwelcome* passes."

"So you chased him off," Karen grumbled.

"Once you come to your senses, you'll thank me," Lucky replied.

Quietly eating her sandwich, Anya conceded that she didn't like Laird either. He might be a psychologist and family counselor, but in her opinion, he could use some counseling of his own.

"How'd you get rid of him?" Zora asked.

Lucky addressed his response to the others, ignoring Zora, as usual. "I may have implied that I'd make his life miserable if he moved in. That's all."

Karen smacked the table. Anya had to grab her iced tea to prevent a spill. "This may be a game to you, Lucky, but I can't make the payments by myself. Now that the renovations are finished, I need a full house. Otherwise, I either have to raise everyone's rent sky-high or sell."

For years, Karen—now in her early forties—had cared for her ailing mom while medical expenses ate up their savings. They'd had to defer all but the most essential maintenance on their five-bedroom home. A few months ago, though, following her mother's death, the counselor had taken out a loan to upgrade the electrical, plumbing and appliances. Then she'd solicited her friends and coworkers to move in for what Anya had to admit was a very reasonable monthly rent.

"It's perfect timing. I understand Anya's lease is up for renewal." Lucky didn't mention Zora. Anya wondered how the two of them expected to share a house. The potential for conflict added to her distaste of the idea of moving in with them.

"You can have the bedroom on the side," Zora wheedled. "I'll take the noisy one in the front."

Everyone stared at Anya. The combined pressure was so

strong, she half expected her chair to tilt. Fortunately, she was used to resisting pressure. "Zora and I will discuss this in private," she said.

"Coward," Lucky teased.

"Sharing a kitchen shouldn't be a big deal because you hardly ever cook," Zora pointed out. As Anya had explained to her friend, she'd grown up shouldering more than her share of household duties in her large family. Heating a can of soup and eating a premade salad felt like a heavenly indulgence.

"And I gather the rent will be considerably lower than what you're paying for your apartment," Melissa added.

Anya calmly started on the second half of her sandwich. *She had* shared her objections with Zora, and the polite refusal she'd voiced several times previously ought to be enough for the others.

Karen drummed her fingers on the table. "Contrary to what you may believe, a wetland is not a swamp. It's a vibrant ecosystem. A healthy wetland actually reduces the mosquito population thanks to the thriving birds, frogs and fish."

"And other insects that feed on mosquito larvae," added Lucky, who'd clearly heard this speech before.

"I just love frogs, fish and insects." Anya's irony didn't extend to birds. She did enjoy those, except maybe pigeons in the vicinity of her car.

Zora widened her eyes in mute appeal. Fortunately, there was little danger of her jumping ship on Anya. Until recently, Zora, an ultrasound technician, had occupied a pariah-like status around the hospital because she'd stolen a popular nurse's husband a few years back. Then, a year ago, Zora had needed a place to go after her husband cheated on her, too, and Anya had agreed to move in with her. Zora had burst into tears of gratitude and they'd had each other's backs ever since.

"I can give you until Sunday night to decide," Karen said. "Monday, I'm posting the vacancies on the bulletin board."

"Oh, come on, Anya," Lucky said. "You haven't given us a good reason. My bedroom's downstairs. You ladies will have plenty of privacy on the second floor, and I can do guard duty."

Anya ignored him and moved on to her sweet-potato chips.

The others shifted to regard someone approaching, as if the short, uniformed woman with thick glasses might be their salvation. Instead, Eva Rogers zeroed in on Anya.

Smiling and holding up her phone, Eva said, "Just got a cancellation. Dr. Cavill-Hunter can fit you in at 6:45. How's that?"

"Fine," Anya replied, trying to keep the bite out of her voice. The other nurse should have more discretion than to approach a patient in front of others, but Anya was grateful for the appointment.

"See you then." With a wave, Eva sauntered off.

Around the table, four very interested faces turned to Anya. "Is anything wrong?" Lucky asked.

"It can't be routine or there'd be no reason to jump at a cancellation," Karen observed.

"Need me to come along for moral support?" Zora asked.

Anya stood. "That's the other reason."

"The other reason for what?" asked her roommate.

"The other reason for not moving into the house." Anya picked up her tray. "Gossip."

She left without waiting for their reactions. Although she'd rather not offend anyone, she had bigger issues to deal with.

Chapter Two

"How is this possible?" Sitting on the examining table, Anya hugged herself through the thin gown.

Mercifully, Dr. Adrienne Cavill-Hunter had broken the news without Eva in the room. Anya's skin was prickling with apprehension so one skeptical look, or even a sympathetic murmur, and her blood pressure might soar to dangerous levels.

The blonde obstetrician rolled her stool over to sit beside Anya. She had chosen this doctor not only because she saw patients in the evening, but for Adrienne's quiet, rational manner.

"Are you taking any over-the-counter medications that might interfere with your birth control pills?" the doctor inquired.

Now, there was a question Anya hadn't considered. It was almost reassuring in its medical focus. And it didn't imply that she'd screwed up by missing any pills.

"The only thing I took was St. John's wort after spending Christmas with my family," she said.

The obstetrician tilted her head questioningly. "Why St. John's wort?"

"It was kind of a depressing experience, and I heard it might help." Anya had chosen the herb, widely available in capsule form, after reading that it was as effective as standard antidepressants with fewer side effects. "Can it interfere with birth control pills?"

"Yes, it can." Dr. Cavill-Hunter—who'd expanded her name after her marriage last month—answered in a level, nonjudgmental tone. "St. John's wort decreases the level of estrogen in the body, which reduces the effectiveness of the pill."

Anya smacked her forehead. "That's why I'm pregnant."

"Not entirely," the doctor said wryly.

True, there'd been no immaculate conception. If only she and Jack had used a condom, too. But in the heat of the moment, they hadn't been able to find one.

Now here she was, stuck in a massive, life-changing situation that Anya couldn't wrap her mind around, except for one important point. "I can't have a baby by myself."

"Many women do," the doctor said gently.

"Not me." Just supervising her three younger sisters had often overwhelmed Anya.

She still had nightmares about one afternoon when she was twelve. After her mother's arthritis had worsened, it had been Anya's responsibility to walk the seven-year-old triplets home from school each day. But Anya's period had arrived unexpectedly and she had to borrow a pad from a teacher, causing her to be late. When she finally arrived at the elementary school, there'd been no sign of Andi, Sandi or Sarah. For a painful half hour, as she traced the path they should have taken home, frightening scenes from TV newscasts had rolled through her mind. What if someone had taken them?

Realizing they might have stopped for a snack at their grandmother's house around the corner, Anya had run there and rung the bell with her heart pounding. Her grandma's gaze had been reproving, but she'd been greatly relieved to find her sisters safe.

Until she faced her father's fury later that night. *You need to take your responsibilities seriously. Why can't we depend on you to do things right?*

Dr. Cavill-Hunter asked a question, jerking Anya back to the present. The doctor had asked about the father and was waiting for an answer. Anya said sharply, "We aren't even dating. It was a mistake. Do you have any resources about adoption?"

"You can take several avenues in that regard." Choosing her words carefully, the doctor continued. "But there's no reason to rush this decision. This is a shock. It's wise to consider what it means to have a child and what kind of family support you might receive."

Anya shuddered at the thought of her family. Returning to Colorado this past Christmas to visit her parents and six siblings had reawakened painful old feelings and reminded her forcefully of why she'd moved to California. "Forget that."

The obstetrician didn't argue. "All right. You can choose a private adoption—either open, with continuing contact, or closed. Or perhaps you have a family member who might take the child."

"No family." Nor did Anya care to deal with a social worker. This was her decision, and she wouldn't be lectured or questioned about her motives. "Can you recommend a lawyer?"

"The hospital's staff attorney could give you a list of family attorneys in the community." The obstetrician cleared her throat. "I'm adopting a child myself, a relative. We're using a lawyer named Geoff Humphreys."

That name rang a bell. "His associate is handling Zora's divorce." She'd have to tell her roommate anyway, so that seemed convenient. "Thanks for mentioning him."

"There's something else." The doctor laced her fingers. "As I'm sure the attorney will inform you, the father has to sign a waiver of parental rights before the child can be released for adoption."

"He what?" Anya would pull all her hair out by the roots before she'd involve that—what was the legal term she'd read?—*casual inseminator.*

Okay, that wasn't fair to Jack, although other nurses *had* described him as a playboy. In her observation, his dramatically good looks simply attracted a lot of women. In her case, despite their joking around in the O.R., he'd always kept a respectful distance. Until New Year's Eve.

That night, while they were dancing at the party, she'd imagined she saw a spark of tenderness in his gorgeous, sparkling green eyes. That, combined with a couple of unaccustomed drinks, had worked magic on her nervous system. Plus, she'd been feeling lonely and estranged from her family after that unhappy Christmas visit.

Jack had been wonderful in bed, fierce and gentle and very skilled. Too skilled, maybe. Anya hadn't had much time for men in her younger years, and her college boyfriend had been sweet but fumbling. Now, her vulnerability scared her. Losing control of her emotions reminded her of how little power she'd had over her life until she left Colorado two years ago.

So over the past few weeks, she'd kept things cool with him, strictly business. He'd gone along at first, as embarrassed as she was, she supposed. Then he'd started flirting again. But she doubted he meant anything by it. He was notorious for avoiding relationships.

And now she needed his permission to choose adoption for her—their—baby? "It's outrageous," she added for good measure.

"It may seem unfair, but that's the law," Adrienne said. "Discuss this with your lawyer. I'm sure he can handle the paperwork."

"So Doctor…Mister Dad gets the news via the U.S. mail?" That was likely to provoke unpleasant repercussions. "I'll deal with him some other way."

Judging by the obstetrician's expression, she hadn't missed the reference to a doctor. She let it go, returning to the pregnancy.

"Based on the dates you gave me, you're about six weeks along, which means you're due in mid to late September," she said. "In case you're interested, the baby's eyes and limb buds are starting to appear at this stage."

Too much information. Anya performed the mental equivalent of closing her ears and skipped to a more bearable topic.

"Six weeks? It's only been five weeks since we…since conception."

"We measure pregnancies from the date of the last menstrual period," the doctor reminded her.

"Oh. Right." All this theoretical knowledge seemed quite different when you were the patient, Anya reflected glumly. "I haven't had any morning sickness. Well, maybe a tiny bit. I thought it was some chorizo I ate."

"Let's talk about a healthy diet during pregnancy," the doctor said, seizing on the topic. "Or are you already familiar with all this?"

Being a scrub nurse, Anya didn't deal with maternity on a regular basis. Also, in her state of shock, she could scarcely recall her own phone number, let alone the rules for moms-to-be. "Refresh my memory. Do I have to eat anything weird?"

"Depends on what you consider weird."

"Seaweed?"

Adrienne smiled. "That won't be necessary, although seaweed is quite nutritious. It's a rich source of antioxidants and vitamins."

Anya wrinkled her nose.

"You can skip it, though," the doctor said. "Be sure to include plenty of fruits and vegetables in your diet. No alcohol or tobacco, no raw fish such as sushi, and avoid soft cheeses. They can carry bacteria."

"I can't eat Brie?" That sounded cruel to Anya. Another mark against Jack. Someone ought to deprive him of Brie for the next eight months.

Oh, don't be childish.

"If the milk's pasteurized, it should be safe," the doctor said. "Cut out caffeine, or at least cut back. No undercooked meat or paté, and limit your fish consumption to twelve ounces a week in case of mercury contamination."

This discussion set Anya's stomach churning. "Can you give me a list?"

"I'd be happy to." From a drawer, the obstetrician fetched several pamphlets and a prescription pad. "Also, we advise that you avoid changing kitty litter because of toxoplasmosis, a disease that sometimes infects cats and can harm the baby. Do you have a pet?"

"Just an African violet." Which Jack had given her. "I hate him," Anya burst out.

The doctor paused, brochures in midair. "The father? Understandable."

"It isn't his fault," Anya conceded. "But that only makes me even madder. I want revenge on somebody, and he's nominated."

"You might write down your revenge fantasies," Dr. Cavill-Hunter responded. "You can always shred them later."

"Can I post them on the internet?" Anya didn't seriously expect an answer. She was simply venting. "Is this what people mean by pregnancy hormones making you cranky?"

"I'd say it's a legitimate emotional response to a difficult situation."

Did the doctor have to be *this* rational? Right now, Anya would prefer a friend to share her righteous wrath.

The rest of the office visit passed in a fog. The doctor answered routine questions. Eva produced a packet of sample vitamins and pregnancy-related goodies and set up the next appointment. Tactfully, she refrained from commenting.

All the while, Anya's emotions seethed. *Revenge. Revenge. Revenge.* Only how did you do that? Especially because she was the one who'd messed up her contraception.

Worse, she had to get the father's stupid John Hancock on the adoption paperwork. Her anger shifted toward the idiots in the state legislature, who she presumed had mandated this. Busybodies. Nanny government.

Don't think about nannies.

In the lobby, her mood didn't improve on finding that the pharmacy had closed minutes earlier. Not that she needed to fill the vitamin prescription in a hurry, but it left yet another pain-in-the-neck detail to take care of.

As she turned away, a twinge of nausea ran through her. Suddenly morning sickness was striking in the evening.

As Anya pressed her hands over her stomach, reality hit like a blast of icy wind. She was pregnant. Carrying a child. About to become a mother. Frequently, she assisted at surgeries for women desperate to conceive and willing to undergo complex, expensive treatments. How unfair this situation was to them—*and* her.

Anya wished she could bless one of them with this miracle because it had happened to the wrong person. She was utterly unready to take on the tremendous job of raising a helpless little person. She was sure to screw up.

Now she also had to deal with the practical side of pregnancy. She faced nearly eight more months of fluctuating hormones and a variety of body aches and pains. How long could she keep working as a surgical nurse? What would her parents say?

Nothing. Because she didn't intend to tell them. To them, it would be yet another sign of her immaturity, of her not being able to do anything right.

Grumpily, she shouldered open the glass exterior door and stopped at a real blast of cold air. February. Ugh. Accustomed to mild Southern California midday temperatures, she'd worn only a light jacket.

Behind her, the elevator doors slid apart and heavy male footsteps smacked across the lobby. "Hold up!" A pushy man—*was there any other kind?* her hormones demanded—reached above her head to hold the door.

It was Jack. Of course. Could this day get any worse?

As always, he smelled like soap and masculinity with a splash of lime. His dark blue coat fit his broad shoulders and strong body as if designed for him. Oddly, she realized, his scent had a soothing effect on her stomach, making her crave more of his nearness. All the more reason to hate him. She trudged on.

He halted on the front walkway. "Anya!"

"Yes?" She wondered what the correct etiquette was for

this situation. You couldn't just blurt, *"I'm pregnant, so sign the parental waiver,"* could you?

That would be efficient but not very diplomatic. Out loud, she said, "We should talk." There, that was better.

Before she could say anything else, though, he asked, "Can you give me a ride?"

They lived in the same complex, so why not? Plus, they'd have a chance to talk away from prying ears. "Okay. What happened to your car?"

"I loaned it to my uncle." He walked alongside her toward the parking garage.

"Where's *his* car?"

"In the shop, as usual." Jack's body partially blocked the wind, cocooning Anya. "He was supposed to pick me up after my office hours, but we had a family emergency."

Anya had never heard about any other members of Jack's family, aside from Dr. Vintner. "I hope it's nothing serious." Much as she'd like for him to suffer, she only wanted him to do so on her terms and without involving innocent third parties.

"Long story."

"Yeah, don't bother to tell me," she grumbled. "Never mind that I'm doing you a favor."

Anya couldn't believe she'd said that out loud. She never snapped at doctors. She hardly ever crabbed at anybody, in fact, except Zora, who could take it.

When they reached the car, Jack put his hand on her arm. The warmth lit a tiny flame inside Anya, a reminder of how comforting it would be to nestle against that strong chest. *Sigh.*

"You're right. I'm being rude." He withdrew his hand as she clicked open the car. "I'll give you the details on the way."

She'd meant to use the ride to talk to *him.* Maybe instead she'd drop her bomb as they parted company at the apartments. Good idea. Not exactly primo revenge, but a satisfying poke all the same.

"I can't wait," she said.

"HAVE YOU HEARD the story about Rod's kids?" That seemed a good place to start, Jack decided as he adjusted the passenger seat to accommodate his long legs.

Backing out of her parking space, Anya frowned. "I didn't know he had any."

Better cut this story short. They only lived a five-minute drive away. "Two daughters. Or so he thought."

"What do you mean?" The pucker between her eyebrows was adorable.

Jack took a moment to organize his thoughts. As they left the garage, he noted only a few cars in the circular drive. Traffic dropped off rapidly in the evening because there was no emergency care aside from labor and delivery at Safe Harbor. Five years ago, the former community hospital had been remodeled to specialize in fertility and maternity treatments, along with a range of gynecological and child services. Most recently it had expanded into treating male infertility, too.

On the opposite side of the compound stood a now-empty dental office building. Someday, with luck, the hospital would acquire it for additional office space. Then Jack could treat patients at more convenient hours.

He resumed his tale. "When my aunt Portia demanded a divorce and my uncle sought joint custody, she revealed that she'd cheated on him." Jack would never forget the heartbreak on Rod's face as he'd shared that discovery. "Neither of the girls was genetically his."

"How awful." She turned the car onto Hospital Way.

"It was a mess." Jack had been living in Nashville, Tennessee, at the time, completing medical school at Vanderbilt University. However, he'd spent most of his holidays with his aunt and uncle.

Technically Tiffany and Amber were his cousins, but he'd always thought of them as nieces. He'd loved playing with them and watching them grow into toddlers and preschoolers. Then they'd been yanked out of his life, leaving a painful void for him, too.

"Your aunt married the girls' father?" Anya tapped the brake at a red light on Safe Harbor Boulevard. The broad avenue bisected the town from the freeway to the harbor that gave the community its name.

"He was long gone, but she found someone else, a rich guy unable to have kids of his own who wanted to adopt hers. They pulled one legal maneuver after another to keep the kids from Rod." Jack still burned at the memory. "Rod was supporting the girls financially, and he went into debt fighting for them in court. If he'd been their genetic father, he'd have stood a chance, but as it was, he lost all rights." And was living in a small apartment and driving an unreliable car as a result.

"What an ordeal." When the light changed, Anya transitioned onto the boulevard, passing a darkened veterinary clinic and a flower shop that supplied the hospital gift boutique.

"We haven't seen the girls for six years. Then, this evening, Rod got a call from my older niece, Tiffany. She ran away from her home in San Diego and asked him to pick her up at the Fullerton train station." That was about a two-hour journey from San Diego.

Anya swung onto a side street. "How old is she?"

"Twelve." He only had a few photos of Tiff from years ago, a little girl with Orphan Annie red hair and a big smile. "It's hard to visualize what she must look like now."

"Twelve is awfully young. Why'd she run away?"

"No idea." His phone rang. Plucking it from his pocket, Jack saw his uncle's name on the screen. "Hey."

"Change of plans. I'm taking Tiffany to her grandmother's house." Rod must be speaking into his wireless device because it was illegal in California to hold a cell phone while driving. "Less risk of legal complications that way. Can you meet us there? You remember where Helen lives?"

"Vaguely." Portia's mother had joined the family for holiday celebrations and had once hosted a Fourth of July party at her bungalow. Jack recalled Helen as a kind, quiet woman overshadowed by her forceful daughter.

A girl's voice piped up in the background. "Is that Uncle Jack? Hi, Uncle Jack!"

"Hi, pumpkin."

"Hi to you too, squash-kins," his uncle said drily. "I mean, as long as we're using vegetables as terms of endearment."

"Very funny. What's the address?"

Rod provided it. Jack's phone showed it to be in the northwest corner of Safe Harbor near the freeway. "Anya, I have another favor to ask."

"Anya's driving you home?" His uncle sounded peevish.

"Who's Anya?" Tiffany piped in. "Can I meet her?"

"End of conversation," Jack said and clicked off. This was far too confusing, and, besides, he needed to focus on winning Anya's cooperation. "How about lending me your car after I drop you at home?"

"How far away is this?" she asked.

"Just a few miles." The alternative was to call a cab, which meant waiting heaven knows how long. In Southern California, where private vehicles outnumbered people, taxi drivers concentrated their efforts on servicing airports and hotels.

And he didn't have the time to waste. No doubt Helen was already dialing her daughter. Portia and her husband, a private equity investor reported to be worth close to a billion dollars, would take a private plane or helicopter to collect the runaway, which left only a window of an hour or so for Jack to connect with her.

Anya hadn't spoken again. "I don't want to lose this chance to see Tiffany." The ragged emotion in his tone surprised Jack. "It's important she understands that she's welcome here and that we love her. I'm afraid that next time, *if* there's a next time, she might go off on her own."

The fate of young runaways in metropolitan areas had been the subject of a recent lecture at the hospital. Staff pediatrician Samantha Forrest had presented a horrifying picture of predators trolling for young girls and boys who'd landed on the streets.

Now that he thought about it, he'd seen Anya at the lecture, too. Surely she understood his concern.

She appeared to be mulling the request as they reached their complex—a half-dozen two-story apartment buildings separated by tree-shaded walkways. In the carport area, Anya halted, her expression shadowed in the thin lighting.

"I'd like to meet her," she said.

"Not a good idea." This was private family business.

"She might talk more freely to a woman than to a couple of guys," Anya said.

"Her grandmother's there."

"I wouldn't discuss anything personal or uncomfortable around *my* grandmother," she replied. "Jack, I remember what my sisters were like at that age. You and your uncle are great guys, and I'm sure her grandmother loves this girl like crazy, but it's important right now that she be able to open up. What can it hurt to have me there?"

Anya did have a point. And he had to admire her willingness to step into such a delicate situation. Jack glanced at her profile: shapely nose, full mouth, firm chin. He needed her help and, besides, he wanted to spend more time with her. Why not seize the opportunity?

"Thanks. I'll navigate, okay?" he said and relaxed as he saw her nod.

They were on the same page for once. That was a nice change.

Chapter Three

Spotting Jack's hybrid sedan in front of a tidy bungalow, Anya knew this must be the place. She wedged her car into a slot at the curb.

What a pretty neighborhood, she thought as they got out. Some of the houses had a fairy-tale air, thanks to their gingerbread trim. Although of a simpler design, the grandmother's cottage had appealing, old-fashioned shutters and an extended porch lit by a sconce-style lamp.

But as Anya hurried to catch up with Jack's rapid pace, she noticed spiderwebs festooning the corners of the front windows. Surely the elderly lady would keep those wiped clear if she were physically capable of it.

The door flew open and a young girl's eager face appeared, her red hair in thick braids. "Uncle Jack!" She threw her arms around him with such enthusiasm that he had to step backward.

"Tiff? I can't believe that's you." After hugging the girl, he took a long look. "You've grown into a young lady."

She smoothed down her navy blazer and tan skirt, evidently a school uniform. "Come in."

"Somebody's blocking my path," he teased.

"Okay, okay." As Tiffany danced inside, her gaze fell on Anya. "Is this your girlfriend? She's pretty! And you're handsome, isn't he, Anya?"

"Most of the nurses seem to think so," she replied, slipping into the room behind them.

Inside, Rod's eyes glittered in the light from the chandelier as he greeted them. Surely those couldn't be tears. Anya had never seen the sardonic anesthesiologist show so much emotion.

The rectangular room encompassed both living and dining areas and had antique-style furnishings. Dusty curio cabinets displayed a charming collection of china plates and cups, while a built-in counter in the dining area held a nativity scene. As the girl's grandmother approached, her small, arthritis-curled hands revealed why she hadn't packed the holiday decorations or removed those outside spiderwebs. Why didn't her married-to-a-billionaire daughter spring for a housekeeper?

"Anya's a nurse who works with Rod and me," Jack explained as he introduced her to the grandmother, Helen Pepper. Slim and silver-haired, Helen wore a mint-green embellished top and pull-on pants that would be easy for those gnarled hands to manage.

"I'm very glad to meet you," she told Anya earnestly.

Anya took the extended hands gently. "You have a beautiful home."

"Anya was kind enough to give me a ride," Jack added. "Since Rod commandeered my car."

"When I heard my little girl's voice on the phone, I couldn't think about anything but rushing to the rescue," his uncle admitted. "It's a good thing the CHP didn't clock my speed on the freeway."

"I'm sorry I had patients, or I'd have driven you," Jack said. "Tiff, I want you to know that Rod moved heaven and earth to try to gain custody, or at least visitation. These past few years have been torture."

Tiffany nodded vigorously. "I was convinced Mom and Vince must have lied to me."

"Lied about what?" Jack asked.

"Well, I didn't get it at first. I was only six." The girl took a deep breath. "They told Amber and me our dad rejected us because we weren't really his."

The anguish on Rod's face tore at Anya's heart. "They dared to say that after I nearly went bankrupt fighting them in court?"

"That's not only a lie, it was cruel to the girls," Jack observed.

"I'm sorry I didn't speak up sooner," Helen said. "I always felt like I was walking on eggshells when I visited them. Please, everybody, have a seat."

She gestured the group into the living room, its walls brightened by colorful framed floral embroideries. She must have loved creating them before arthritis crippled her hands, Anya thought.

"Why did *you* stop visiting, Grandma?" Tiffany nestled beside Rod on the couch. "You hardly come anymore."

Helen lowered herself gingerly to the sofa. "My hip got so bad, I can't travel." To the others, she said, "I don't mean to complain. Portia hired a limo to bring me for Thanksgiving and Christmas."

"Big of her," Rod muttered.

It seemed to Anya that everyone was avoiding the central question of why this child had run away. However, being a not-very-invited guest at a family crisis, she held her tongue.

"How's your little sister?" Jack beamed at his niece, apparently as overjoyed to see her as she was to see him, Rod and her grandmother. "Amber must be ten now. She was a bold little thing. I'm surprised she didn't come with you."

"Don't give them ideas," Helen said tartly.

"Oh, she isn't bold anymore," Tiff said. "She's shy."

"Unlike somebody I know." Rod quirked the girl a smile. "Sweetheart, as Jack said, I fought for both of you."

"I figured you must have." Tiffany lifted her chin proudly. "I kept remembering you reading us bedtime stories and cracking jokes, and the older I got, the weirder it seemed that you stopped caring about us."

"I always cared!"

"How'd you get his phone number?" Helen asked. "I'm

sure your parents don't keep it around, although I guess kids can find anything on the internet these days."

"Mom and Vince only let us use computers for school-work." Tiffany made a face. "They won't let me have a cell phone either. My friend's big brother dug up Daddy's phone number."

Rod tweaked one of Tiffany's braids. "You should have called before you left home, squirt. Taking the train by your-self, that's scary."

"It was fun," the red-haired girl proclaimed. "And if I'd called, you might have said no."

Jack regarded her sternly. "Tiff, what if he'd been out of town? Dangerous people hang around train and bus stations watching for runaways. Please don't take a chance like that again."

"Then you'd better give me *your* number, too," she replied, then added mischievously, "just in case."

"Sure." Fishing a prescription pad from his pocket, Jack began writing on it. "Honey, call me before you put yourself into a potentially dangerous situation, okay?"

"I'll try."

"Don't just try." He also gave her a business card. "That's my office number. If for any reason you can't get through on my cell, make sure the receptionist understands it's an emergency."

He certainly was acting fatherly, or like an uncle, Anya thought. Another woman in her situation might be thrilled, but to her it raised a whole bramble bush of unwanted pos-sibilities. If he cared this much about his nieces, how might he feel about his own child?

"I hate to bring this up, but I have to call your parents and let them know you're safe," Helen said.

"Not yet!" Tiffany begged. "I'll go home on Sunday, okay?"

"It's only Thursday, and you've already missed a day of school," her grandmother chided.

With obvious reluctance, Rod backed Helen up. "They've

probably notified the police. We'll all be in trouble if we don't report your whereabouts."

"They're mean." Tiffany slouched down. "If my grades aren't perfect, they ground me for a whole weekend. They make me play soccer because that was Vince's sport. I had to drop dance class, which is my favorite."

"Too many organized activities," Helen commiserated. "It's not healthy."

Anya wondered how Tiffany would have responded to *her* family's demands. At twelve, Anya had hurried home every day after school with her seven-year-old triplet sisters, assisted her disabled mother, cleaned the house and fixed dinner.

Her older brothers had spent their after-school hours assisting Dad in the feed store. The only escapee had been her older sister, Ruth, who'd married and moved out by then. But she'd soon had kids of her own to care for.

"Children deserve a chance to develop at their own pace," Rod was telling Tiffany as Anya tuned back in. "But if you were still with me, you'd probably complain about how strict I am, too."

Anya admired his effort to be fair. He could easily seize on this chance to whip up his daughter's resentment toward her parents.

"No, I wouldn't because I'd know you loved me." The girl's lips trembled. "When I asked them if I could visit you, Vince said if I ever mentioned you again, he'd send me to a boarding school in Switzerland."

Rod looped an arm around his daughter's shoulders. "Honey, I'd hate for that to happen. But after the court ruled in his favor, Vince adopted you. I have no legal rights."

"He treats Amber and me like he owns us. Like we're pretty objects for him to show off to his friends."

We're still missing something, Anya thought. The girl was unhappy, but why take action *now?* "Why did you run away today?" she ventured. "Did something happen?"

"Good question," Jack murmured.

"It's because of last Sunday." The girl sniffed. After a deep breath, she resumed. "They make me take piano lessons even though I'm terrible because their friends' kids play instruments. I had a recital on Sunday and I messed up."

"What do you mean 'messed up'?" Helen asked.

Tiffany's hands clenched. "I forgot part of my piece in front of all those people. It was embarrassing. As soon as it was over, Vince dragged me outside and yelled at me where everybody could hear. He called me stupid and lazy." Tears rolled down her cheeks. "Daddy, no matter how hard I practice, I still suck. When I try to memorize music, it falls out of my brain."

"It's good to play an instrument, but not if it makes you miserable," her grandmother noted.

"I was great in dance class!" Tiffany burst out. "And I enjoyed it."

"That's why you ran away?" Jack asked.

"I had to see Daddy," the girl said. "I knew he'd love me for who I am."

Rod drew her close. No question about it; those were definitely tears brightening his eyes.

Anya understood how it felt to long for the freedom to be oneself. In a sense, she, too, had run off, although she'd waited until she was an adult with a nursing degree.

Rod's gaze met Helen's, his frustration obvious. "I wish I had the power to intervene, but legally, I don't."

"I should get a choice about who I live with," Tiffany insisted.

"When you're older, you might," her grandmother said.

"How much older?"

"Fourteen, I believe." Jack recalled that information from the lecture about runaways. "But you'd need your parents' consent and your own money."

"That'll never happen!" Tiffany flared. "And what about Amber? They're mean to her, too."

"In what way?" Rod asked sharply.

"Since she's a good swimmer, Vince took her to this competitive coach. Now he and Vince both yell at her when she doesn't do well at meets," her sister said. "She hardly talks to anybody anymore except me. When I told her I was short on money to buy my ticket, she gave me her savings."

"Amber knew about your plans?" Rod sighed. "They'll squeeze the truth out of her. They could have me arrested if we don't report right away that you're here."

"We love you guys," Jack put in. "But nobody's above the law."

"If they stick me in boarding school, I'll run away from there, too." Fire flashed in Tiffany's eyes. Anya shuddered at the prospect of the girl wandering alone in some foreign city, an easy target for a predator.

"Please don't put yourself in danger," Rod said.

"If I can't live here, they ought to at least let me visit," Tiffany responded. "I'm going to tell them that when I get home."

"Oh, dear." Helen's shoulders slumped. "I heard Vince say to your mother…"

"What?" Tiffany demanded.

"That I'm a bad influence because I indulge you girls. And once Vince's mind is made up, he's a bulldozer. I'm afraid he'll cut me off completely."

Vince was clearly a control freak. He couldn't stand sharing the girls with anyone.

"My opinion of that man isn't fit for polite company," Rod growled.

"I did talk to a lawyer in town," Helen said. "I could file with the court for visitation rights. But they'd fight it, and you know how much money Vince has. He'd bankrupt me before he'd give in."

Unless they found a solution, Tiffany faced a difficult and possibly disastrous adolescence, Anya thought. Although it wasn't her place to interfere, she did have an idea. "May I make a suggestion?"

Mixed expressions greeted this remark. Rod spoke first. "I appreciate your concern, Anya, but you're not familiar with any of the people involved."

"She was a teenage girl herself not long ago. Let's hear what she has to say." Jack's encouragement finally drew a nod from his uncle.

Anya addressed the girl. "They won't let you visit your dad, but your grandmother isn't getting any younger. You and your sister are old enough to spend a week or two with her during vacations. And then you can discreetly visit your dad."

"Vince won't let us do anything that isn't his idea," Tiffany replied bitterly.

"Surely your mom has some influence. Play the guilt card," Anya persisted. "Grandmothers are precious, and I'm sure she could use two helpers for spring cleaning. It would give your parents a break, too, during vacation."

"They already get a break. They stick us in camps, like music camp and swim camp and soccer camp." Despite the objection, a note of hope brightened the girl's voice.

"I would love to have them here. They're growing up so fast." Helen gazed fondly at her granddaughter. "And it would be wonderful to do some spring cleaning together."

"I'd like that. Amber would, too," Tiffany replied. "Could we visit Daddy and Uncle Jack while we're here?"

"Not officially," Rod told her. "If your parents get wind that I'm involved, they'll forbid you to come. They might even file a restraining order against me."

Jack leaned forward. "I'll bet we could arrange something if we're careful, though."

That was exactly what Anya had had in mind. She wondered if she should speak again or let the others carry the ball from here.

Helen clasped her hands in her lap. "But if Portia and that husband of hers found out I let you spend time with the girls, they'll cut off all contact with me."

"I suppose that's a risk," Jack conceded.

Anya cleared her throat. Everyone turned to her, with varying degrees of curiosity and skepticism.

"As I said, you have to be discreet," she ventured. "But, Helen, surely you have friends who could take the girls on outings. It wouldn't be your fault if they happen to run into their dad."

"You're a sneaky little thing," Rod said appreciatively.

"I grew up in a family that tried to run my life even after I was grown," she explained. "I learned the less I told them, the better."

"Some of the hospital staff have school-age children," Jack remarked. "There are lots of possibilities for playdates at a park or the beach."

Rod grinned. "If I ran into them, naturally I'd offer to spring for lunch."

"Thanks for the idea," Helen told Anya. "I don't suppose you have children, do you? You'd be a splendid parent."

"Not yet." With a twist of pain, she remembered the news she'd received this evening. *I will have a child for about five minutes—until her forever mom claims her.*

A dozen years from now, how would her child feel about being adopted? Anya supposed different kids had different responses. Tiffany had been torn up about Rod's supposed abandonment, but that was because they'd formed a bond. A birth mother who relinquished her baby wasn't rejecting her. Exactly the opposite. You had to do what was best for the child.

"I have another idea! Amber and I could go to the movies with Anya and Jack. Like a double date." Tiffany clearly assumed they were a couple, despite their denials. "And he could cook dinner for us. Do you still cook, Uncle Jack?"

"Rumor has it," he replied cheerfully.

More soberly, Rod said, "None of this is guaranteed. But you should make your case, Tiff. The fact that you ran away might show them they can't keep you under lock and key. Let's hope Amber hasn't mentioned that you planned to contact me."

"I swore her to secrecy." The girl toyed with the end of her braid. "She knows Vince would go ballistic."

"When you talk to them, don't forget to lay on the guilt,"

Anya reminded her. "Emphasize how unfair they're being to your grandmother."

"Their poor *aging* grandmother," Helen said lightly. "Who can't do a proper spring cleaning anymore."

"Not that anyone could tell." Anya wasn't about to mention the spiderwebs on the front windows. Even if the detail reinforced Tiffany's case, it would only embarrass her grandmother.

The girl bounced with excitement. "I'll act totally pathetic. This is great! Thank you, Anya. I can't wait till you're my aunt."

Heat rushed to her cheeks. "Jack and I aren't dating, sweetie. We just work together."

Rod studied her. Anya hoped he hadn't changed his mind about her so drastically that he might play matchmaker. She hadn't meant to be *that* helpful.

"Now that we have a plan, I'll go call your mother," Helen said.

Taking that as her cue, Anya stood. "It's been great meeting you and Tiffany."

"Do you have to leave already?" the girl asked. "I like you."

"I like you, too." And truthfully, Anya hoped she'd see Rod's daughter again. "But I have to hit the hay. Surgical nurses start work at 7:00 a.m. That means rolling out of bed by 5:30 a.m."

"Does Uncle Jack roll out of bed by 5:30 a.m., too?" his niece asked mischievously.

Anya blushed. "I wouldn't know."

"You're grown-ups. That means you can sleep together, right?" Tiffany teased.

"Where'd you pick up that idea?" Rod demanded. "I thought your parents monitored your media access."

"Everybody knows about that stuff." Tiffany patted his arm. "Don't worry, Daddy. I don't have a boyfriend yet."

"That's one thing I approve of," he said with mock gruffness.

Anya said her goodbyes. "Back in a sec," Jack told the others, then followed her outside.

"We have something to discuss," she began as they walked toward her car.

"Maybe tomorrow."

She'd prefer to get this over with. "It's important."

He didn't seem to hear her, though. "What was my aunt thinking, shutting Rod out of the girls' lives? Rod's their father in every sense that counts. You can't sever a bond like that, no matter how many lawyers you hire."

In this state, Jack wouldn't take her news well, Anya conceded. "Tomorrow night, then. Let's find a moment to talk, okay?"

"I remember flying home from college right after Tiffany was born," he continued, oblivious. "Holding her in my arms… She was a little cutie with her red hair. I got this wild rush, like it was my job to protect her from the world. Isn't that nuts? I was twenty years old."

"Kind of a strong reaction." In the glow of a streetlamp, Anya clicked open her car lock. "You're only their uncle. Or cousin. Or whatever."

"Yes, whatever," he said dourly. "But it doesn't matter that we aren't genetically related. We're family. And families mean more to me than to most people."

She stopped. "Why?"

"Because for most of my childhood, I missed out on having one." Jack dug his hands into his pockets.

He hardly struck Anya as the product of a deprived upbringing. "You grew up in foster homes?"

"Not exactly."

"What does that mean?"

"My dad was a firefighter who died in a fire when I was three." Jack stared down the dark street. "My mother wasn't the domestic type, and after Dad died, she stopped trying to be. She adopted one cause after another and travels all over the world, saving the subjugated women of India and Africa.

And South America. And Central America. And probably the South Pole."

"Surely she took you along." Anya had no idea how anyone could raise a child under those circumstances, but it might be exciting and educational.

"She dragged me here and there until I reached kindergarten. Then she dumped me on my grandparents." Bitterness underscored his words.

At five years old, his mother had left him? That was harsh. With a shiver, Anya tried to relate his mother's actions to her own situation. To her, it seemed an entirely different matter. But Jack might not see it that way.

"Grandparents are family, too," she said.

"Mine weren't even prepared to have Rod, a surprise midlife baby. He's thirteen years younger than my mom, and they certainly weren't eager to add a grandchild to the mix." Jack seemed lost in his painful past. "Physically, they took care of me, but I grew up feeling as if I wasn't wanted there. It was lonely."

The opposite of me. Anya had often longed for less family. "Wasn't your uncle like a brother?"

"A much older brother. He was a teenager when I was in grade school," Jack said. "It was later that we got close."

She shook her head. "I had no idea. Are your grandparents still around?"

"They died a few months apart while I was in high school." A hurt look shadowed his face. "It felt like the end of the world to me. They may not have been perfect, but at least I had a home."

"What about your mom?" Surely the woman had stepped up to the plate at such a critical point.

"After the funeral, she offered to fly me to Central America, where she was living in a jungle hut or something like that," Jack said tightly. "She was vague about her circumstances, which I took to mean she'd rather I stayed here."

"What did you do?" Anya wished she could soothe his

sadness. She'd always pictured Jack as a secure person from a solid, supportive background.

"I moved in with Rod. He was in medical school by then and too busy to spend much time with me, but we got along. I received my father's survivor benefits from Social Security, so that covered my share of expenses, and I did my best to be useful."

"That's why you learned to cook?"

"Along with other household skills." He shrugged. "That's how my childhood went. Better than for a lot of kids, but not exactly storybook." Jack glanced toward the house. "That's why it tears me apart to see Tiffany and Amber growing up like this. Being rich doesn't compensate for feeling unloved and unvalued."

"Surely their mother loves them."

"Not enough to put their interests ahead of hers," he said grimly.

Anya had no intention of discussing *that* subject. Instead, she sent forth a small feeler. "I don't suppose you want children of your own, considering how unhappy you were."

Deep green eyes bored into hers. "If I'm ever lucky enough to have them, I'll be there for them one hundred percent. They'll be the most important things in my life."

What a devoted father he'd make, Anya thought, but how realistic was his promise? As a surgeon, he had to work long hours. The person who'd really be there morning, noon and night was the mother.

Still, seeing his hurt, feeling his unhappiness, Anya couldn't help wanting to fix things for him. But she knew where that path led. She had the best of intentions but eventually her patience wore out, and she made dangerous mistakes.

She'd tried to be the perfect substitute for her mom with her younger siblings and to help at home as her mother's rheumatoid arthritis grew progressively worse. Molly had put on a cheerful face for her husband and the triplets, but Anya had noticed the swollen joints and profound fatigue, the weight loss and the discouragement as one promising medication after another proved disappointing.

Anya had been exhausted by the extra work and—much as she regretted it—sometimes resentful. During her senior year in college, she was studying for exams one weekend and had decided to ignore her mother's call for assistance from downstairs, just for a few minutes. *Please, let someone else help her this once,* Anya had thought. Unaware that everyone else had gone out, she'd concentrated on her textbook until she heard a sickening crash.

Trying to go to the bathroom alone, Molly had fallen and sprained her hip. Aching for her mother and filled with guilt, Anya had spent the next few days sleeping in her mother's hospital room to make sure no such accident happened again. She'd also endured furious lectures from her father about failing those who relied on her yet again.

Then on the exams she'd received her lowest grades ever, losing a chance at a grant for a graduate program. Anya had given up her goal of becoming a nurse practitioner with her own practice. Instead, she'd taken a job at a hospital in Denver, continuing to make the hour-long commute from her small town until she'd gained enough experience and enough self-confidence to move out of state.

It was only two years later, and Anya wasn't ready to tackle a lifelong commitment to a child or a man. Her baby would have as close to an ideal childhood as she could arrange, though—with an adoptive family. As for how Jack might react when he learned about her pregnancy, she'd rather not be there.

She'd learned the hard way that avoidance was often a wiser tactic than blunt honesty. She'd admitted to Dad what had happened that day with her mother and had received a tongue-lashing.

Yes, she'd let Jack calm down on his own rather than lash out at her out of shock. In fact, the more distance she put between them, the better. Suddenly, Karen's house seemed like a haven.

"It was great meeting your niece," she told him.

The tension eased from his body. "You were great. Thank you."

"Glad to do it." As she slid into the car, Anya added, "By the way, my roommate and I are moving."

"Moving?" Dismay replaced his warmth. "What about your lease?"

"It's up for renewal, and this will be cheaper," she said. "We're only going a few miles, to Karen Wiggins's house. See you at work!"

Quick escape: turn on the ignition, pull out from the curb, wave blithely and *go!* In the rearview mirror, she saw Jack staring after her, openmouthed.

As she drove home, Anya processed the fact that she'd just committed to living with four other people, including Lucky, who was annoyingly nosy. And she still had to deal with informing Jack about his impending fatherhood.

Look on the bright side. Literally. In Karen's airy house, her African violet had a better shot at survival.

And so did Anya's hard-won peace of mind.

Chapter Four

"Manager or police?" Jack asked.

His uncle studied the dented blue van blocking their carport spaces. "I'm guessing the driver hasn't gone far. It'll be faster if we wait."

"I'd rather call someone, but you're probably right." At 11:00 a.m. on a Sunday morning, Jack's stomach was growling for brunch at Waffle Heaven. "I figured now that you have your car back, we'd be bulletproof. If one doesn't start, we could take the other. Then this jerk blocked us both."

"Shall we punch him when he shows up?" Rod asked drily.

"You do the punching," Jack said. "A surgeon's hands have to be protected."

"It takes dexterity to insert my tubes and syringes," his uncle replied. "How about I sit on him while you administer the beating?"

"What if he is a she?" Jack asked.

"Let's do rock paper scissors," his uncle proposed.

"To decide whether we call the police or to decide which of us messes up our hands?"

They broke off their nonsensical discussion when they heard voices from around the corner of the nearest apartment unit.

"Angle it to your left! No, your other left," a man ordered.

"It's tilting!" squawked a woman.

"Hang in there, Anya. Zora, get over here!"

Shoes shuffled on the sidewalk. "Okay, I have it."

They came into view on the walkway, navigating the narrow path between low-growing palms and bushes. With Anya and Zora was the male nurse Jack had met a few days earlier. Even though the temperature had barely reached the low sixties, he was wearing a sleeveless undershirt, displaying his expansive tattoos.

Behind him, Anya helped her roommate support the other end of a faded purple couch. She'd tied back her dark hair and donned an oversize T-shirt that ought to be shapeless. But on her, every movement reminded Jack of the tempting curves underneath.

"That," announced Rod to the group, "is a truly ugly sofa. Dare I hope you're taking that purple monstrosity to the Dumpster?"

"It isn't purple," said Anya. "It's orchid."

Her roommate's thin face poked out from behind the couch. "It's for the second-floor landing." She blew a curl of reddish-brown hair off her temple. "Nobody has to see it but us."

"Hauling it upstairs is going to be a fun job," Lucky muttered. Served him right for playing rooster in the henhouse, in Jack's opinion. "Are we blocking you doctors?"

"Yes, and we're hungry," Rod answered.

Show no weakness in front of Anya. Especially not while this guy was hefting furniture and rippling his muscles. "I'm not that hungry. We can pitch in." As if to defy his speech, Jack's stomach rumbled. Hoping no one had heard, he marched over to boost the women's end of the couch. They released it willingly.

Reaching the van, the men maneuvered it inside. A few minutes of grunting and shifting later, they'd fitted it in place. By then, Anya and Zora had disappeared between the buildings.

As Jack jumped down, the male nurse said, "I'll get the van out of your way. We don't want to inconvenience you lords of the realm."

Did the man resent all physicians or just the two of them

specifically? Jack had learned—more or less by chance—that Lucky worked for the distinguished head of the men's fertility program. He doubted the fellow leveled snide remarks at the famed Dr. Cole Rattigan. But apparently an anesthesiologist and an ordinary ob-gyn were fair game.

"Don't bother," Jack said. "We're fine."

Rod rolled his eyes. "What if they run out of waffles?"

"Honestly!" Jack growled.

"Go ahead. I can handle this," Lucky assured them.

Jack refused to let Anya see him as a lazy slug who whisked off for a leisurely meal while others, especially her, labored. "With a few more hands, you'll finish faster."

Lucky rolled his shoulders, producing loud cracks. "Suit yourself."

The women reappeared, arms full of mismatched towels and sheets wrapped in clear plastic bags. "Amazing. The ladies copied our color scheme," Rod said.

Zora peered dubiously at the linens in hues ranging from pink to purple to olive-green. "This is a color scheme?"

"Dr. Vintner has a dry sense of humor." Anya lugged her towels to the open van.

On the upper level, Lucky took them from her arms. "Didn't I mention we should bring out the chairs and table before the small stuff?"

The women exchanged glances. "Huh," said Anya. "Did he?"

"Maybe, but these were on top of them," Zora responded.

"And you couldn't put them on the floor?" Lucky asked.

The guy was blowing his opportunity to appear heroic, Jack thought. And although the man's peevishness appeared to be aimed at the redhead, Anya was the one who spoke up. "Don't make a federal case out of it. Pile them on the couch."

With an annoyed click of the tongue, Lucky obeyed.

Rod, still planted on the sidewalk, smiled pleasantly and said to him, "It's nice when roommates get along so well."

"I'm sure they'll work it out," Jack told him. "Once they've moved in and all."

"They might end up with blood on the sofa," his uncle answered. "Which would be an improvement."

Another tenant, backing out of the opposite carport, glared at them while maneuvering around the van. Lucky waved in a friendly manner, and the man tilted his head in grudging acknowledgment.

"Out of curiosity, how many bathrooms does this house have?" Rod inquired, eyeing the towels.

"Three and a half," said Zora.

"For how many people?"

"Five." Lucky jumped down from the van.

"That's not bad, but you'll have a traffic jam if you work the same hours." Rod adjusted his fedora to block the sunlight.

Anya sighed. "I'd have killed for that many bathrooms when I was growing up. We had two for nine people."

"One of our bathrooms is in my suite downstairs," Lucky said. "You're welcome to use it whenever you want."

"Thanks." She gave the nurse a vague smile.

Jack tried not to scowl. "Why don't we bring down the rest of the furniture?"

"Sounds like a plan." Anya gave Jack a vague smile, too.

Half an hour later his muscles were throbbing, but he would have rather worked to the point of collapse than admit defeat.

Fortunately, he was in the right place when Anya, approaching the parking lot with a box marked *Dishes,* halted abruptly, the color draining from her face.

"Are you okay?" Jack rushed to relieve her of the box but had to dodge a near-collision with Lucky.

"I've got it." The male nurse snatched the container from Anya's shaky grasp.

Zora approached, struggling antlike with a crate much too large for her. "Anya? Are you sick?"

"Go on," her roommate told her. "I'm fine."

"Well, okay." Zora staggered toward the truck. Lucky ignored her.

"Sit down." Jack took Anya's elbow. "I'm speaking as a doctor."

"Yes, a nurse couldn't possibly figure out what she should do." Lucky sent him a poisonous glare and carted off the dishes.

"I can manage." All the same, Anya leaned on Jack as he escorted her to a wrought-iron bench bordered by flowering bushes.

From around the corner, Rod appeared, carrying a toilet plunger and a pack of bath tissue. "Doing my bit," he announced, waving the lightweight items in the air and strolling on his way.

Jack gladly refocused his attention on Anya. How vulnerable she looked, sitting there twisting the hem of that huge T-shirt. "Can I get you some water?"

"No, thanks. I just drank half a glass." She sucked in a breath, as if gathering strength from the fragrance of the flowers. Despite the cool air, she must have overheated from her exertion.

To distract her, Jack said, "I've been meaning to tell you how terrific you were with Tiffany." They hadn't had a chance to talk privately since Thursday.

"How'd things work out for her?"

His niece's freckled face popped into his head. He'd been thinking about Tiff a lot these past few days. "When her parents learned she was safe, they were relieved for about thirty seconds before they became furious."

"Understandable, I suppose," Anya said. "They must have been worried sick."

"Helen said they blistered the phone. She refused to let them talk to Tiffany until they calmed down."

"Good for her." Anya tucked a wedge of dark hair behind her ear. She'd lost her clip, he noticed. "Did they drive up?"

"They flew into Orange County in their private jet." John Wayne Airport, the closest to Safe Harbor, accommodated both commercial and private aircraft.

"That's a short hop." Anya swallowed, still struggling with whatever was bothering her.

"Twenty minutes in the air, I gather." Judging by how tense she'd become when he'd just sat beside her, touching her wouldn't be welcomed, so Jack folded his arms and went on talking. "However, with all the arrangements, it took them about two hours, roughly the same as if they drove. But that wouldn't have satisfied Vince's sense of importance. That gave us time to order pizza and play a round of Monopoly."

"Who won?" Anya asked.

"Rod." Jack smiled at the memory of his uncle battling for turf with Tiffany, both of them relishing each small victory and flourishing every Get Out of Jail Free card. "He's a tough customer."

"He didn't cut a twelve-year-old any slack?"

"Kids can't deal with life if parents pave every step of their path," the anesthesiologist responded, sauntering back from the truck.

"I don't imagine her parents are making *her* life easy," Anya said.

"A reasonable point." He stepped aside for Lucky and Zora to file by. "However, there's a difference between berating a child, as they do, and teaching her that concentration and strategy pay off."

Hoping his uncle would move on so he could have Anya to himself again, Jack narrowed his eyes. "Yes, Monopoly is an excellent metaphor for life."

"Also, I like to win." With a grin, Rod departed.

"You didn't run into the parents, did you?" Anya's cheeks had regained some of their healthy pink color. "Considering the legal issues, that would have been awkward."

"We aren't suicidal," Jack assured her. "Helen asked Portia to phone when she landed, so we knew when to clear out."

"Then how do you know what happened when they got there?"

"Helen called." Rod had said the older woman had been near tears on the phone.

"Was it bad?"

"Vince stormed into the house and called Tiff a spoiled brat." Although Jack had never met the man in person, he'd seen pictures. Vince came across as large and intimidating, even in a headshot.

"He sounds awful." Anya's dark eyes smoldered. "What a bully."

"Tiff's not easily cowed." Jack was proud of his niece. "She had to work hard at appearing contrite, according to Helen. Then she took your advice and cried to her mom about how much she'd missed her grandmother. That it was cruel to deprive an old lady of her grandchildren. Also, she mentioned something about spiderwebs and dust."

"Did it work?"

"Helen thinks her daughter was swayed, but there's no telling what Vince will decide." Jack's aunt had always struck him as a strong person—maybe a little too strong, in view of the way she'd treated Rod—but she seemed unwilling or unable to stand up to her second husband. "Even if he agrees, they might choose to fly Helen to San Diego rather than letting Tiff and Amber come here."

"Let's hope not." It was Rod, toting a small reading lamp. "The girls need a break before those people crush their spirits."

"Tiffany doesn't strike me as crushable," Anya said. "But if she runs away again, she might end up who knows where."

Jack had no intention of allowing that to happen. "I made it very clear that if she can't reach Rod or Helen, I'd meet her anywhere, anytime."

Her hand fluttered to his arm. "You really care about her. That's so sweet."

He fought down the instinct to gather her close. "Of course."

Rod cleared his throat, but apparently reconsidered whatever he'd been about to say and vanished toward the parking lot. For once, he'd picked up on the vibes around him and showed a trace of sensitivity. *And I'm sure I'll hear about it later.*

Anya lifted her hand. "Sorry."

"Nothing to be sorry about," Jack told her.

"Listen." In the dappled sunlight, she raised her face to his. The soft light emphasized the velvet texture of her skin and the fullness of her lips. "We should meet for coffee. Or tea. Or juice."

Finally, she was ready to move past this tough patch in their relationship. "Any beverage will do." Encouraged that she'd taken this step of her own volition, Jack cupped her hands in his. "Now that you're moving to Karen's house, we won't be running into each other outside of work. I'd like to remedy that. I miss you."

She swayed closer, then slid her hands free and scooted back. If he'd been paying attention to their surroundings, he'd have heard the footsteps, too. Jack would gladly have kicked Lucky and Zora, except that might have made them drop the TV they were carrying.

Agonizing seconds passed. When they were alone again, he asked, "What day is good for you?"

"For what?"

"Drinks."

"Oh, that." Anya studied him as if seeking the answer to an unasked question. "Just suppose…what if Tiffany and her sister had to move away somewhere that you and Rod would never see them? I mean, if it was best for them. Like, witness protection."

What a bizarre idea. "There are no circumstances under which my nieces would not need their father," Jack responded vehemently.

"Oh."

She seemed to shrink away.

What was that about? Surely she knew his anger wasn't directed at her. "I could meet you tomorrow afternoon when you get off." Jack worked an overnight shift on Sundays in labor and delivery, so he had Mondays free. Well, free aside from sleeping.

Rod bustled past on the walkway, whistling and keeping his gaze trained ahead. He didn't have to be so obvious about ignoring them, but it was better than if he'd stopped to gab.

"No, the whole thing is a bad idea." Anya stood up. "We work together. Let's keep it professional."

"Wait a minute." She was the one who'd proposed to meet for a drink. "Is this a game?"

"I beg your pardon?"

Jack brushed off his slacks as he stood. "I realize you weren't feeling well…"

"Probably low blood pressure," she said.

"Regardless, that's no excuse for jerking me around." He'd interrupted his breakfast plans and overtaxed his muscles, which would now probably hurt like hell during the long night ahead. That was all fine—she hadn't requested his assistance, and he didn't begrudge a few aches and pains—but it was unfair to suggest they meet for coffee and then behave as if he had pressured her. "If you'd rather I kept my distance, fine. But don't issue invitations you don't mean."

"I didn't…it wasn't like that." A familiar pucker appeared between her eyes.

Jack nearly softened. She had an astonishing ability to stir his protective instincts. But no one had appointed him her guardian. She had plenty of friends, and if she'd rather drink coffee or simply hang out with the other nurses, male or female, that was her business.

"I'm glad you're feeling better," he told her. "If it's low blood pressure, you should eat something."

"Crackers." She swallowed. "I think we packed them. But that's okay. Karen and Melissa promised to fix sandwiches."

Lucky strode by. "The first of many meals. I don't suppose you've seen the updated kitchen? It's impressive."

"No." Jack was sure he had a much better idea of how to make the most of a kitchen than Lucky did.

"And all that space!" the man crowed. "Once we settle in, it will be a fantastic party house."

"Knock yourself out." Jack had endured enough veiled taunts for one day. Also, he realized, the apartment must be nearly empty by now. "I'll let you folks finish on your own. Enjoy your sandwiches."

"Thanks for the help," said Anya.

"Don't mention it."

He'd reached the parking lot before he remembered that the van still blocked their cars. Then he spotted Rod's distinctive fedora. His uncle was facing a statuesque lady in formfitting green slacks and a halter top. Golden-brown hair floated around a determined face as she waved.

"Hi," Jack called. What was the Realtor's name? Della? Danielle? It always reminded him of old-fashioned countertops. Formica. No, that wasn't right.

"Danica was just mentioning she had a couple of very lonely apple pies," Rod informed him.

"There's more than I can eat," Danica confirmed. "It's my mother's closely guarded recipe. Homemade crusts, too."

"With whipped cream, they'll be better than waffles," Rod said. "There is whipped cream, isn't there?"

He noticed a mischievous glint in her eye, hinting that the whipped cream might be put to all sorts of creative uses. "Absolutely. And espresso."

He'd struck out with Anya, so why not? "Sounds wonderful," Jack said. "Very kind of you."

"My pleasure."

The real estate agent linked one arm through Rod's and the other through his as if laying claim to them both. That didn't last long, though, since it was impossible to climb the exterior steps in that formation. As they were separating, he caught Anya's expression from behind the truck.

She looked...hurt. Or was he kidding himself?

Much as Jack enjoyed her company, he was done behaving like a teenager with a crush. If she chose to retreat from

what they'd shared and return to acting strictly professionally he respected that.

Besides, he was starving.

Chapter Five

Empty of furnishings, the apartment had a pathetic air, Anya thought as she took a last look around. Matted patches of carpet revealed the shapes of their sofa and chairs. But after the management had the place professionally cleaned, those marks would vanish, leaving no sign of the two women who had spent a year within these walls.

When she'd agreed to pair up with Zora, Anya had been happy to bid farewell to the motel suite she'd been living in since her arrival from Colorado. Anya had found a sympathetic soul in her roommate, who'd been licking the wounds of her husband's betrayal. The women had formed a team as they popped corn, shared movie nights and, playing on their names, joked about being experts on everything from A to Z.

Now that transitional period of their lives was ending. Maybe that explained Anya's rush of nostalgia. Also, she would no longer enjoy the awareness that just around the corner of the next building dwelled a guy with a devilish grin and the most skillful hands she'd ever encountered, in *or* out of an operating room.

She hadn't meant to drive him to that rapacious woman who flaunted her surgically enhanced breasts at every opportunity. Right now, they must be sitting at that woman's table with their legs bumping underneath. Anya hoped Rod was bumping his legs in there, too.

And she still had to break the news of her pregnancy to Jack. That comment about his nieces needing their father, no matter what the circumstances, didn't bode well for gaining his consent to adoption. Yet surely he wouldn't raise a baby by himself. And he couldn't force Anya to take on a role for which she was completely unprepared.

Their child deserved better. Surely he'd see that eventually, but she dreaded the confrontation. His attitude only reinforced her belief that she should entrust the task of informing him to someone else.

After checking her bedroom for overlooked objects, Anya peeked into the bathroom. The medicine cabinet was empty, no leftover shampoo in the tub…oh, wait. There on the windowsill sat the remarkably robust African violet. Far from withering away, it was thriving. Perhaps, as she'd read on the internet, it really did prefer humidity and filtered light.

She'd intended to toss it in the trash, but it would be cruel to kill a blossoming plant. Lowering it, Anya admired the dark fuzzy leaves and tiny purple flowers. "You deserve another chance, no matter who gave you to me," she murmured as she exited the bathroom. "It isn't your fault Jack knocked me up."

A gasp from the kitchen was followed within milliseconds by a crash. Dismayed to realize she'd been overheard, Anya stared at a shocked Zora as she rushed into the kitchen.

Freckles stood out against her roommate's face. "He what? You're what?"

"Forget you heard that," Anya commanded, despite the futility of such a request.

"See what you made me do!" Zora transferred her distress to the shattered millefiori vase, its delicate colors and swirling, kaleidoscope-like neck reduced to shards on the kitchen floor.

"I thought you gave that away." The beautiful vase had been an anniversary gift from the treacherous Andrew, who'd bought it on a business trip to Italy.

"Like you said, there's no sense blaming an object just because a jerk gave it to you." Zora scraped up the broken pieces with paper towels.

"You have to get over him," Anya told her.

"He's still my husband," her friend retorted. A few months ago, Zora had gone so far as to throw a divorce party in the hospital cafeteria, proclaiming how happy she was to be free. But clearly she was neither happy nor, technically, free.

Anya refused to act as an enabler. "Andrew hasn't signed the final papers only because you haven't forced him to. He enjoys keeping you dangling. It's a power trip."

"Maybe he hasn't signed them because he still has feelings for me." Zora dumped the shards into a plastic trash bag.

Lucky stomped through the front door, which they'd propped open. "Did I hear what I think I heard? You're hanging on to that cheater? You're an idiot."

Zora shot him an unladylike gesture. Anya wished Lucky would quit meddling in their business. Just because he'd overheard their conversation didn't mean he had the right to pass judgment. Besides, whereas Anya's criticisms were prompted by concern for her friend's well-being, his motive was less charitable.

Most of the hospital staff had forgiven Zora for her husband-stealing once nurse Stacy Layne had happily remarried. But Lucky had taken the situation to heart because Stacy had married his beloved boss; therefore, he resented any and all harm that had ever been done to her.

"Let's lock up, okay?" Anya said. "Melissa and Karen must be wondering if we had an accident on the drive over."

"Just double-checking the premises." Finding nothing further to remove, Lucky marched out. Their arrangement was for him to drive the rented van while the women transported personal and fragile items in their cars.

"I'll return the keys to the manager," Anya offered brightly, eager to escape.

Zora blocked the doorway. "We haven't discussed your pregnancy."

"We'll talk about it later."

"When did this happen? *How* did this happen?"

"New Year's Eve, and in the usual way." There—she'd

answered the questions. Quickly, Anya added, "Not a word to anyone."

"You can't expect to hide it for long."

"That's not your problem. And I'm hungry. You shouldn't make a pregnant woman go without food."

Scowling, Zora went out. Still holding the African violet, Anya locked up and took both sets of keys to the manager.

I should have held my tongue. Well, Zora would have found out sooner or later. So would everybody else, Anya conceded. At least about her pregnancy. Not necessarily about the father.

As for Jack, she'd figure out a way to handle this promptly and efficiently. Unlike Zora, she didn't plan to drag out the paper-signing until the bitter end.

Carefully, Anya wedged the plant into a cup holder in her front seat. Stroking its furry leaves quelled the nausea rising again in her stomach, just as Jack's scent had soothed her earlier. Something about male pheromones and lime had a therapeutic effect on her morning sickness.

Wondering where she'd find the right spot for the little plant, she headed for her new home.

"It was the jasmine," Zora said. "Or maybe the honeysuckle."

"No, we had stuffy noses," Anya corrected her as they stood in front of Karen's house.

The two-story stucco home, freshly painted white with blue trim, glowed in the afternoon sunlight. Most of the other structures on Pelican Lane had been removed over the years, reportedly bought up and razed by supporters of the adjacent marsh. Isolation only added to the place's dignified beauty.

Trellised roses and bougainvillea, along with other flowering plants, tumbled across the yard that wrapped from the front lawn to the back of the house. What a luxurious spot—if only it didn't smell like rotten eggs. Maybe the perfumed flora or the lingering paint smell had disguised the stink a few weeks ago when they'd first considered Karen's offer, but Anya would put her money on their head colds.

Beyond the house and off to their right, toward the Pacific, stretched a green and brown expanse where saltwater and freshwater met. In the estuary, birds nested, nature lovers in sturdy shoes hiked the dirt paths and coyotes prowled, while plants and mollusks decomposed. And reeked.

The African violet quivered in the breeze, as if in sympathy with the dying vegetation. Anya had decided to carry it inside immediately because harsh light through her windshield might damage it.

"Paula doesn't like it here," she told Zora.

"Who?"

Anya indicated the plant. "African violet's proper name is Saintpaulia, after the German baron who took credit for discovering them in Tanzania." She'd checked out the subject online.

"I'll bet the natives didn't think he discovered them," Zora muttered.

"I'm sure you're right."

"Anyway, why did you name your plant?" her friend asked.

"Because it has personality."

"No, it just has memories of Jack. Speaking of which, does he know about this?"

"Oh, look. Here comes Lucky." Anya wasn't making that up. He'd parked the van in the gravel driveway, blocking the unpaved turnaround where they'd left their car. He had to take it back to the rental place tonight, so it would be gone before anyone needed to leave.

"We can unload your stuff later," he called on approach. "Let's eat."

"Okay." Anya fell into step alongside Zora, ignoring a skeptical expression from her friend that warned this conversation was only on hold.

Despite the foul smell, Anya hadn't lost her appetite. Quite the contrary. Pregnancy had carried her to new realms of hunger.

As the wide front porch creaked beneath their feet, Karen

opened the front door. Wearing a long woven skirt and top, she had a relaxed air. "The gang's all here! Come on in."

Anya wiped her shoes on the doormat before entering. Even so, she was glad they didn't traipse through the living room, with its striped sofa and polished curio cabinet, or into the formal dining room. She'd hate to mess up the newly vacuumed carpets.

Instead, they veered left around the staircase and traversed the rumpled family room. Near a pair of sliding glass patio doors, a comfortably chipped table was set with a sandwich platter.

"Finally!" Melissa, dark blond hair loose around her shoulders, set down a fruit salad. "Karen and I almost started without you."

Where to put Paula? Anya set the plant in an empty spot on the floor, away from the traffic pattern. "It's only till I finish lunch," she told it and went to wash her hands.

Then, taking a paper plate from a stack, Anya joined the others, grateful for the healthy selection of food. When she came up for air, she surveyed the circle of new housemates: tanned Lucky, devouring his second sandwich; Karen, blooming with good cheer now that she'd rented out all her rooms; Melissa, who'd piled her plate with fruit, and Zora, sitting as far from Lucky as possible.

It occurred to her that, in this house, she'd be progressing through the formative months of her baby's gestational life. Instead of a family, she'd be relying for support on a group of people who were—except for Zora—casual acquaintances. How would they react when they learned of Anya's pregnancy?

A longing to burrow into Jack's arms and rely on his powerful paternal instincts twisted through her. He'd take care of her, wouldn't he? *And then he'd assume he's the boss of me. I'd be stuck raising a kid and trying to please a guy and chewing my fingernails to the quick like I used to.*

No, she wouldn't because Anya had a choice now, unlike when she'd been growing up. She'd been the fourth child in the family. Her sister Ruth, older by nine years, had been tired of helping supervise their twin brothers and, when Anya was born, had openly resented the newcomer. Anya had spent her toddler and preschool years tagging along after her parents as they worked in their feed store. Naturally, there'd been chores, from collecting chicken eggs in the morning to sweeping the floor after dinner, but they hadn't been burdensome.

At age five, those relatively carefree years had ended when her mother had given birth to triplets. Although the older siblings occasionally babysat, everyone assumed that Anya would pitch in with diaper duty and clean-up. And as arthritis sapped her mother's mobility, more and more of the care of her three little sisters fell to Anya.

Everyone had worked hard, so she hadn't complained. Maybe she should have been more cantankerous, like Ruth, who'd argued a lot with their parents and married at nineteen. Or quicker to shrug off domestic duties, like her two brothers, although they *had* assisted Dad in the feed store. But, sensitive to the deepening lines on her father's face and to her mother's silent pain, Anya had carried on.

She'd expected the pressures to ease when she entered college and the triplets threw themselves into high-school activities. However, the family had figured Anya, as a nursing student, was the natural person to assist their increasingly disabled mother and to babysit Ruth's growing brood when difficult pregnancies sidelined her. The few occasions when Anya had spoken up, her family had simply dismissed her complaints. The more she tried to distance herself, the bigger the guilt trips they laid on her.

Though there'd been sweet moments, too. When she received her nursing degree, the triplets—juniors in high school at the time—had thrown her a surprise party. It had been their version of the now-abandoned "capping" ceremony in which nurses used to receive their white caps. Because modern nurses don't wear caps, the girls had bought an array of funny hats for the whole family to wear while they cut the cake and sang silly songs.

But as her career progressed, so did Anya's desire for independence. She developed a passion for surgical nursing, and it was frustrating to be summoned home for one thing after another on top of the hours she put in doing her family's housework and supervising her mom's home medical care. The last straw was when Anya was forced to trade shifts for an "emergency" at home, losing a chance to assist at a major transplant operation. She'd arrived home to learn that the urgent situation was that her dad needed her brother to do stock inventory and so he couldn't drive Molly to physical therapy.

Mom had apologized profusely, but it wasn't her fault. The rest of the family had taken Anya for granted, refusing to change *their* schedules or recognize that Anya's work was just as important as theirs. She'd realized they never would, and the only way to have her own life was to move away. In frustration, she'd signed up for a nursing registry and moved to California. Later, she'd learned of an opening at Safe Harbor and she'd leaped at the chance to apply.

Most of her family still didn't understand why she'd left, although she'd explained herself frankly as recently as last Christmas. The holiday had been a miserable series of criticisms and nags for her to move back. Her mom, who might have intervened, had been under the weather while adjusting to new medication and hadn't spoken up.

She kept hoping her father and siblings would finally grasp why she'd left and why she had to stay away. It hurt that they didn't.

Yes, she was better off leaving her family out of this pregnancy and sticking with her new friends.

"Later today I'd like us to draft some ground rules," Karen said, breaking into Anya's thoughts. "Establishing guidelines should make this house-sharing experience run smoother."

"What kind of ground rules?" Lucky asked.

"All sorts of things. For instance, how we'll handle cooking—whether we do our own or if we each cook for a week on and then have a month off." Melissa's smooth reply indicated she'd prepared for this discussion. Although she was a decade younger than Karen, they'd become close friends.

"We should set a schedule for cleaning, too, so no one gets stuck with more than their fair share," Karen said. "What other issues concern you guys?"

"How we divide up community expenses," Lucky said.

"And what temperature we keep the thermostat." Zora always seemed to be cold, even in summer.

"Privacy," Anya said.

"Entertaining—who, when, how loud and how many," Melissa put in.

"Great!" Karen responded. "We'll hold a roundtable meeting as soon as you guys unload your truck."

Anya wasn't sure she liked the sound of that. Her experience with group discussions in her family had been, *Let Anya do it.* "If there's conflict, how do we decide?" she asked.

"We vote on it," Karen replied.

That sounded ominous to Anya. "You mean, the majority always rules?"

Her tension must have been evident to Zora, who asked, "What if there's a chore somebody really hates?"

From across the table, Lucky grimaced. "Opting out of bathroom duty, are you?"

Zora blinked. "What?"

"She was asking because of me," Anya told him. "My family tended to dump the nasty stuff on me."

"Nobody gets dumped on." Karen's narrowed eyes sent Lucky a back-off message. *"Nobody."*

Zora and Anya both folded their arms and added their stares to Karen's.

"Message received." Lucky scooted away from the table. "Let's get to work."

All five of them carried in furniture and other possessions. By evening, Anya was worn out but determined not to show it, especially to Zora. Her hovering was already making Lucky curious.

Through her weariness, Anya struggled to concentrate as,

over a dinner of pizza and salad, they put together a cleaning schedule. Regarding kitchen duty, Karen proposed they take turns as chef, each planning meals, shopping and cooking for a week.

"It's a lot of work, but then we get a month's break," she said. "Also, the cook doesn't have to clean up."

"Is it okay for the cook to buy takeout?" Lucky asked.

"As long as it's not pizza every night," Karen said. "Okay, everyone?" Heads bobbed.

"It's important that we choose healthy foods," Melissa qualified. "Plenty of fruits and vegetables, organic if possible."

"Right. Actually, I'd prefer that we eat vegetarian." Lucky reached for his third slice of olive-and-pineapple pizza.

"That could get boring," Zora said.

"You'd be surprised how many types of cheese there are," he told her. "And I'm willing to include fish."

Anya stirred from her near-stupor. "No soft cheeses and no sushi." Catching the curious looks from around the table, she wished she could recall her words. Too late.

"Surely you aren't...?" Melissa broke off.

"She isn't what?" Lucky asked.

"That's what they tell pregnant women to avoid," Karen filled in.

So much for keeping my secret. "Huh," Anya said.

Her three tormentors turned to Zora, who sent a pleading glance at Anya. Which only had the effect of confirming their suspicion.

"This is an interesting development," Lucky remarked.

"And nobody's business." That wasn't precisely true, though, Anya supposed, because her pregnancy was likely to affect everyone. "It was an accident and I'm giving it up for adoption once the father signs the waiver."

"And who is—" Lucky broke off as, from both sides, Melissa and Karen kicked him. "Ouch."

"That's wonderful of you, to carry the baby for someone else," Karen said. "So many couples are desperate to have children. We wish our fertility program could help them all, but it can't."

"You shouldn't do any cleaning duties that involve chemicals," Melissa insisted.

"Everything's composed of chemicals." Anya had no intention of shirking her fair share of the responsibilities. "But we don't use anything toxic, do we?"

"If we do, I'll handle it," Lucky said. "And at the risk of getting kicked again, I think the father should pitch in. Which brings up the question of who that might be…"

Zora, who rarely flared at him on her own behalf, leaped into action for Anya's sake. "Give it a rest! If Anya wants to reveal the father's identity, that's her decision."

With a duck of his head, Lucky yielded the point but not happily.

"To return to our topic, we definitely shouldn't use toxic chemicals. If I get pregnant…" Melissa exchanged glances with Karen.

"Oh, now, what's this?" Lucky appeared torn between curiosity and disapproval. What right did he have to be so judgmental? Anya wondered. "I hadn't heard mention of a boyfriend."

"I've been considering artificial insemination," Melissa hurried on before he could raise further questions. "Anyway, until then, I'm willing to do extra for Anya's sake."

Zora and Karen spoke almost in unison. "Me, too."

Anya raised her hands. "Stop. This isn't your problem."

"It isn't a problem at all," Karen told her. "It's a privilege."

Tears pricked Anya's eyes. "Thank you." But it wasn't only their kindness that affected her. It was the longing to see the same tender expression on the one face that wasn't here.

She had to tell him about the pregnancy. But if Jack reacted with this kind of loving concern and urged her to keep the baby, what if she wasn't able to stand against him? On the other hand, if she saw condemnation in his face, she'd be so angry she might say something she'd regret.

It was all too much, and right now, Anya's eyes threatened to drift shut.

"You're drooping," Lucky said. "You should rest."

"She should choose for herself when to rest," Zora shot back.

"You ladies are tough customers." Rising, Lucky collected their paper plates. After today, they'd agreed to use ceramic dishes for the sake of the environment, but tonight, everyone was too tired to wash. "I'd better watch my step."

Speaking of that, his foot was dangerously near the African violet, which Anya had forgotten until now. Guiltily, she bent down and snatched Paula to safety. "I'll take this upstairs."

"I'll come with you." Zora stood.

Lucky regarded her dubiously. "It takes two people to carry a tiny little plant?"

"Huh," said Anya.

Lucky grinned. "I think that means I should butt out. By the way, I forgot to say congratulations."

"Thanks," she muttered, making her way around the table.

"I mean it." He spoke in earnest. "Having a baby grow inside you is amazing. It's an experience we guys miss out on."

"If he says that when you go into labor, I'll smack him for you," Zora said.

"No picking on the lone male in the household," he countered. "You women are touchy."

"Maybe yes, maybe no," Melissa said.

Karen collected the leftover pizza. "There are five leftover slices, one for each of us. We can all count. If any one of us comes up short, the thief will be sniffed out, drawn and quartered."

Everyone nodded. Living together might actually be fun, Anya thought as she carried Paula upstairs.

When she entered her cozy corner room, her gaze went to the window, which had a splendid view of the marsh and farther out to the ocean. The winter sunset sent a pale gold sheen over the misty marshland, and as she peered out, a pelican swooped low.

Zora followed her gaze. "Looks like that pelican caught something."

"Judging by the lumps in his pouch, he's collected a lot of somethings." Anya cradled the plant as if to protect it from the distant pelican. "I think she'll be happy on this little table. It catches a lot of light." She positioned the plant, moving aside her e-book reader.

"Getting back to Jack…" Zora began.

"Must we?"

Her friend persevered. "You mentioned having him sign a waiver. What if he refuses to let you give up the baby?"

Anya squared her shoulders. "He can't force me to raise a child, and I doubt he's prepared to be a single father. What other choice is there?"

"Well, remember to stand your ground." Plopping onto the cushioned window seat, Zora slid off her shoes. "Men talk a good story, and then they leave you to pick up the pieces."

"Jack's not like that." She hadn't meant to spring to his defense, but she *did* respect Jack's integrity.

"You think so?" Zora rubbed one foot. "He has quite a reputation as a ladies' man."

Although Anya had heard that, in her observation it was more a case of women flirting and Jack merely being polite in return. With a pang, she remembered that real estate agent, Danica, hanging on his arm and sauntering up to her apartment with him. "Maybe he deserves it and maybe he doesn't."

"How'd it happen?"

No sense dodging again. She'd have to fill in the details eventually. "As you guessed, it was after he drove me home New Year's Eve."

"That's it?" Zora's eyes widened.

What was she expecting, a tale of seduction and intrigue? "This isn't a complicated story."

"I mean, you only did it once?" her friend clarified.

"It happens. Not everybody suffers from infertility," Anya pointed out.

Zora took a different tack. "New Year's Eve—he took advantage of you when you were drunk."

"I only had two drinks, and the attraction was mutual. Plus, I assured him I was on the Pill, which was true." Anya explained about the St. John's wort. "So I'm at least as much to blame as he is."

"Taking a silly herb doesn't make it your fault," Zora said loyally.

"It's not his fault either." Anya preferred to focus on her most pressing problem, though. "I dread telling him."

"You think he'll get mad?"

That reaction might fit Zora's soon-to-be ex-husband but not Jack. "Exactly the opposite. He loves kids with a passion." Anya paced around the room, too agitated to stand still. "What if in a weak moment I back down? I have to stand strong on adoption. One chink in my armor and I'd be boxed into a responsibility I'm not ready for."

Zora began massaging her other foot. "You should let Edmond give him the waiver."

"Who's Edmond?"

"My lawyer," Zora said. "Talk to him. He could present the whole thing to Jack from a guy's perspective."

Zora was right: a man could explain in practical terms what all this meant. And having the lawyer handle it reduced the risk of Anya caving in.

All the same, she had doubts. Breaking such important news via a third party might infuriate Jack.

"Edmond's not some old codger who'll treat me like a fallen woman, is he?"

"No, he's young and good-looking." Her friend smiled. "And he's Melissa's ex-husband. But she still recommends him as an attorney. And since he doesn't want kids himself, you should have his sympathy."

In view of Melissa's powerful desire for children, Anya understood why they were divorced. Still, he must be a skilled lawyer if she *and* Zora spoke well of him, and Anya would need an attorney to handle the adoption anyway. Might as well start now. "I'll call him tomorrow for an appointment."

"Great." Zora slid her feet into her shoes. "Go for it."

"I will." With that weight off her mind, Anya opened one of the boxes that lined the walls and set to work unpacking.

Chapter Six

Friday was a long day for Jack. He'd arrived early for surgery, then took a break for a late lunch and had barely retreated to an on-call room for a nap when he was summoned to Labor and Delivery. With an unexpectedly large number of women laboring at once, all hands were needed.

After delivering five babies, he arrived late for his patient appointments at his shared third-floor office suite and had to remind himself to slow down and give each woman the attention she deserved. But when his last scheduled patient of the day failed to arrive, relief washed through him. He phoned Rod to ask for a ride; his uncle's aging car was in the shop yet again and Rod was borrowing Jack's car.

Jack thought of the less-than-exciting weekend ahead. Patient appointments on Saturday followed by an open calendar. Well, Danica *had* invited him to join her and a group of friends for a movie Saturday night, which might be a good way to meet new people. However, it would be unfair to encourage Danica's interest while Anya's dark, skeptical eyes haunted Jack's dreams.

He'd kept his word about leaving Anya alone. When they saw each other in the O.R., she acted politely distant, and so did he.

He wasn't sure how much longer he could keep that up, though. He'd noticed she'd gone pale several times during surgery. She'd always rallied and performed her duties flawlessly, but it worried him. When he'd asked her about it between surgeries, she'd said she'd stayed up late yakking with her new housemates.

They must be having a great time, Jack thought with a touch of bitterness. Certainly he didn't wish for her to be unhappy. Well, maybe a little unhappy. He wanted her to miss him and be keenly aware that he was honoring their agreement to remain at arm's length.

He was frustrated and more than a little disappointed that she didn't seem to feel either of those things.

Rod poked his head in the staff entrance to the suite. "Ready?"

"More than." Jack gave a farewell nod to the nurse.

Ned Norwalk, RN, a blond fellow noted for his surfing prowess, glanced up anxiously from the phone. "Dr. Ryder? I'm glad you haven't left. Your patient was waiting in the wrong office. She's on her way up from the second floor now."

Rod rolled his eyes.

"How did that happen?" Jack asked.

The nurse set down the receiver. "Apparently she got confused between you and Zack Sargent. Then she forgot to check in, so they didn't realize they had our patient in their waiting room."

"Yes, Ryder and Sargent sound exactly alike, don't they?" Jack grumbled.

"It's more the Zack and Jack part," said his uncle. "Rhymes with Frick and Frack. Did you know they were a team of comic Swiss ice skaters?"

Jack ignored his uncle's riff. "You'll wait for me, right?"

Rod waggled his eyebrows. "Sure. I have some great new apps on my cell."

"Now you're playing games?" His uncle used to scorn that sort of activity.

"Just the ones for preteens." Rod hadn't given up hope of renewing contact with his daughters, although they'd heard nothing from Tiffany in the week since her surprise visit.

When Rod had called Helen, she'd declined to nag or pry

information out of her granddaughter. "Give Tiffany a little credit. She and Amber will figure something out."

After having his hopes raised, Rod wasn't about to back off completely. Instead, he was apparently channeling his energies into getting up to speed on the world of preteens.

"Have fun," Jack told him.

"I'll be in the waiting room." He sauntered off.

The patient arrived. While Ned prepped her, Jack performed breathing exercises to calm his annoyance at her delayed arrival. Every patient deserved his best.

He studied her medical records. In her early sixties, the woman had been in excellent condition during her recent annual checkup, aside from normal symptoms of menopause. She'd declined to take hormones because of concerns about cancer risks.

In the examining room, he found a trim, alert woman, her champagne-blond hair carefully styled. "It's my hot flashes," she told him. "They've started keeping me awake at night, and I practically have to carry a fan around with me. Isn't there anything you can recommend other than hormones?"

"Let's talk about dietary changes." Jack mentioned avoiding caffeine, spicy foods and alcohol, as well as stress, hot showers and hot tubs, and intense exercise. As they talked, he noted that she showed no confusion, so perhaps the office mix-up had been a simple mistake rather than a sign of the brain fog sometimes referred to as mentalpause.

"You might try soy products," he added. "Some women find them helpful."

"One of my friends recommended an herb." She consulted her notebook. "Black cohosh?"

"It has been associated with cases of liver damage, so I don't recommend it." To present more options, Jack added, "There are no studies that prove acupuncture helps, but some women like it. And on the plus side, it probably can't do any harm."

She jotted down his recommendations. "Okay. I think I'll start by cutting out the spicy Indian and Chinese food."

"You eat those a lot?"

"Three or four times a week."

Hoping that would help, Jack said goodbye to the woman and returned to the waiting room, empty save for his uncle. "Now you understand why I chose anesthesiology," Rod said, sticking his phone in his pocket. "Regular hours and limited patient contact."

"But you miss the highs," Jack pointed out. Performing surgery and delivering babies provided a thrill that never faded. He'd also learned that simple discussions, such as the one he'd just had with his patient, could result in major quality-of-life improvements.

Hot curries and Chinese food three to four times a week? He suspected that might give *him* hot flashes.

"Highs tend to be followed by lows," his uncle advised.

"It's worth it."

"Not to me."

The outer door opened. No other doctors were on duty at this hour, so somebody must be lost, Jack thought, an impression reinforced when a man in a tailored suit entered. In his early thirties, he might be a pharmaceutical rep, promoting his company's products. "Can I help you?"

"Is one of you Dr. Jack Ryder?" The fellow pushed up his glasses.

"Are you a process server?" Rod demanded. He'd been hit with a ridiculous number of summonses during his legal battles with Portia.

The man blinked. "Not exactly."

That wasn't promising. Might as well get it over with. "I'm Jack Ryder."

The man extended his hand. "Edmond Everhart, family attorney."

Reluctantly, Jack shook it. "What's this about?"

The man glanced at Rod. "Is there somewhere we can talk privately?"

Rod tipped back his fedora. "I'm his uncle and I'm staying."

Jack appreciated the support. "What's this about?" he repeated.

A thin line forming on his forehead, Everhart plucked a sheet of paper from his briefcase. "My client asked me to give this to you to sign."

That sounded ominous. "Someone's suing me?"

"No." The man's frown deepened. "She didn't discuss this with you?"

"Who?" Jack asked impatiently. "Discuss what?"

"Miss Meeks," the fellow clarified, casting a glance toward the unoccupied reception desk. "Do you have a private office? This is a very personal matter."

Rod, who had little tolerance for dithering, snatched the paper from Edmond's hand and read the heading aloud. "Waiver of parental rights." He studied Jack askance. "Do you know anything about this?"

Unbelievable. "She's pregnant? And she breaks the news with a waiver?" Taking the document, Jack confirmed that it was, indeed, a form to sign away his parental rights. "Is this how the matter is customarily handled?"

The lawyer shook his head. "No. I had the impression you were already informed."

"Obviously not." Jack stood there stiffly, fitting the pieces together. Anya's upset stomach last Sunday and her pallor during surgery—now he understood the cause. But if she was carrying his baby, why push him away? And why send a stranger with this odd request? "I don't understand why she wants me to sign this."

"Miss Meeks has requested I arrange an adoption for her child-to-be." Edmond spoke with a touch of embarrassment, and no wonder. Anya had put him in an awkward position. "When she requested I deliver this form, I assumed you'd agreed to sign it."

It wasn't like Anya to lie. However, her tendency to speak tersely meant that her words might easily be taken the wrong way, especially if she wanted them to be.

While Jack was considering that, Rod filled the silence.

"I'm surprised a lawyer would bring this in person. Isn't that what process servers are for?"

Edmond chose his words carefully. "Some of my clients seem vulnerable. I like to be sure matters are handled with tact."

Vulnerable—yes, that fit Anya. It was hardly an excuse, though. "She's been pretty damn tactless, if you ask me," he muttered.

"No kidding," Rod seconded. "It's harsh, sending a lawyer to inform my nephew that he's going to be a father. Then there's my own trauma in learning, without preamble, that I'm about to be a great-uncle. Don't I have any rights?"

"I'm afraid not." Edmond didn't crack a smile at the absurd question. To Jack, he said, "Miss Meeks strikes me as a reticent person. Perhaps she finds you intimidating."

"I don't see why. But she *has* been avoiding me." For the sake of accuracy, Jack amended that to, "Outside work. She's a scrub nurse—a surgical nurse."

A smile touched the attorney's face. "I know what a scrub nurse is. My ex-wife works in the medical field." He cleared his throat. "I recommend that you and Miss Meeks review this matter face-to-face. I can mediate if you like."

"Are you sure that you *are* the father?" Rod asked Jack. To Edmond, he said, "I had a situation where I supported my children for years before discovering I wasn't their genetic father. And then—well, no sense getting into *that* mess."

Anya had claimed to be on the Pill, Jack recalled. Not that it was infallible and not that he would blame her for a pregnancy that resulted from their mutual involvement, regardless of what contraception she did or didn't use.

But if he signed that document without a DNA test and some other fellow was the real father, it would be a mess. Although Jack doubted there was another man, Anya *had* been evasive lately. "Let's conduct a DNA test before we proceed, just to confirm."

The attorney took this in coolly. "I'm not the doctor here,

but since the baby hasn't been born yet, doesn't that require an invasive procedure?"

"Not anymore," Rod said. "Just snip, snip, snip."

"Excuse me?"

With a quelling glare at his uncle, Jack explained, "He means it's no longer necessary to perform an amniocentesis or chorionic villus sampling on a pregnant woman." Both procedures required inserting a needle into the mother and carried a small risk of miscarriage, infection or amniotic fluid leakage. "An SNP microarray procedure can be done with a simple blood test on the mother as early as the ninth week. Hence, the term *snipping.*"

"What's SNP stand for, exactly?" Edmond asked.

"You don't want to know," Rod said.

"Humor me."

"Single nucleotide polymorphism," Jack answered.

"I see." Refocusing, the attorney went on, "I suppose a DNA test isn't too much to ask, then."

Anya might not agree, Jack supposed. Well, she'd decided to give up their baby without informing him, and he had a stake in this, too. Okay, she *had* informed him via Edmond, but he suspected that was only due to a legal requirement. And if there was even the smallest chance this might not be his baby, he couldn't in good conscience sign those papers.

"Can we hire you to serve her with a demand for a DNA test?" Rod asked.

"You'll have to find another attorney." Edmond spread his hands apologetically. "I can't represent you both."

"But you can mediate for us both?" Jack challenged.

"I would recommend you bring your own attorney to any negotiations. Or a quiet conversation might be appropriate, depending on your relationship with Miss Meeks." The lawyer tilted his head sympathetically. "I'll admit, if I were you, I'd be mad about the way this information was presented, too."

Information? That was a rather impersonal way to refer

to the stunning news that Jack was going to be a father. But that was probably typical lawyer-speak.

"Try royally ticked off," Rod responded. "I'd like to tell Miss Meeks precisely what I think of her so-called reticence."

"Excuse me." From his full height, Jack peered down a few inches at his uncle. "Whose baby is this?"

"Family's family." Rod stood his ground.

"Leave Anya alone. Got it?" Jack might be furious with her, but he'd tolerate no interference. To the attorney, he said, "Thanks for stopping by."

"Sorry the news came as a surprise." As they shook hands, Edmond studied him with concern. "May I make a personal observation?"

"Knock yourself out."

"People don't always act rationally when it comes to having children," Edmond said. "I recommend communicating, listening and weighing all aspects before choosing a course of action."

"Duly noted," Jack said.

"Have a good evening." With a nod to his uncle, who didn't bother to extend a hand, Edmond exited.

Belatedly, it occurred to Jack that Ned might have overheard the discussion. However, a check of the suite showed that the nurse had departed. Also, health care workers were accustomed to keeping anything they learned at the office strictly confidential. He hoped that applied to private conversations of physicians as well as patients.

As Jack turned off the lights and locked up, his brain raced. Anya was pregnant. She was carrying a child, their child. Didn't she understand how much this mattered to him?

It would be unfair to equate her conduct with his former aunt's duplicity. But he also had the dubious example set by his mother, who viewed the world strictly in terms of herself and her selfish wishes, despite her devotion to charity work.

Case in point, when Jack had asked her to find a project where they could spend a summer together providing medical care to impoverished women and children, she'd sent him a list of websites. Then off she'd gone on her latest cause, raising funds to buy whistles so women in Haiti could summon help when attacked.

Yes, Mamie Ryder did a lot of good. But only in ways that suited her.

Rod was waiting by the side exit. "You and Anya had sex. When and where did *that* happen?"

Jack switched off the hall light. "Boundaries," he reminded his uncle.

"Don't dodge the question."

"None of your business." That seemed plain enough.

"Must have been New Year's Eve." Rod strolled beside him toward the elevators. "That would put her pregnancy at about seven weeks. Hmm. Looks like I'll be an uncle by the end of September."

"Great-uncle," Jack amended.

"I am, aren't I?"

"Rod," he began in a warning tone.

His uncle pressed the down button. "Okay. I'll shut up." About two seconds later, he said, "One more thing."

Jack narrowed his eyes.

"If you don't sign the paper and she insists on adoption, what then?" Rod asked.

"How do you feel about turning the living room into a nursery?" Jack retorted. When the elevator door opened, he stepped inside, grateful there was another person in the elevator to stifle the conversation.

He appreciated that his uncle, apparently lost in thought, barely spoke the rest of the way home. Jack hadn't meant to propose they raise the baby themselves; how could they? Yet, how could he give his child away?

Chapter Seven

Feet propped on the worn coffee table in the den, Anya skimmed her email on her phone. Her favorite department store was having a sale—how frustrating since she'd soon be shopping at The Baby Bump instead.

Beside her, Zora swore under her breath at the square she was crocheting, or trying to crochet, from a baby blanket pattern. "I keep messing this up. I wish I could call Betsy. She's the expert."

"I don't need a baby blanket," Anya reminded her.

"Who said it's for you?" her friend muttered. "It's for Harper." Nurse Harper Gladstone and her husband were expecting twins via a surrogate in June.

Lucky peered at them both from his laptop. Although the table was ostensibly part of the kitchen, it bordered the family room. "Speaking of Betsy, how're you getting along with your ex-mother-in-law, anyway? Or should I say, almost exmother-in-law?"

Safe Harbor Nursing Supervisor Betsy Raditch was, in Anya's opinion, much too nice to be the mother of the faithless Andrew. "Why do you care?"

"Zora can answer for herself," he said.

"Why do you care?" Zora echoed.

Their housemate grinned. "You guys are like a brick wall. I can't make a dent."

"That's the idea." Anya missed their old living room, where she and Zora had been able to relax without male intrusion. Also, she was too restless tonight to concentrate on her own task, reading a book.

Edmond Everhart had promised to present the waiver to Jack by the end of the week. She hadn't heard any explosions or seen flames rising from the central part of town, but neither had Edmond called or messaged to say Mission Accomplished.

Had Edmond put it off? He seemed trustworthy, although Melissa refused to discuss her ex-husband in a personal manner, which implied that he'd sinned in some major and irredeemable way. Still, Anya felt a twinge of guilt that she'd let him assume that she'd already informed Jack of the pregnancy. Although she hadn't lied, she hadn't corrected his obvious mistaken impression either.

Lucky flexed his shoulders. On his right bicep, exposed by his sleeveless T-shirt, a colorful dragon writhed. "It's Friday night. Let's throw a party."

"At the last minute?" Zora sniffed.

"Lame," Anya told him.

"We should plan a housewarming, at least," he returned, unruffled.

"Bring it up on Sunday," Zora said. All five housemates had agreed to hold weekly meetings to coordinate schedules and nip any problems in the bud.

"Fine. But you guys are way too buttoned-up," Lucky said. "Live a little."

"I thought you got enough of that lifestyle with your old roommates." Anya had heard him complain more than once about his party-hearty pals.

"They were noisy slobs," he said. "And inconsiderate when I was trying to concentrate on my thesis." He'd almost completed work on a master's degree in medical administration.

"If your thesis is so important, why are you talking to us?" Zora asked.

"I'm taking a break."

The doorbell rang. "Who could that be at eight o'clock on a Friday night?" Zora dismissed her own question when she added, "Maybe a friend of Karen's." Karen, whose longtime friends occasionally dropped by unannounced, was attending a play at South Coast Repertory with Melissa.

"I'll get it." Lucky pushed back his chair.

But Anya had a pretty good idea who it might be. "Stay there," she commanded and hurried to the front hall.

When she opened the door, there towered Jack, dark hair mussed and green eyes as hard as emeralds.

The first time she'd seen him, she'd had to catch her breath. Then she'd found out she'd been chosen to assist this brilliant surgeon with movie-star looks, and a tremor had gone through Anya's knees. In the year since then, he'd grown more handsome, more confident and more terrifying, especially when he was angry, like now.

The impulse to apologize nearly wrenched a "sorry" from her lips. She bit down so hard her teeth hurt. Okay, he had good reason to be mad, but ultimately, there was no debate. He had to sign the waiver.

She ought to warn him that they had an audience within earshot. But Anya couldn't force out the words. Guilty twinges about sending Edmond in her stead, and about taking St. John's wort, quivered through her. Or possibly that was morning-and-evening sickness.

He was waiting for her to speak first. Finally, she managed to say, "I gather you met Edmond."

"I can't believe you did that." When Jack glared, his body seemed to grow to mammoth size, like a genie released from a bottle. "How do you think I felt when a *lawyer* informed me I was going to be a father? Oh, and here, sign away your rights on the dotted line while we're at it."

"You don't have any rights. It's a legal dodge dreamed up by male legislators to oppress women." Anya had no idea if that was true—it might have been a court ruling. But the point was the same.

"You think I'd dismiss having a child that lightly?" he demanded.

"Think about the alternative," she retorted. "Have you

ever raised a baby? I helped raise three of them. They stole my adolescence. That was enough."

"I didn't realize it was such a burden." Her anecdotes about her sisters, which she'd shared in bits and pieces during their operating room discussions, had often been humorous.

"They're sweethearts," Anya conceded. "But when they were little, I used to cry myself to sleep thinking about the stacks of diapers and the endless chores around the house."

Jack's manner softened slightly. "I can imagine that colored your assumptions rather darkly. But you're not an adolescent and we aren't discussing your sisters."

"To me, adoption is the only reasonable choice," she told him.

"We're having a child," he replied quietly. "This is not something you just throw away."

Providing a child with an adoring family hardly constituted throwing it away. But that wasn't the point. "What's your assumption—that I'll raise it because you say so?" Anya asked. "That I'll be a robot you can order around for the next twenty years?" She'd lived through that experience already. Once was enough.

"Of course not." Jack shifted uncomfortably. "How about inviting me in?"

Because there was nothing to be gained by rudeness, she moved aside. As he entered, Jack peered around and gravitated to the now-empty living room. Good. All the same, their voices could carry.

"I should warn you…" she began.

He took up a stance in front of the curio cabinet. "I won't sign the waiver until I'm sure the baby is mine."

His statement drove all other considerations from Anya's mind. "You think I sleep around?"

"I didn't mean that." Jack stuck his hands in his pockets. "But I'd like confirmation."

"Don't be ridiculous."

"It's a simple blood test," he said.

"You have incredible nerve!" Her earlier hesitation evaporated in the face of this insult.

"Then my consent will have to wait until after the baby's born so we can test it on its own." His level tone proved just as maddening as his outrageous demand.

"I can't wait that long. I need to choose an adoptive family who'll pay my bills." The attorney had explained that it was customary for the adopting parents to pay expenses related to the pregnancy, such as medical care, maternity clothing and other necessities.

"I'll pay your bills," Jack told her.

"I don't want your money!" Accepting his support would put her completely at his mercy.

Even though his hands were in his pockets, she could see them form into fists. "Why do you refuse to acknowledge that I have a stake in this pregnancy?"

"Because any stake you have is nothing compared to…" Anya broke off because her stomach was in full rebellion. *Please don't let me throw up in Karen's living room.* Losing her balance, she grabbed an end table, an unfortunate choice. The thing wobbled and then tipped, sending her and a lamp crashing to the floor.

"Anya!" Jack rushed to catch her, too late to prevent a painful bump on her hip. Still, his strong arms prevented any further tumbling.

Had she broken Karen's lamp? Mercifully, it appeared intact on the carpet.

Footsteps thudded. Around the corner rushed Zora and Lucky, colliding by the stairs. "Back off, you big oaf!" Darting under his arm, Zora hurried forward.

Lucky stayed in place, surveying the scene. "I guess this answers the question of who the dad is."

Jack's lip curled. "You told them you were pregnant before you told me?"

"It slipped out." Anya wiggled free from his grasp. Her stomach had subsided, thank goodness, but her temper hadn't. "You see what I have to go through? My tummy hurts, my feet hurt and I can't imagine how I'll feel when I'm as big as this house."

Zora helped her up, with Jack taking the other side and assisting her to the couch. "Men have it easy," her friend added.

"He wants me to take a DNA test," Anya said.

"She hired a lawyer to break the news to me," Jack defended himself to their audience of two.

"Pretty cold," Lucky agreed from across the room. "Seriously, Anya, a lawyer?"

"I can't believe you're taking his side." Zora straightened the table while Jack gingerly lifted the lamp. "Or maybe I should expect that. After all, guys stick together, don't they?"

"There are no sides," Jack said. "I'm here to help Anya, not hurt her. But getting back to our topic, how else can I declare legally that I'm the father? I'm not her husband or even her steady boyfriend. If I sign those papers without proof that I'm the father, I could be guilty of defrauding the adoptive parents. If some other guy shows up later and claims paternity, it would be a painful mess."

Judging by Lucky's nods, that argument must make sense from a male perspective. Anya was insulted all over again. However, much as she resented Jack's attitude, the alternative—waiting until she gave birth before choosing adoptive parents—was unacceptable. "If I take a DNA test, you'll relinquish your rights?"

That stopped him briefly. "I'll consider it."

"Not good enough."

"Once the baby's born, he can get a court order for the test," Lucky reminded her.

"What kind of judge would let him stick a needle in a helpless baby?" Zora flared.

"All newborns have a few drops taken from their heels to screen for serious medical conditions," Jack informed her. "It's no big deal."

The discussion swirled around Anya as if she weren't there or weren't the primary person carrying this baby. It reminded her unhappily of her family's behavior at Christmas as they discussed why she ought to move back to Colorado.

Suddenly queasy again, she gripped the arm of the couch. No one had bothered to ask if she'd like a cup of tea or anything else.

That gave her an idea.

FRUSTRATED, JACK wondered how to penetrate the guard Anya had raised around herself. He'd stated his case, including his willingness to support her. Now he had to deal with her roommate fluttering around, raising objections. Thank goodness the male nurse had grasped his point. The guy was improving on closer acquaintance.

Jack's request was perfectly rational, and Anya would realize that if she weren't so—well, not irrational but far from completely objective. Pregnancy hormones were well known to affect moods.

Stop thinking like a doctor, and pay attention. What was it that lawyer had recommended? Oh, yes, communicating, listening and weighing all aspects.

Focusing on Anya, Jack saw that she'd gone pale again and was hanging on to the arm of the couch. "You obviously feel lousy," he said. "Should I get a basin?"

Her chin came up. Although he wished she were less stubborn, he admired her spirit.

"Ice cream," she told him. "Lucky ate the last of it earlier."

"There was only one scoop," protested her housemate from his post by the stairs.

"Two scoops. The one in your bowl and the one you ate standing over the sink," Zora corrected. "Lucky should go out for more."

"Jack can do it." Resolve strengthened Anya's words. "If I have to go through this, you shouldn't get off scot-free. It's only fair that you share some of the burden."

"You mean earn the right to a DNA test?" he asked drily.

"I wouldn't exactly put it that way," Anya said, "but you should be willing to help out."

"I can make grocery runs." He nodded. "What else?"

"Foot massages would be nice." She regarded him as if testing the waters.

That might be fun. "I'm happy to." And after the stories she'd told him about the work she'd done for her sisters and mother, Jack supposed it was about time someone—namely, him—did the same for her. "Sure, bring it on. Whatever you need."

"My favorite flavor is butterscotch," Lucky said.

"Chocolate," Zora put in.

"Take a hike," Anya told them both. "It's vanilla with caramel ripples."

"Hold on." Jack had no intention of becoming the household puppet. "I'm helping Anya and only Anya. But how long before you take the blood test?"

"You're the doctor," she said. "How soon is it feasible?"

That would be at about nine weeks. "Rough estimate, two weeks from now. Do we have a deal?"

"Maybe." To the others, she said, "This is between Jack and me, guys."

With a shrug, Lucky retreated. Zora wrinkled her nose, but she, too, departed.

Sitting beside Anya and taking her hands in his, Jack found them unexpectedly warm. Blood volume increased during pregnancy by as much as 50 percent, but mostly in the later stages.

You're thinking like a doctor again.

"Let's agree on terms," he said.

"Terms?"

No sense risking a misunderstanding. "If I do as you ask, do you promise to take the test as soon as your OB approves?"

"Yes. And then you promise to sign the paper," she countered.

Jack's chest squeezed. He remembered Tiffany and Amber as toddlers, running to him with hugs and butterfly kisses, playing horse by climbing onto his back and tumbling off with shrieks of glee.

But that wasn't the same as being a single father. Parenthood was a commitment that should take priority over everything else. How could Jack meet the child's emotional and practical needs while building his medical practice and paying off educational loans? It would be different if Anya were willing to participate, but alone, how could he provide the kind of loving, attentive home this little one deserved? As much as it hurt, he couldn't.

"If you're still absolutely determined to seek adoption at that time, I'll sign."

"Define *absolutely*."

Her response startled a chuckle from him. "You missed your calling. You should have been a lawyer."

"Don't change the subject." She left her hands in his.

"You have to be willing to discuss the issue frankly," Jack said. "No avoidance."

"That's my survival strategy," she protested. "Duck and run."

"Like hiring an attorney to break the news to me."

She flushed. "Sorry about that."

"So you agree to be straight with me about adoption? If your feelings change, I have a right to know."

Slowly, Anya nodded. "Okay, after we get the results of the DNA test, I'll think it over carefully. But if you fail your part and don't take care of me to my satisfaction, you'll sign after two weeks *without* a DNA test. Because if you won't even inconvenience yourself that much, you have no business insisting I raise a child."

"*Help* raise a child."

"Mothers do two-thirds of the work even under the best of circumstances."

"It depends on the father, but let's stay on topic." Although tempted to demand an objective standard for judging his cooperation, Jack had to admit that would be difficult. And he didn't believe Anya intended to cheat him. He'd already insulted her enough by requiring a DNA test to confirm his paternity. However, he still had to be clear about this bargain they were striking. "I'll let you decide whether I've kept my part of the bargain, but your demands have to be reasonable."

"Define…"

"…*reasonable,*" he finished for her. "No jerking me around."

"Such as?" she demanded.

"No phoning in the middle of the night for something minor like rubbing your feet, unless you allow me to move in with you." Jack hadn't been angling for any such thing, but now that he thought about it…

"That won't be necessary," she said quickly. "What else?"

"No interrupting my work unless it's an emergency."

"Of course not." Anya regarded him indignantly. "I'd never interfere with patient care. Even if I keel over during surgery, you keep at it. Somebody else can cart me off."

"We'll see." Jack hoped nothing like that would happen. "Have we covered everything?"

"I guess so." Anya released a long breath.

He transferred her right hand into his and shook it. "Done. Jack Ryder agrees to approximately two weeks of catering to Anya Meeks's pregnancy-related needs. In return for which she agrees to take a DNA test."

"And then he agrees to sign the relinquishment."

"If she's still set on adoption," he concluded. "Can we stop referring to ourselves in the third person now?"

She chuckled. "This is a funny bargain."

It felt strange to Jack, too—but rather pleasant. "As long as we're both satisfied, I deem these negotiations successful."

"You actually listened to me," she said with a touch of wonder.

"That surprises you?" He hadn't meant to ride roughshod over her in the past.

"It's not what I'm used to." She tilted her head. "What now?"

"Vanilla," he said, rising.

"With caramel ripples. Better get extra," she warned. "My roommates are a hungry lot."

"Anything else you need at the store?" Jack asked. "Fresh vegetables? Yogurt? Milk?"

A few minutes later, shopping list in hand, he decamped. Darkness had fallen over the marsh, punctuated by chirps and whirring noises above the thrum of the ocean. A sea breeze had eased the rotten egg smell, and a pale winter moon hung low in the sky.

Jack's instincts warned that by agreeing to sign the waiver, he was embarking on a path that would affect him for the rest of his life. Until now, in many ways, he'd been in control of his destiny, or he'd imagined he was.

Not anymore.

The idea of losing his child, knowing those special moments and precious photos would belong to another family, nearly made him rush inside to retract his offer. Yet these days, birth parents weren't necessarily kept in total ignorance of their child's well-being. The right parents could notify him and Anya about the baby's health and progress. He'd know for certain that his child was loved and happy.

A lump formed in Jack's throat. He'd never expected to face such a difficult situation. And not only in regard to the baby.

The sight of Anya stumbling, flailing in vain for a grip and falling, had wrenched at him. She was in this vulnerable state partly because of his actions.

Fortunately, there was an upside to their pact. Although he couldn't be here every minute to catch her, their agreement meant he didn't have to keep his distance either.

His spirits rising, Jack set out for the market.

"At the very minimum, as that Edmond fellow recommended, you ought to hire your own lawyer."

Jack shook his head. "That risks turning this into a battle."

"There's nothing wrong with protecting your rights." Rod's phone sounded. "Now who could that be? Probably another salesman for solar panels."

In Jack's hand, his phone also beeped. "I hope this isn't a citywide emergency." He checked the readout. "Nope, it's Anya."

Rod had vanished into the kitchen. Good.

"Hey," Jack said into his phone. "What can I do for you?"

"You don't have to be at Labor and Delivery until 8:00 p.m., right?" she said.

"Yup. And I'm ready for action." He'd been almost disappointed at the lack of a request yesterday.

"We're having our weekly house conference at four," Anya said. "It was supposed to be after dinner, but it got moved up. Anyway, I forgot I'd promised to bring a snack, and I'm kind of tired. I wondered if you were willing to run out to the store again."

This was exactly the kind of thing Jack had volunteered for. "Glad to. What kind of snacks did you have in mind?"

"Chips and dip will be fine."

"No problem." It was almost three now. Jack had plenty of time to swing by the Suncrest Market.

"You can just drop the stuff off," Anya added.

Eager to get rid of him, was she? He'd see about that. "Sure."

As they ended the call, Jack was already figuring out a healthier alternative to chips and dip. He might not be able to raise his child, but he could provide a healthy start for him or her. Celery sticks with cheese or peanut butter, perhaps. Or fruit would be excellent.

"Good news!" Rod reappeared, grinning. "That was Helen. The girls are arriving next weekend for a three-day visit."

"Great." It was too early in the year for spring break, Jack noted. "What's the occasion?"

"A week from Monday is Presidents' Day, and there's no school. The kids've been nagging hard, I gather, and their parents caved." Rubbing his palms together, Rod added, "Helen liked my idea that they volunteer at the animal shelter on Saturday."

"Where they'll run into you," Jack said.

"Purely by chance," his uncle tossed off blithely. "I'll bet we can think of other ways for them to stumble across me, too."

"You bet—as soon as I get back." Sticking his phone in his pocket, Jack explained about the errand.

"Just one sec." From the hat tree that held his assortment of toppers, Rod selected a gray fedora.

"You're coming with me?" That might not be the best idea, in light of Rod's attitude.

The older man tipped his hat by way of an answer.

"No digs at Anya," Jack ordered.

"I'll be on my best behavior," his uncle answered easily.

Jack didn't find that statement reassuring. "Exactly what constitutes your best behavior?"

"I'm there for your protection," his uncle said. "In case you haven't noticed, it's not safe for you to be alone with those people."

"We work with those people," Jack reminded him.

"Different context." Rod pocketed his keys from the side table. "What's on the menu?"

"Celery and…hmm." An idea occurred to Jack that might let him stick around for the house conference. He'd love to hear what those folks were up to.

It was worth a try.

ANYA'S HOUSEMATES STARTED wandering into the den at a quarter to four. From the kitchen, Karen called out that there was hot apple cider with cinnamon sticks. "Help yourselves."

"Jack should be here any minute." Anya felt a little guilty about passing her responsibility to him, even though he deserved it after his ridiculous demand for a DNA test.

"Let's get started," Lucky said once they'd filled their mugs with steaming, aromatic cider. "We're all here, and we can take a break when the food arrives."

Their first item was a disagreement about the kitchen. Karen and Melissa preferred that all dirty plates, cups and tableware be placed immediately in the dishwasher. Zora and Anya were accustomed to accumulating items in the sink between meals.

"It's more efficient than having to open the dishwasher a dozen times a day," Zora said.

"Except someone else might need to use the sink," Melissa pointed out. "I had to put away your coffee cups this morning so I could bake muffins."

Anya had enjoyed the blueberry muffin Melissa had shared with her. "I guess that's reasonable."

Zora shrugged. "Okay. It isn't a big deal to me."

Lucky had stayed out of this one, Anya was glad to see. She'd been concerned that he might try to boss the women around, but it appeared he'd learned better. Or perhaps he simply didn't care about this particular matter.

"Next item." Karen tapped her list. "Do we each stock our own toilet paper, or should we purchase it in bulk? And what about paper towels? We can't very well have separate rolls for each of us."

Before anyone could answer, the doorbell rang. Anya rose quickly. "That should be for me."

As soon as she opened the door, a green T-shirt stretched across Jack's muscular chest dominated her field of vision. Next, she noticed the well-filled grocery sacks he carried on each side, while, behind him, Rod Vintner's arms encircled a third bag.

She stepped out of their path. "You didn't have to buy out the store."

"I figured this late in the day, we might as well bring dinner." Jack moved past her into the family room. "Don't let me interrupt," she heard him announce. "We brought cold cuts and bread for sandwiches. I'll set these out in the kitchen."

Anya found herself face-to-face with Rod. His flicker of reproach vanished so fast she wondered if she'd misinterpreted it.

"Tiffany and Amber are visiting next weekend," he said in a mild tone. "I'm sure your suggestion helped. Thanks."

"I'd love to see them." From the way he lingered in the entryway, she sensed he had more to say. "What?"

His gaze dropped to her abdomen. "Congratulations." The curl of his lip indicated she *hadn't* mistaken his reaction to her.

"Don't start on me," Anya warned.

Rod gave a jerk of surprise. "What did I say?"

"It's what you were thinking." No doubt this man who'd lost all rights to his daughters held a strong opinion about the future of his great-niece or nephew.

"Now you're a mind reader?" The man feigned innocence about as effectively as a toddler with chocolate smeared on his face and a plundered cookie jar behind him.

"Yes," Anya said. "Watch it."

At the hospital, he might be a lordly doctor. Well, semi-lordly; anesthesiologists didn't have the same cachet as surgeons. But in *her* house, he'd better behave like a good guest.

After a tense moment, Rod yielded. "My nephew would agree."

"He's a wise man."

She rejoined her housemates in the den. After greeting the small assembly, Rod trailed Jack into the kitchen.

Anya sneaked a glance at Lucky, half expecting him to complain about the intruders. Instead, he leaned back with a satisfied air. *Oh, right.* It was his week to cook, and they were relieving him of the duty.

The roommates returned to the topic of paper goods, agreeing it would be sensible to pool their money and buy in bulk. Karen promised to set up a kitty to which they would all contribute each month.

During the discussion, Anya remained keenly aware of Jack's quiet presence as he set a series of platters—breads, cheeses, sliced meats—on the table. He'd gone to a lot of trouble.

The others wrapped up the meeting quickly, no doubt enticed by the sight and smell of food. Rod seemed to take pride in arranging a stack of pastries pyramid-style on a plate. "No meal is complete without dessert," he informed the residents as they poured in from the den.

Anya decided against reminding Jack he was supposed to drop off the snacks and then depart. That would be ungracious. Besides, her housemates were clearly relishing the treat.

From a cabinet, Karen took a stack of plates. "There's plenty of apple cider left if you doctors would like some."

"I've seen you at the hospital but we haven't been formally introduced," Rod said to Karen. "I'm Rod Vintner."

She smiled. "Karen Wiggins. I've seen you, too." Her pleased expression hinted at an attraction.

Rod beamed right back at her. "You do such interesting things with your hair. I liked the dark color with the pink stripe, but this reddish-blond is nice, too."

"It's called strawberry." She stood in the middle of the kitchen, unaware that everyone else was waiting for her to set down the plates.

"Why don't we eat in the dining room?" Melissa asked. "The table's larger."

Her words stirred Karen into action. "Great idea."

"I'll bring the silverware." Lucky lifted the entire organizer from a drawer.

"We can use the kitchen table as a serving buffet," Zora added.

Everyone pitched in. Jack gravitated to Anya's side. "I get why you moved here. It's like being part of a big family."

No, because they aren't ordering me around. "It's better than a family," she said softly. "We respect each other."

"Don't families do that?" Jack murmured. "Good ones do, surely."

"I suppose." Because no one appeared to be listening at

the moment, she added, "Jack, this whole setup—I wasn't expecting you to bring dinner."

"The surprise is half the fun." He snagged a plate from the pile Karen had set down. "Can I fill this for you?"

It felt weird, having someone offer to wait on her. Weird, but nice. Too nice. "Thanks, but I'm not an invalid."

"Understood." Jack handed her the plate and stood back to let her serve herself. Both he and his uncle were in good spirits. They might not have been invited, but she was glad now that they'd joined the group for dinner.

In the dining room, Karen opened the curtains. Late-afternoon sunlight played over the backyard—the brick patio, the lawn and the plot of cool-weather vegetables. Around the perimeter, bougainvillea, honeysuckle and climbing roses obscured the fence with a wealth of pink and orange blossoms. Beyond them stretched the marsh with its subtle shadings of brown and gold.

"It's beautiful here." Rod gazed out admiringly. "There's only one drawback."

"The smell?" Karen said.

He tilted his head in agreement. "You must get used to it."

"Yes. I grew up here," she said. "And I'm grateful for this full house so I can afford to stay."

The seven of them took seats around the oak table, which Melissa and Zora had set with place mats. Jack wound up between Lucky and Melissa, which should have pleased Anya, but she missed him. She was wedged between Rod and Karen, who talked over and around her.

That felt familiar.

A smile played across Jack's face as he observed his uncle and Karen. Anya shared his pleasure at seeing sparks ignite between the couple.

She'd moved here to put distance between her and Jack. It didn't seem to be working out that way.

At the moment, though, she was rather enjoying the warm feelings she had when he was near and the sound of Jack's laughter at a remark of Lucky's. Her cheese-mustard-and-sprouts sandwich was delicious, too. A woman could get used to being coddled.

During a pause in the conversation, Rod remarked, "You folks ought to throw a housewarming party."

On Anya's other side, Karen said, "What a great idea!"

"I was going to propose that at the meeting," Lucky said. "Thanks for reminding me."

They settled on a barbecue next Saturday afternoon, with each of the residents preparing a dish and guests bringing desserts. For entertainment, they would play croquet on the lawn and set up board games in the den and living room.

"My daughters will be here from San Diego," Rod told Karen. "As long as they're in town, is it all right to invite them and their grandmother?"

"Of course!" She looked as delighted as if he'd offered to bring the cast of her favorite TV show. "How old are they?"

"Ten and twelve," Rod said.

Anya figured they'd enjoy the party more if they had a role to play. "They could dress up as waitresses—wear frilly aprons and serve hors d'oeuvres."

"How adorable," Zora said.

"Anya's good with kids," Lucky noted. "She could supervise the hostess brigade."

"She's *great* with kids," Jack affirmed. "Tiffany's crazy about her."

Their praise flowed over Anya like perfumed lotion. And being around girls that age would be more like play than work. "Sure, I can do that."

"Who else shall we invite?" Karen asked. "Let's make a list."

After they'd drawn up the names of coworkers and friends they wanted to invite, Rod asked Karen for a tour of the house. "This is my dream home," he added.

"I'd be happy to show you around."

Lucky cleared his throat. "Not to rely on stereotypes about rich doctors, but I would have assumed you'd have a place of your own by now."

"Long story." Rod helped Karen from her chair. "I'll tell you while we walk, if that's okay." He'd cut Lucky out of the explanation, which served the guy right, in Anya's opinion.

Lucky accepted the situation with good grace. "Since it was my turn to cook and you guys saved me the trouble, I'll clean up."

"I can help," Zora said. When the others stared at her in surprise, she added, "He's always accusing me of shirking my share of the work. I'm just proving him wrong."

"I do not," Lucky protested as he arose.

"Yes, you have, several times," Anya told him.

"Really?"

"I'll help, too," Melissa said. "It's dangerous to leave you two alone. There might soon be chalk-marked bodies on the kitchen floor."

Rod and Karen sauntered into the living room. Jack followed, so Anya went along, too.

"That's quite a collection." Rod examined the colorful plates in the curio cabinet, each bearing the design of a different geographic location. "You must love to travel."

"Most of these belonged to my mother, from when she was younger." Karen's voice thinned. "I did love to travel with her, but my ex-husband broke most of my plates that I bought on our trips."

"That's awful!" Anya had heard that her friend was divorced, but she didn't know any of the details.

"He was a nasty— Well, I'd rather not use an ugly word." Karen hugged herself, a movement that emphasized her slender figure.

"I'm sorry." Rod touched her shoulder lightly. "I didn't mean to bring up bad memories."

Karen moved toward the stairs. "We've been divorced for ten years. It's old news."

"My wife left me six years ago," Rod told her as they climbed, his voice drifting back to Anya. "She was a nasty piece of business herself."

"He isn't exaggerating," Jack said from beside her. "I can vouch for that."

Anya poked him in the ribs. When he swung toward her questioningly, she indicated the older couple, who'd reached the second-floor landing. "They could use some privacy," she murmured.

He gave her a conspiratorial wink.

While Rod and Karen ambled left toward the master suite, Anya detained Jack in the wide upstairs hall. "That's Safe Harbor in the 1930s." She indicated a sepia-toned photo of bare bluffs overlooking a harbor smaller than its present formation, with a scattering of vacation cottages where shops, a hotel and restaurants now stood. "Karen says it was dredged and enlarged later."

His gaze dropped to the purple couch from Anya and Zora's apartment. "I'm glad to see you guys were able to haul that sofa up here in one piece."

"If you notice any blistered paint, it's from Lucky's cursing." Keenly aware of being alone with him, Anya fought the impulse to draw closer to his warmth. Chattering more than usual to fill the void, she said, "He doesn't even use it, since his room's downstairs."

"Being on this floor with three other women must be like living in a dorm," Jack mused.

It isn't all women right now. Ignoring her mental digression, she said, "I never lived on campus. I'll bet it's fun."

"It is. Almost everyone lives on campus at Vanderbilt."

He'd mentioned before how much he'd enjoyed the excellent premed and medical training in Nashville. However, there was one question he hadn't answered. "Why did you decide to become a doctor?" Anya asked. "Was it Rod's influence?"

"Partly. If not for him, I'm not sure I'd have believed it was possible. But that wasn't the main reason." Jack's expression grew thoughtful. "My mother told me once that my dad had longed to be a doctor but couldn't afford medical school. He turned to firefighting instead as another way to help people. He died after re-entering a burning apartment building to find an elderly woman who was still missing. The roof collapsed on him."

Anya touched his arm. "What a terrible loss."

"That's the risk firefighters accept."

"What happened to the woman?"

Jack shook his head ruefully. "Turned out she wasn't even there."

She searched for a more pleasant subject. "Why'd you go so far away to medical school? I mean, being a California resident, it would have been cheaper to go to a UC campus, and they're world-class."

"I wanted to experience a different part of the country and a different climate." Jack stroked the back of her hand, which still rested on his arm. "Since I won a partial scholarship, the cost was comparable to in-state tuition, and Vanderbilt has an outstanding program."

"Lucky you." His caress quivered through her. "I'd hoped to pursue a master's degree to become a nurse practitioner." In rural communities and inner-city areas that lacked doctors, nurse practitioners often provided vital primary care to infants, children, adults and the elderly, which had originally been her plan. "But without a grant, I had to stop at my RN."

"Why'd you decide to become a scrub nurse?" He watched her with keen interest. Not just making idle conversation, Anya realized.

Being the center of his attention felt wonderful; it showed that she mattered to him. "I got a job at a hospital and started helping in the O.R. The more surgeries I assisted with, the more I loved it. I developed my skills on the job."

"So you found your true calling more or less by chance," Jack said. "Maybe not getting a grant was a lucky break."

Anya laughed. "I never thought of it that way."

He indicated the three bedroom doorways. "Which one's yours?"

"Back corner."

"I'll bet it has a great view."

Taking the hint, she led him into the room. "Ignore the

mess, okay?" She'd left a stack of clean laundry on the bed to be folded.

"You consider this a mess? I like what you've done with the room. It's nice." Hardly high praise, but then, her plain, inexpensive furnishings didn't merit compliments.

She found Jack's nearness even more enticing in these intimate quarters. Everything about him appealed to her, from the chest-hugging T-shirt to the light in his green eyes.

Longing shimmered through Anya. As a diversion, she hurried to the window. "It's especially pretty at sunset."

"It sure is." Jack came to stand close to her, not quite touching, and the air heated between them. His arm circled her waist, drawing her close.

Anya relaxed against him. Jack turned her toward him and touched his lips to hers, and the longing that rushed through her underscored how much she'd missed him.

Pleasure tingled through Anya as she stroked his thick dark hair. New Year's Eve hadn't been a tipsy aberration. She'd longed for him from the moment they met. And now she longed for more.

As they eased away from the window, they bumped into a small table. Wrenched from her reverie, Anya grabbed the small plant rocking on its drip plate. "Oh, no!"

Jack barely glanced at the African violet. "No harm done. It was nearly dead anyway."

"That's what's so awful." She stared in dismay at Paula. Robust and blooming a week ago, the plant now drooped in its pot. "I can't believe it's in such bad shape. I didn't even notice."

"You said you expected to kill it," he reminded her, his cheek against her hair.

Anya tried to figure out what she'd done wrong. "I must have overwatered it. I was afraid it would dry out, away from the bathroom."

"It'll recover."

"Are you kidding? It's a goner." Guilt flooded Anya as she fingered a wilted leaf. If she couldn't care for a plant, how could anyone expect her to raise a child? Not that she planned to. "I hope it isn't suffering."

Jack released her with a sigh. "I'm sorry the plant is so upsetting. I should have given you a silk one."

"Would you throw her away for me?" She couldn't bear to dump poor little Paula in the trash.

"No problem." Lifting the plant and drip pan, he bore them from the room and she followed.

Belatedly, Anya reflected that she'd spoiled their tender moment. But that was just as well. What if someone had walked in on them? Worse, what if someone *hadn't* walked in on them?

In the hall, Rod and Karen were talking earnestly on the couch. They broke off as Anya and Jack approached. "Good tour?" Rod asked Jack.

"The best."

His uncle studied the plant. "You have quite an effect on growing things."

"One scowl and it withered away," Jack said cheerfully.

As they descended the stairs, Anya heard Karen and Rod's conversation shift to next weekend's housewarming party. Karen was bubbling with enthusiasm about meeting Rod's daughters, and he had a new lilt to his voice.

If she hadn't insisted that Jack wait on her, he and Rod wouldn't have been here tonight, Anya thought. For Karen's sake, she was glad they'd come. But talking about her dreams and witnessing Jack's sadness about his father had made her even more vulnerable to him. She'd nearly welcomed him into her bed all over again.

If not for the baby, she'd love to spend more time with Jack. But she remembered she'd too often acquiesced to her family even as an inner voice warned that it was a mistake. She had to listen to that voice this time. She wasn't ready to be a mother. Her spirit rebelled at the prospect of taking on the responsibilities—the fears, the worries, the inadequacies— she'd only recently escaped. And with that frame of mind, she'd be a poor mother anyway.

As she reached the ground floor ahead of Jack, Anya's hand drifted to her abdomen. Startled, she snatched it away.

She couldn't do anything about work or next weekend's party, but aside from that, she would stop requesting Jack's assistance. The less time they spent alone together, the safer she'd be.

Chapter Nine

Jack hefted his tray and surveyed the nearly full hospital cafeteria. Tables outside on the patio, warmed by heat lamps in the brisk February afternoon, sat empty. Inside, he spotted several tables occupied by his fellow surgeons and other specialists, including Rod.

So he couldn't claim that there was nowhere else to sit, but then, he didn't require an excuse. *Just march over there and plunk yourself down.*

Aware that he was breaching an unwritten rule of cafeteria etiquette, he navigated the maze of tables to join Anya and three of her housemates. "Hope this chair isn't taken," he said and sat beside her.

Whatever she'd been discussing with Lucky, Melissa and Karen, the conversation died. No sign of Zora. Probably had an ultrasound to perform.

From his tray, Jack handed Anya a small salad. "That's yours."

"I didn't ask for anything," she said rather ungraciously.

It was Thursday and she hadn't made a single request since last weekend. "It's my job to take care of you. You should eat more vegetables."

Melissa nodded wordlessly. He'd scored points with someone.

"Well, thanks." Anya poked a cherry tomato with her fork. "How'd you know I like ranch dressing?"

"Who doesn't?" Jack responded.

"I had you figured wrong," Lucky observed.

"Oh?" While Jack wasn't keen on conversing with the fellow, he could hardly avoid it. Especially because he'd invited himself to their table.

"I took you for a stuck-up talks-only-to-God surgeon," the tattooed nurse responded.

Jack didn't bother to ask what he'd done to deserve such an assessment. "I condescend to mingle with the masses occasionally."

Karen brushed crumbs from her blouse. "You have to drop this reverse snobbery if you plan to be an administrator, Lucky."

"Is that your goal?" Jack tackled his teriyaki chicken with an appetite stoked by a long morning in the O.R.

"He's earning a master's in administration," Melissa explained.

"I graduate this summer."

Lucky's air of pride was deserved, Jack acknowledged. "Then what?"

"Then I hope a suitable position opens up here at Safe Harbor."

"Otherwise he might have to move," Karen noted.

"Good luck." *Enough about him.* Jack turned to Anya. "While we're on the subject of Saturday's housewarming party…"

"We aren't." She started eating the salad.

"Give Jack a break," Karen said.

Had Karen always been a sympathetic soul or only since her new friendship with Rod? In any case, Jack appreciated the support.

Anya waved her fork. "You're right. Jack, what were you about to say?"

He dredged up the excuse for barging in he'd decided on earlier. "That was a great idea you had about the girls acting as servers, Anya. I heard the thrift store rents costumes, so I swung by there and reserved two cute waitress outfits. I can pick them up tomorrow."

Anya's nose scrunched. "Might be awkward."

"Why?"

"Didn't Rod tell you?" Karen asked. "Our boss, Jan, and her husband are bringing their daughters, too."

"They're nine and ten," Melissa put in.

Jack adjusted his plans in a flash. "I'll rent extra costumes. They had more, and as for the sizes, it shouldn't matter if they're a bit loose."

"Especially if there are apron strings we can tighten," Karen said.

"I'll make sure of it."

"You'd be a great dad," Melissa said. Catching the dismay on Anya's face, Melissa raised her hands apologetically. "I just find Jack's attitude refreshing. My ex-husband hated the idea of parenthood. I wasn't keen on it, either, at first, but working in the fertility field, being around babies, I developed this intense desire. More than a desire—a conviction that having children is why I was put on this earth."

"And he didn't stand by you?" Jack found it hard to imagine a man abandoning his wife on such a fundamental level.

"He went out and had a vasectomy without telling me." Melissa's classic features tightened into an angry mask.

Abruptly, Jack made the connection: the attorney who'd brought the waiver to him was Edmond Everhart—same last name. He'd seemed a decent enough guy, but to Melissa, an action like that must have been tantamount to a betrayal. And once a person betrayed your trust, Jack didn't see how they could regain it.

"When I was in my twenties, I'd have liked to have been a mother," Karen said wistfully. "Then my ex's drinking got out of control. Even if you divorce, children bring all kinds of legal and emotional ties to the other person. I couldn't bear being yoked to that man for life."

"Wow, this is a heavy discussion," Lucky said.

"Does it make you uncomfortable?" Jack teased.

"What are you, a psychologist?"

"He sounds like one sometimes," Anya said. "In a good way."

Jack chuckled, surprised by her response. "Glad you think so."

"Well, you deserve a compliment now and then." She indicated her empty salad plate. "It was kind of you to bring this."

"Uh-oh, better watch out for knives in your back, Anya." Melissa indicated a nearby table where a couple of young nurses were glaring in their direction.

"What's their problem?" Jack asked.

"You didn't see them eyeing you and toying with their hair?" Karen asked. "I was afraid that leggy one was going to trip you when you walked by her."

Jack frowned. Why would a nurse trip him?

"She means they were flirting." Lucky blew out his frustration. "Man, the rest of us guys kill ourselves trying to get that kind of response, and you don't even notice."

"I have more important things on my mind."

Lucky turned to Melissa. "Speaking of more important things, what's on Saturday's menu?"

"It's my week to cook, which puts me in charge of the meal planning," she explained to Jack. "We're barbecuing burgers and hot dogs. Veggie burgers, too, for Lucky. You guys are fixing the side dishes."

"Pasta salad," Karen volunteered.

"Fruit." Anya left it at that.

"Green salad." Lucky gazed around the table. "We're short one person. What's Zora bringing?"

"Something," Anya said.

Jack laughed. Now that he was growing accustomed to her terseness, he rather liked it. Especially when it came at someone else's expense.

A clatter of dishes signified the departure of the nurses at the other table. One rolled her eyes at him, as if questioning his judgment. The leggy one pointedly ignored him.

He hoped none of them were invited to the party. It would be a lot more fun without their ridiculous tactics.

Too bad he couldn't get the same kind of attention from the one person he really wanted to receive it from.

"THEY'RE SO CUTE!"

"How darling!"

"I want to put it on right now!"

Four little girls swirled around Anya in the den, holding up lacy white aprons and caps, shiny black under dresses and frilly white socks. Tiffany, the oldest, seemed as entranced by the notion of playing dress-up as did her ten-year-old sister, Amber. With their red braids and freckles, the two were a matched set, save for height.

No such hesitancy came from stepsisters Kimmie and Berry Sargent. They looked nothing alike—nine-year-old Kimmie had elfin features, whereas Berry was tall for her ten years, with a smooth dark complexion inherited from her late mother. Anya had heard that Berry's stepfather, Zack Sargent, had been raising her as a single dad when he re-encountered his first love, Jan, and they'd blended their families.

The girlish chatter reminded Anya of the special moments when her triplet sisters used to rush to her with their joys and concerns. Supervising them hadn't been *all* hard work and feeling trapped. She was proud to think of them graduating from college this spring. Could they really be that old?

"My friend showed me how to carry a tray like a real waitress," said Berry, the tallest of the young group. "You hold it to the side with your hand open underneath. Oh, she said to load the heavy stuff in the middle so it doesn't tip."

The other girls looked impressed, all except for Kimmie, who was hopping up and down with excitement. "Where can we change?"

"In my room," Anya said. "Berry, after we change, I'd love for you to show us all how to carry the trays."

"Me, too?" teased Jack, who'd arrived in a black vest and slacks and a crisp white shirt. The man could easily pass for the maître d' at a five-star restaurant, where that devilish grin would net him plenty of tips. If the surgery business ever dried up, at least he had a fallback, Anya mused.

She straightened his rakish bow tie. "There you go."

"Thanks." His gaze caught hers for a shimmering moment.

"We love the clothes, Uncle Jack," Tiffany said.

"I'm glad." He beamed at his nieces.

Anya draped her waitress outfit over her arm. She hadn't expected him to bring one for her, too, but was glad he'd thought of it. "Girls! Follow me upstairs, and hold on to the railing. No shoving."

They snaked through the crowded house, the girls dodging under grownups' arms and bumping their elbows. It was a miracle they didn't leave a trail of spilled drinks.

In Anya's room, the girls dived into their outfits. Their high spirits were infectious; even quiet Amber giggled when Kimmie tied her apron around her head so it flowed down the back, saying, "Don't you guys just love this cool hat?"

Seeing Tiffany about to follow suit, Anya waggled her hand for attention. "Aprons around the waist, please. Hats on heads. Socks on feet." Her no-nonsense tone did the trick.

As she donned her black dress and apron, Anya saw that she'd left her laptop sitting on the low table, open to her social media page. She was about to click it off when she noticed her grandmother's stern, beloved face on the screen. Grandma Meeks had never been the cuddly, brownie-baking type of grandmother, but it had been she who'd recognized Anya's aptitude for nursing.

"It's not all bedpans and massages," she'd declared when her granddaughter initially dismissed the suggestion. "In my day, nursing was considered a challenging career, and it still is. And you can save lives while you're at it. Can't beat that!"

Her grandmother's enthusiasm had inspired Anya to volunteer at a nearby hospital. She'd been surprised how much she enjoyed the setting, and after talking to some of the nurses, she'd realized Grandma had been right. Then she had the idea to become a nurse practitioner and run her own practice, which had excited her even more. In retrospect, it would probably have been a tougher path than she'd imagined, but at the time, the prospect of gaining her independence while filling an important medical need had fired her with purpose.

But as Jack had pointed out, it had all worked out in the end.

While the girls finished dressing, she read the post on the site. It was from her sister Ruth. Grandma Rachel would be celebrating her 80th birthday in April. The whole Meeks family was invited—or rather, commanded—to gather in their Colorado town for a big blowout.

A string of responses bore the names of Anya's siblings, aunts, uncles and cousins. Many offered suggestions and hardly anyone had demurred. It would be a shame to miss this event, Anya conceded, but she'd been planning to avoid her family until next Christmas because she didn't want them to know about the pregnancy. Now what was she going to do?

Downstairs, she found Jack in the kitchen, arranging hors d'oeuvres on trays that Karen had produced. "Young ladies!" he commanded the four little waitresses, who quit poking each other. "Who wants to serve outdoors?"

"What if someone hits us with a croquet ball?" Berry asked.

Jack peered out the window. "I don't see anyone playing right now. As for the badminton game, those plastic shuttlecocks wouldn't hurt a fly."

"Berry and I can go outside," Kimmie said. "That's more fun and we don't mind the smell."

"Speak for yourself!" Kimmie's sister scrunched her face.

"Put a drop of perfume on your upper lip," Tiffany advised.

"I'd rather stay in."

"I'd rather be outside," Amber piped up.

Hearing the girls' preferences, Anya took charge. "Here's how we're doing it. Berry, you show everyone how to carry a tray. Then you and Tiffany can stay in the house because you're taller and it'll be easier for you to avoid smacking into everybody. Amber and Kimmie, you'll be the outdoor team."

Heads nodded. Soon they were balancing the trays, following Berry's example.

After they marched out to perform their duties, Jack gave Anya a thumbs-up. "I'm impressed. You had them all figured out."

"It's best to pair them by age, anyway," Anya told him. "This way they can make new friends. And it's important to take what they want into consideration."

He lounged against the counter, his gaze lingering on her until heat rushed through her body. "You make a sexy waitress."

"And you're a smashing head waiter." Her fingers itched to loosen that tie and undo the buttons on his starched shirt.

He was moving toward her when a small throat clearing from the corner drew their gazes to Helen Pepper, who'd been dozing on a chair. Jack paused, and Anya eased away.

"You're both wonderful with children," Helen said as if she hadn't noticed the vibrations between them. "Today you've brought the sparkle back to Amber's face. She's been much too quiet since she arrived."

"Anya's the one who understands kids," Jack told her.

"It's self-defense." Anya took a chair across from the older woman rather than talk down at her. "I practically raised my three younger sisters after my mom became disabled. But as for my maternal instincts, they're pathetic. I even managed to kill an African violet."

Helen chuckled. "They're delicate plants. I murdered an entire bed of begonias and that practically requires a blow torch."

"Overwatering?" Anya asked.

"Taking a vacation and forgetting to arrange for any watering at all." With an indulgent air, Helen patted Anya's hand. "Don't worry. You would never mistreat a child, even by accident. You're a natural mother."

Anya was eager to skip that subject. "Can I get you something to eat or drink?"

"Those little sandwiches look delicious."

Jack presented a platter with a low bow. "At your service, madam."

"You're so handsome—all the girls must adore you." She patted his cheek before selecting a couple of sandwiches. "But take my advice and stick with Anya."

"I agree," he said. "There's no one like her."

A spurt of joy caught Anya by surprise. Did Jack really want her for who she was, rather than just because she was pregnant with his child? At unguarded moments, he still had the power to melt her with his tenderness and sensitivity, and as for this buzz tingling through her...

Embarrassed, she realized Helen was observing her reaction. "I'd better go check on my waitstaff."

"I'll come with you." Jack set the platter aside.

To Anya's relief, Rod popped in to speak to Helen about the girls, distracting Jack. Rod had a store of questions, which the older woman seemed more than willing to answer.

Anya lingered with the trio just long enough to confirm what Tiffany had said during her previous visit—that the girls were unhappy but not suffering from physical abuse. Then she slipped away to check on her outdoor team.

The smell from the marsh didn't bother her today thanks to the appetizing scents wafting from the barbecue where Melissa was grilling burgers. The aromatic smoke also mitigated the queasiness that occurred whenever Anya went more than an hour without eating.

Or without inhaling Jack's aftershave lotion. No, it must be something about male pheromones, she corrected herself.

The crack of a mallet against a wooden ball warned Anya to move off the lawn or risk having her ankles smacked by a croquet ball. She stepped into the drift of the game's onlookers, where the girls were circulating.

Anya was glad to see that Kimmie's bouncy manner had rubbed off on Amber, who laughed readily at her new friend's antics. The girl deserved a family that brought out her happy side, Anya thought.

Though things might be getting a little *too* high-spirited, Anya realized as Kimmie tripped over a rough patch of lawn and was forced to put a hand down to break her fall. The remaining hors d'oeuvres on her tray went flying.

"I'm sorry." Kimmie was crestfallen.

"Don't worry about it," she soothed the girl. Anya took both their trays, while other guests disposed of the dropped food in a nearby trash can. "Dinner will be ready soon. You guys go have fun."

With a squeal of glee, Kimmie led Amber on a dash into the house. How cute they were, Anya mused.

An image of a little girl with dark hair and green eyes toddling across a lawn flashed through her mind. *My daughter. Jack's daughter.*

This little person was growing inside her right now. Anya's chest tightened. A sweet moment, a baby kiss, the feel of chubby arms around her neck—those were precious, but, she reminded herself sharply, a real mother had to be prepared for the sleepless nights, the anxieties and irritations, the loss of privacy, the weight of unending chores and that sense that your best was never good enough.

If more women had Anya's experiences growing up, world population growth would cease to be a problem, she mused as she toted the trays through the sliding doors into the den. And adoption would be far more common.

Pausing to let her eyes adjust to the dimness, Anya noticed Zora in a corner, holding up a square of mangled crocheting. Betsy Raditch, short caramel-brown hair fluffed around her head and half-glasses perched on her nose, examined Zora's work and made a comment that Anya couldn't hear. Her friend mouthed a grateful thank-you for the advice.

Anya had always liked the nursing director, who brought calm efficiency to her job. She always seemed approachable despite a long list of duties.

Too bad the woman had, in a sense, lost two daughters-in-law, Stacy and Zora, of whom she'd grown fond. Now Andrew had announced his engagement to a woman he'd met on a business trip to Hong Kong. Maybe three times would be the charm, but Anya doubted it.

"I can't imagine why he hasn't signed those divorce papers." Anya heard Betsy's words through a lull in the ambient chatter. "It's unfair for him to keep you dangling like this."

"Maybe he's changed his mind about marrying that, that... woman." Zora's voice trembled. Anya hoped her friend wasn't clinging to the absurd notion that Andrew still had feelings for her. The man cared about nobody but himself.

"I have no idea what my son is thinking," Betsy said. "He's got too much of his father in him, but I shouldn't be talking about that."

And I shouldn't be eavesdropping. Anya scurried off before anyone caught her.

As she entered the kitchen, she halted, her path to the counter blocked by Lucky's muscular shape. He was removing a bowl of salad from the fridge, too intent on his task to notice her.

Beyond him, Jack remained clustered with his uncle, Karen and Helen. "I've done everything I can think of," Jack was saying. "Why can't she see the obvious? You were right, Helen. She's a natural mother. She'd be perfect with this baby."

Resentment flamed through Anya. Never mind that she was eavesdropping again; anybody could overhear Jack discussing her future as if she was common property and he had the right to make decisions for her.

Lucky closed the refrigerator door. His eye roll made it clear he hadn't missed what was being said, nor her infuriated expression. "I'll get out of the line of fire."

Ignoring him, Anya dumped the trays into the sink with a clatter. When Jack looked up, she didn't bother to hide her scowl.

"Anya." He paled. "Sorry. That was tactless. But..."

"You made a promise to sign away your rights." Having

to confront him in front of Rod and Helen and Karen added to her fury.

"Only if you're still as determined..." he began.

"I'll take the DNA test next week. The lab will need a specimen from you, too." Though he probably knew that, being an ob-gyn. "Once I've kept my part of the bargain, a deal is a deal."

Without waiting for a response, she stalked out of the kitchen.

Chapter Ten

By the following Friday, the entire hospital staff knew about Anya's pregnancy and Jack's paternity, a situation for which Jack blamed himself. Sitting with her in the cafeteria, although he'd only done it once, had attracted plenty of attention, and his big mouth at the party hadn't helped either.

Everywhere he went, conversations stopped, then resumed behind his back. And his uncle's moodiness about the girls' departure prevented him from running interference with his usual acid rejoinders. Not that he'd been around much anyway.

In Jack's opinion, it was a good thing Rod had taken to spending his spare time with Karen. She had far more patience than Jack to listen to Rod's concerns about Tiffany and Amber and his frustration that he couldn't count on future visits.

Despite Anya's annoyance with Jack over his comments at the party, she had kept her share of the bargain. They had both submitted blood samples, with the DNA results due next week. By mutual consent, they would receive the news together at Adrienne Cavill-Hunter's office. Having an objective third party would hopefully help them figure out their next step.

Anya gave no indication that she'd changed her mind about adoption, not that they'd had much chance to discuss the matter. Before the party, Jack could have sworn she was mellowing toward him, and observing her shepherding the flock of little girls had been a treat. If only he'd clamped down on his opinions and avoided that painful moment in Karen's kitchen, maybe she'd have begun to see for herself how wonderful she was with children.

Sensitive to the undercurrents, the nursing supervisor had taken to assigning other staff to assist at Jack's operations. He supposed that was wise. But he missed Anya's tart comments and rare, endearing smiles.

The closer they came to learning the DNA results, the more powerfully he felt drawn to babies. He gazed in fascination at the tiny people he helped bring into the world. Their arrival had always been a miracle, but now he understood how his patients could love a child from the moment of conception, putting its well-being first even when complications endangered their own lives.

And the day of reckoning was fast approaching. How could Jack go back on his word—yet how could he sign away his rights to an infant he already loved?

The questions plagued him even into surgery, though once he got under way, he was able to focus on the procedure. Today, his scrub nurse was the always-reliable Erica Benford Vaughn, who usually assisted Dr. Tartikoff. Short and deft, she was quick to anticipate Jack's needs as he performed a laparoscopic myomectomy. This microsurgical operation removed uterine fibroids—noncancerous tumors that could cause significant pain—while preserving the patient's uterus for future childbearing.

Jack loved working with the Da Vinci robotic system. Seated at a console with a 3D high-definition camera providing an on-screen view inside the patient's body, he manipulated the master controls. The system transmitted each careful movement to the tiny instruments with precision, allowing him to operate with the smallest possible impact on the patient.

Despite the equipment's invaluable aid, the surgery still depended primarily on the surgeon's skill as well as that of his support team. He stayed alert for any complications.

As always, the surgery involved the assistance of numerous other staff, but Jack paid little attention to the conversational remarks swirling around him, mostly concerning the staff members' young children and their fun-but-sometimes-maddening extracurricular activities.

Erica, while focusing on Jack's requirements, shared insights about her lively year-old son, who'd begun refusing to use his high chair. "Jordan would rather stand on a regular chair, which means spilling food everywhere. He's driving Lock crazy." Lock was her husband, a private investigator.

"He isn't driving *you* crazy?" Rod asked from nearby, where he was monitoring the patient's vital signs on his equipment.

"Oh, I sit back and enjoy the show." She chuckled. "Lock was so keen on being a dad that after I got pregnant, he was ready to raise Jordan by himself if I refused to marry him. As if he had any idea how hard it would be!"

"It wasn't a planned pregnancy?" Jack wouldn't normally ask such a personal question, but she'd raised the topic herself.

"Definitely not. Initially, I insisted on adoption." She cut him an embarrassed glance, which meant she'd heard about his situation.

"Your husband must have had experience with children," commented the circulating nurse. "Had he taken care of a younger sibling?"

"Not at all." Erica double-checked her tray, where she'd readied the tools to attach to the robot's arms. "He was kicked around foster homes until he finally landed in a good one. His younger foster brother helped whip him into shape, from the way they tell the story."

"So why would he want to be a single dad?" That didn't sound logical to Jack. Surely the man had grasped what a major challenge he'd be facing.

"His birth mom entrusted him to the wrong adoptive couple," Erica explained. "They got hooked on drugs, which is how he ended up in foster care. That's why Lock has such a low opinion of adoption."

The circulating nurse bristled. "I'm sorry for him, but that's unfair. My husband and I adopted *our* children, and we love those little guys more than anything."

"I'm sure that's more typical," Erica agreed.

Jack fell silent, concentrating on his work. In the back of his mind, though, her comments presented a tantalizing possibility. *Could* he raise the child himself? He'd dismissed the idea previously, assuming it was unrealistic.

He had a tendency toward perfectionism. That was essential for a surgeon, but it had drawbacks in relationships and especially in parenting.

The idea jolted him. Had he been demanding too much of himself? Maybe he *could* succeed as a single dad. Kids needed a lot of love and careful supervision, and he would certainly provide those.

"If you and Lock hadn't married, would he have raised Jordan alone?" Jack asked Erica.

"I doubt it," she said. "Not after I insisted he go through some hands-on training."

"How did he do that?" If there was a boot camp for daddies, Jack might give it a try.

"I arranged for us to babysit Dr. Tartikoff's twins." Her words glimmered with amusement. "Two little tykes at once. It was very demanding. That convinced Lock he couldn't raise a child without backup, especially considering his odd hours as an investigator."

"Then you fell in love and decided being a mom isn't so terrible?" the circulating nurse teased.

"That was part of it. Also, we both had to face up to some personal issues." Erica didn't specify what those were.

Her words echoed in Jack's mind. He, too, worked occasional odd shifts, but most of them were regularly scheduled. Although he knew childcare was no simple matter, several women on the staff juggled medical careers with single parenthood. Plus, if he required emergency help, Rod had experience with diapers and that sort of thing.

He'd probably be willing to fill in, especially once he fell in love with the baby.

So it might be possible for him and Rod to create a loving home that met a child's needs. Jack would never want his little one to grow up as lonely as he had been. But plenty of single mothers raised children successfully despite busy work schedules and financial pressures. And he had the most important quality: a heart full of love for his child.

Before he suggested any such thing, however, Jack would need to learn more about single fatherhood—talk to other parents, do research on the web—and draw up a plan to persuade Anya to give him custody. Or, if upon further investigation he found he wouldn't be able to give the child what he or she needed, then he had no business urging Anya to be a single mom either.

ANYA DIDN'T UNDERSTAND why she'd been so distracted—next week's meeting with Dr. Cavill-Hunter was unlikely to bring any revelations. She knew Jack was the father of her baby, so the only question the DNA test would answer was the baby's gender. And ultimately, that changed nothing.

Jack had promised to sign the papers. So why did she have this nagging worry that he might spring a surprise on her? Surely he wouldn't go back on his word.

Sitting at the breakfast table, she set down the Sunday entertainment section of the *Orange County Register* and stared out the glass doors at the misty March morning. The fog lay so thick, she could barely see past the fence that marked the border of Karen's yard.

Only Zora remained at the table, sharing her box of cereal but saying very little. Anya had no idea where everyone else had disappeared to or why her friend was acting so subdued. Zora had been preoccupied since the party, and Anya realized with regret that she'd failed to ask why her friend was so downcast. *Just because I have problems doesn't mean I should ignore Zora's.*

"You going to tell me what's the matter?" she asked.

Zora's head jerked up. "Why do you assume anything's wrong?"

It wasn't like her to dodge a question. "First, you aren't talking a mile a minute." Usually, her friend's chattiness provided a pleasant counterpoint to Anya's reticence. "Second, if you pull on your hair any harder, you'll yank it out by the roots."

Zora stopped twisting a strand around her finger. "I thought I'd have heard from Andrew by now."

"About what?" *Don't be dense.* "You prodded him about signing the divorce papers?" Perhaps Betsy's comment had borne fruit.

"I stopped by his house Monday." Zora folded her arms defensively.

"And?" Anya prompted.

"That woman wasn't there." Her friend's tight jaw emphasized the thin planes of her face. "She flew back to Hong Kong."

What difference did that make? "That's where her family lives, isn't it? She might be preparing for her wedding."

"She can't be!" Zora exclaimed. "He doesn't love her, not the way he loves me."

As a rule, Anya allowed people to indulge their delusions, but Zora was in desperate need of a reality check. "And you believed him when he swore he never loved *Stacy* the way he loved *you.*"

"Maybe he didn't." Zora fiddled with her napkin. "Don't forget, I knew him before she did. We were inseparable all through high school. I never understood why he dumped me."

"That's not exactly an indication of true love," Anya noted dryly.

"He was young and confused," her friend answered. "When he met Stacy in college, he had a crush on her for a while, that's all."

"Awhile?" The couple had been married for several years, from what Anya had heard.

"A couple of years. Then we ran into each other at our high school reunion and—well, you've heard the story."

"He sold you a bill of goods and you fell for it." Anya winced at the harshness of her analysis, but it was far kinder than Andrew was likely to be. "Zora, he cheated on Stacy and he cheated on you. That's the kind of person he is. He's not capable of loving anyone but himself."

She stopped on seeing angry denial on her friend's face. Anya had to admit, she only knew Andrew by reputation. No, that wasn't true; she also knew him by the pain he'd caused Zora far too often this past year.

"You're wrong!" Despite Zora's defiance, a hint of uncertainty trembled in her voice.

A light tap from a nearby doorway reminded Anya that Lucky's room lay on the far side of the wall. He poked his head out. "Sorry to intrude, but I couldn't help overhearing."

Zora slammed the table, rattling the dishes. Thankfully both cereal bowls were empty. "Don't you start on me, too!"

He raised his hands in protest. Shirtless, Lucky was quite a sight. On his right shoulder, a cartoon woman in skimpy armor wielded a sword that extended along his arm. On his left side wriggled a colorful dragon. "Wouldn't dream of it. I just wondered if you noticed the envelope Andrew dropped off for you last night."

"What envelope?" Zora peered around.

In the den, Lucky scooped up a manila envelope from the coffee table. "I heard someone at the door, but by the time I got there, he was already pulling away from the curb. Maybe I should have left it at your place on the table, but I figured it might get soiled." He handed it to Zora.

She swallowed hard, staring at her name handwritten on the front.

"You ought to know…" Lucky grimaced. "There was a woman in the car with him."

Anya didn't ask what the woman looked like. It scarcely mattered whether his fiancée had returned or whether he'd picked up someone new. "Thanks. Now go away," she told Lucky.

"Yes, ma'am." He ducked out. No argument. The guy was making impressive progress in adapting to his roommates.

Why was Zora staring at the packet as if it contained an order for her execution? "It's the divorce papers," Anya guessed.

"It can't be."

"Why not?"

Her friend shot a glance at Lucky's door. Although he'd closed it, their voices carried, as they'd just learned. "Upstairs."

After clearing the table, the women went to Zora's room, which faced the street. Despite the foggy morning, the glare was intense due to the western exposure.

While Zora tilted the blinds, Anya perched on her friend's floral bedspread. The room was about the same size as Anya's but had more feminine décor, including a ruffled bed skirt and dainty pink throw pillows.

Breathing fast, Zora opened the envelope and drew out the papers. Despite having waited months for this, she stared at the signature white-faced.

"Sit," Anya ordered.

Her friend collapsed onto a chair. "I can't believe it."

"Why not?" Anya repeated her earlier question.

"Because we…" Tears started down Zora's cheeks.

Anya mentally cursed Andrew. "You had sex."

"He said he'd made a mistake, leaving me." Her friend's hands clenched in her lap. Anya leaned forward and plucked the papers from her grasp. While she doubted a few wrinkles would invalidate them, the last thing Zora needed was to have to get them signed again. "He told me he missed me terribly."

Anya laid the papers atop the bureau. "And you believed him."

"I must be really stupid." Zora's gaze pleaded for understanding.

"He took advantage of you." *Again.* "That's the kind of

jerk he is." *And speaking of stupidity...* "You used contraception, right?"

Zora's blank expression gave her the answer. "I never
thought about it."

"You're an ultrasound technician," Anya pointed out. "You
spend all day showing people their unborn babies, and pregnancy never occurred to you? I'm not trying to be mean. I
goofed, too, but..."

"But you were on birth control pills and I'm not," Zora
finished. "Well, that was Monday, so it's too late for me to
use a morning-after pill."

"You're not late already, are you?"

"No." Zora blew her nose into a tissue. "I'm sure I'm not
pregnant. We tried for a whole year to have a baby and it
didn't work."

"There. You're safe." Anya was relieved for her friend.

Judging by the fact that Zora was shredding the tissue,
though, *she* wasn't relieved. "On the other hand, my stomach's bothering me."

Uh-oh. "Bothering you how?"

"Churning." Her friend stared at her in dismay. "Not only
in the mornings, though. That means it's from tension, right?"

Their gazes met. "Or not."

They shared a silent moment of dread. Then Zora asked,
"How early do those pregnancy tests work?"

"We might be able to get results this soon." Despite choosing not to test herself, Anya had read the label on one of the
kits at a drugstore. "They work as early as seven days past
ovulation."

"I don't track my ovulation."

"When's your period due?" Anya asked.

"Like, yesterday." Wistfully, Zora said, "Betsy would love
to have a grandchild."

"You mean you'd keep it?" Anya couldn't imagine that,
not only because of her own feelings toward motherhood but
even more because of her friend's messy relationship with her
ex-husband. "How do you suppose Andrew would react?"

A sodden tissue hit the wastebasket. Zora snatched another. "He won't bring me ice cream and cute costumes, I can tell you that."

There was no comparison between Andrew and Jack. Appreciation flooded Anya for the kind, caring guy she'd chosen. *Except you didn't choose him, and this is way off topic.* "You aren't still fantasizing that Andrew loves you, are you?"

A deep sigh. "I guess not." Zora perked up a little. "If I keep the baby, he'll have to pay support. That's fair, right?"

"And you'll be tied to that creep for life. He'll keep you dangling, paying late and playing other games, just like he did with the divorce papers." Hoping Zora would abandon this crazy line of thought, Anya added, "Not to mention how much the baby would remind you of him."

Her friend wrapped her arms around herself. "Don't tell me you haven't imagined your baby resembling Jack. He *is* handsome."

"We aren't talking about me."

"But he'd take care of you," Zora persisted. "Jack's like the prince in a fairy tale."

"Get real!" Anya's idea of happily-ever-after did *not* involve being locked in a castle, wearing glass slippers that hurt her feet and curtseying every time his Highness entered the throne room. "Back to *you.*"

"If I want to keep my baby, that's my business," her friend said.

Anya saw no sense in arguing. "Okay. Besides, your period will start, and that will be that."

"I want to know *now.*" Determination transformed her friend from weepy to demanding.

"As in, this very instant?"

"Yes."

Might as well get it over with. "I'll drive you to the drugstore," Anya said.

Less than an hour later, they were back in the bedroom, side by side on the bed, staring at a pink stick. Not faint pink either. Bold and definite.

"Oh, pickles," Zora muttered.

"Pickles?" Anya would have chosen a stronger word.

"I can't use bad language where the baby might hear."

Anya started to laugh. Zora glared, and then she, too, dissolved into giggles. They fell into each other's arms, laughing until they cried.

"Don't take this the wrong way, but I'm kind of glad we're in this together." Her friend sniffled.

"Me, too." From the day they'd met, they'd been in sync with each other—not that Anya had anticipated anything like this. "You have to tell Andrew."

"I'll send him an email." A faint smile broke through. "And copy it to his mother."

"We should warn his fiancée so she understands what kind of man he is," Anya said.

Zora shrugged. "He'll give her a snow job and she'll buy it like I did. Besides, she'll find out sooner or later."

"Before the wedding would be helpful."

"I'll let Betsy break the news."

Now that they knew for sure—or almost sure—that her friend was pregnant, Anya hoped Zora would think carefully what was involved in raising a child alone, with or without financial support. "Just to get the facts, you should talk to your attorney about adoption."

Zora shook her head. "This may be the only baby I'll ever have. I want a little person to love."

Would Anya ever have another child? She hadn't considered her pregnancy in that light.

Still, it was one thing to long for a baby, as Zora apparently did. For Anya to hang on to her child simply because this might be her only shot at motherhood would be far more selfish than relinquishing it.

Yet later, alone in her room, she wondered what it would be like to stay on in the house after the babies were born. She'd been picturing having fun with Zora the way they always had, dancing and catching the latest movies and sampling ethnic food at Orange County's many street fairs.

Instead, there'd be a little person toddling about, cute and demanding and requiring all Zora's attention. How was Anya going to handle watching another baby grow and flourish after giving up her own child?

Chapter Eleven

She wasn't meeting his gaze. Shifting uncomfortably on the waiting room couch, Jack studied the tumble of dark hair that masked Anya's face.

When he'd entered a few minutes ago, she'd already been sitting there, glaring at her phone. If she'd seen him out of her peripheral vision, she gave no sign. Surely she couldn't be angry already; she hadn't heard what he had to say. What was so infuriating?

The nurse had called in another patient ahead of them, leaving them alone. At 6:30 p.m. on a Tuesday, the medical building was nearly empty, and no one was at the reception desk.

Jack decided not to waste this chance to speak to Anya. He'd been anticipating her arguments for days, educating himself about childcare options, talking to staff members both single and married about their biggest parenting challenges and winning Rod's support, however tentative. If they could get a running start on the issues, they might avoid a painful argument in front of Adrienne.

Not that Jack figured he had much chance of escaping Anya's wrath. He *had* promised to sign the waiver.

Moving closer, he noticed that, at this angle, her little nose seemed to have wrinkled in disgust. "If it's that bad, why are you reading it?"

"Excuse me?" Anya glanced up, eyes startled, full lips parted.

He restrained the urge to brush back the sweep of her hair. She hadn't assisted him in the operating room for a week, which might have been good for his concentration but left him feeling hollow. "You look ready to smash that thing."

"It's not the phone. It's my sister Ruth." She held up the device, displaying a social media site. He couldn't read the post, but the accompanying photo showed a woman slightly older than Anya with sterner features on a similar heart-shaped face.

"What's this dragon done?" Jack asked.

Her faint answering smile faded quickly. "The whole family's gathering in Colorado for my grandma's 80th birthday in April. Ruth arbitrarily assigned me to supervise all the babies and children."

Anya might be suited to the job, given her skill with youngsters, but it was unfair to drop such a big job on her without her consent. Another objection also occurred to Jack. "How does she expect you to arrange all that when you're out of state?"

"Oh, she's decided I should arrive a few days early." Anya scowled at the screen. "And all my cousins have started weighing in with their head counts. So far there are four infants, six toddlers and I've lost count of the school-age kids."

"Why can't they watch their own children?"

"Because Ruth's a control freak." Anya heaved a frustrated sigh. "But if I get into a squabble with her, she'll lay a guilt trip on me in front of everyone. Plus, my cousins will feel entitled to debate this, as if I were their property."

Much as Jack would have liked to produce a simple solution, he didn't have one. Besides, his job was to defend and protect Anya, not mediate a family dispute. "That's too heavy a burden for you, especially in your condition."

"They don't know about my pregnancy and I'm not sure I'm going to tell them." She closed down the website. "Ruth's pregnant, too, with her fifth child. I can't expect any sympathy from her."

Jack took her hand. "Whatever you decide, let me know how I can help."

"I'll have to miss Grandma's birthday party." Sadness shaded her gaze. "It's too stressful."

"Don't you want to be there? Turning eighty is a big deal." Having lost his grandparents when he was young, Jack envied her chance to attend such an event and connect with relatives. But then, Anya couldn't enjoy the occasion if she was buried in babies.

"I'll plan a trip to see Grandma later, when we can spend more time together." Unhappily, Anya added, "It'll have to be after the baby's born."

"Won't your sister raise a storm over your decision not to attend?"

"I won't announce it for as long as possible." Anya stuck the phone in her purse.

She'd mentioned that avoidance was her survival tactic. Jack was beginning to understand why. "That'll give her even more ammunition to fire in your direction," he warned.

"By now, Ruth ought to realize she can't boss me around," Anya replied. "If she's surprised by the consequences, that's her problem."

The nurse, a short woman with thick glasses, opened the door to the inner sanctum. "Dr. Ryder? Miss Meeks?"

They both rose. Instead of an examining room, though, the nurse escorted them to a small office with *Adrienne Cavill-Hunter, M.D.* on the door. "The doctor will be right with you."

"Thanks." Jack held a chair for Anya.

As she slid into it, he noted that her snug T-shirt revealed a still-flat stomach and well-defined breasts enlarged by pregnancy hormones. His body sprang to alert, remembering the feel of them beneath his lips... *Quit staring. And quit thinking about that.*

While they waited, Anya studied a wall chart depicting the stages of embryonic growth. Jack didn't need a reminder that, at ten weeks of development, their baby was about an inch and a half long. This week marked the end of the embryonic period, after which the term *fetus* was used.

It amazed him that the little creature was already becoming the distinctive individual who might live into the next century. He wished he knew exactly when personality manifested itself. Maybe genetics and epigenetics were already kicking in with whatever talents or traits would distinguish this wonderful child.

Jack wished Anya shared his sense of delight. From long habit, she'd schooled her expressive face into a mask. Anger stirred in him at the family members whose tactics had trained her to hide her emotions.

After a light tap, Adrienne breezed into the office, a white coat open over her tweed slacks and tailored blouse. She shook both their hands, then produced printouts. "These are for your files, but I'd suggest not reading them until we review a few details."

Anya set the papers in her lap. "Such as what?"

"Let's start with your reason for taking the DNA test. The probability that Jack—Dr. Ryder—is the father," Adrienne said.

"Yes?" Although he'd more or less taken the answer for granted, Jack felt a tremor of suspense.

"It is 99.9 percent likely."

His muscles relaxed. This was his baby. Unlike with his uncle's kids, there remained no risk of confusion or deception.

"You don't have to tell me," came Anya's tart response. "As far as I'm concerned, it's 100 percent. He's the one who questioned it."

Jack ducked his head in embarrassment. "I didn't mean it that way. But it seemed important to eliminate any doubt."

Adrienne maintained an air of professional detachment. "This test also reveals the gender of the baby. That's why I suggested you delay looking at the results, in case you prefer not to know."

Eager as he was to find out, Jack was willing to wait until he was alone if necessary. "Anya?"

She fingered the paper. "Go ahead. What is it?"

"It's a girl." Adrienne waited for their reactions.

"Oh." That was all Anya said. No indication if that made any difference.

Jack hadn't cared about the gender, but now the child in his mind came into even sharper focus: a little girl with brown hair and expressive eyes. No one would force her to hold herself back, to guard against emotional manipulation. She'd grow up with parents—*a parent*—who loved her and encouraged her to be herself.

It was still possible she'd be raised by strangers, but he hoped not. If only he could persuade Anya to stop distancing herself from the situation. "You're allowed to have feelings," he told her.

She folded the paper. "I do have feelings."

"So do I." *Here goes.* "I realize I promised to waive my parental rights—"

She gripped her purse. "Don't you dare go back on your word!"

Jack made what he hoped was a conciliatory gesture. "I have an alternate proposal."

Leaning against her desk, Adrienne folded her arms. She didn't bother to hide her curiosity, but Jack was sure he could count on her impartiality.

Anya swallowed. "I'm listening."

It was impossible to tell whether anger seethed beneath the surface. Still, having anticipated an immediate fight, Jack appreciated the opportunity to present his case. "I acknowledge that you aren't prepared to raise a child, with or without my help."

She cleared her throat. "That's right."

"So I'll raise the baby myself." Fingering the notes crammed in his pocket—the mere touch seemed to jog his memory—Jack outlined his plan: daycare at the hospital's child center, a licensed private sitter during his overnight shift in labor and delivery and off-hours backup provided by

Rod. "I don't underestimate the challenges, but lots of single parents cope, and I will, too."

"I can recommend a licensed sitter that my husband and I trust with our little boy," Adrienne said. "However, I strongly advise counseling. This is a major decision."

"I hate counselors," Anya said. "They make you confront things."

"You can have as much or as little involvement as you like, Anya," Jack said. "If you want to make things official, you can sign a waiver of parental rights."

"I should point out that you can't waive your financial obligation to the child," Adrienne warned her patient. "A lawyer can give you the whole picture."

"Your attorney, Edmond, seems reliable," Jack agreed. For some reason, he trusted the fellow.

Anya's shoulders hunched. What did that mean, he wondered.

"There's no need to decide now," Adrienne said. "The baby isn't due for over six months."

"I want this settled." Anya regarded Jack sternly. "What if something happens to you? With an adoptive family, she'd have two parents."

"Adoptive couples aren't immune to issues like divorce, illness and death," he reminded her. "And I'll appoint a guardian, just in case."

"Your uncle?" she asked dubiously.

"He's willing, and he has parenting experience." Jack returned to the main issue. "Honey, I love this baby. Maybe that sounds crazy because she isn't born yet, and I wasn't expecting to be a father, but I love her."

"An adoption means a clean break," Anya said slowly. "If you raised her, you'd still see me as backup."

"I promise I won't."

"What if she gets sick?" she challenged. "What if Rod isn't around when you need him? I'd be mommy on call."

"That's not true."

"How can you be sure?" She didn't sound argumentative; she appeared almost regretful, in truth.

Jack struggled to marshal his arguments. But what if she was right?

"This decision deserves more consideration," Adrienne repeated. "You don't have to resolve it now."

Her presence, initially helpful, was beginning to chafe on Jack. "If you have a patient waiting, you can go."

"I allowed extra time for this consult," the doctor assured him. "I'm fine."

Too bad. Jack could see Anya's uncertainty, but if they delayed this conversation, her default position—just say no and run for cover—would kick in.

To him, the fact that she hadn't immediately rejected his plan indicated that her determination to give the baby up had softened. All the same, Jack respected her right to say no.

And her objections had merit. How *could* he be sure he'd keep her out of the picture while raising their daughter? There was no way to try things out in advance. Or was there?

The last time they'd had a serious disagreement, Anya had put him to a test of sorts to earn the right to have her take the DNA test. Jack hadn't minded shopping and handling other chores; he wished she'd requested more, in fact. Although he couldn't prove that he'd keep his end of this new bargain, a good-faith attempt might reassure her. And it'd be a learning experience for him, too.

He dove in. "Let me prove that I won't lean on you. That I can handle extra pressure at home and not give in to frustration or dump my problems on you."

"How?"

"A few weeks ago, you gave me a challenge," he reminded her. "Let's agree on another one. I'll cook for your entire household for two weeks. That includes shopping and paying for the food."

Adrienne blinked. "That's quite an offer."

"I don't see what difference it would make," Anya said doggedly.

"Some nights I'll be tired and cranky, and I'll have to field the demands of a bunch of people." As he spoke, Jack reflected that he wasn't sure *how* he'd deal with the sometimes irritating group of housemates. But if he couldn't, maybe he wasn't cut out for single fatherhood. "It'll be a test for my own information as well as yours."

She seemed to be weighing his offer. "Why two weeks?"

"Two weeks from now is the earliest we can schedule an ultrasound, right?" He looked to Adrienne for confirmation.

"That's correct, doctor," she said.

Jack plowed onward. "At that time, maybe the best course of action will be clear to both of us." He didn't believe he'd change his mind. But when Jack had asked for Rod's cooperation, his uncle had pointed out that being a parent was harder than most people expected.

The nurse knocked, then looked in. "Doctor? The next patient is prepped."

Jack got to his feet. "Thanks, Adrienne. You've been great." And she had, despite his internal carping.

"Good luck to both of you," she said. "Since it's after hours, Eva will have to get back to you about scheduling the ultrasound."

"It's okay if Zora does it," Anya told the nurse. "If that simplifies the scheduling."

Eva nodded. "Okay."

Was Anya agreeing to his proposal? Jack wondered as he accompanied her out through the waiting room. Or was she saving her refusal for when they were alone?

ANYA'S HEART CONTRACTED. She was carrying a little girl like Tiffany or Amber or like Anya's two-year-old niece, Kiki, a sensitive child who seemed lost among her three siblings. After Christmas dinner, Kiki had nestled in her aunt's lap, content to watch the world go by from the safety of Anya's arms.

What a sweetheart. But Anya hadn't missed the exhaustion on Ruth's face by the end of the day, when she and her husband shepherded their children home. Cuddling a toddler for a few hours shouldn't be mistaken for a taste of motherhood.

As for Jack's plan to embrace single fatherhood, it reeked of good intentions that would only go awry. So why hadn't she put her foot down back there?

He promised to relinquish his rights. Keeping his word was a matter of honor.

As the elevator discharged them into the lobby, Anya admitted that there'd been an escape clause in his earlier promise. His words were engraved in her memory: *If you're still absolutely determined to seek adoption, I'll sign.*

Each day, she became more keenly aware of the baby taking shape inside her. Plus, now that Zora was planning to raise *her* child—although she still hadn't broken the news to the father—Anya was troubled by the prospect of having to live with an ever-present reminder of the baby she'd given up.

Jack had promised she could have as much or as little involvement in raising the baby as she liked. Of course, she preferred zero, but that meant she'd have to avoid Jack because seeing him would mean seeing their daughter, too.

It was hard, struggling through a thicket of possibilities. Also, in the short term, Jack's offer to cook for the house was tempting.

Zora's cooking duties started on Sunday, with Anya's the following week. They could both use a break.

Adoption. Adoption. Adoption.

But why did she have to repeat that mantra if she truly believed in it?

You only get to make this decision once. Then you'll bear the consequences for the rest of your life.

Yet Jack's nearness had the oddest way of calming Anya. The thought of having him around the kitchen was almost irresistible.

Surely by the date of the ultrasound, she'd have a clearer idea of what course to choose. *You're procrastinating.* Well, so what?

In the parking garage, Jack accompanied Anya to her car.

Even beneath the meager lighting, his earnest, vulnerable expression pierced her defenses.

"You deserve a shot," Anya said.

"Really?"

"Better grab the chance before I rethink this."

Joy blazed from his eyes. "Thank you."

"That's all it is—a shot," she cautioned.

"I understand."

They stood close enough for her to feel the ripple of energy he generated, a force that drew everything nearby into his aura. The first time she'd experienced it, in the operating suite before their first surgery, she'd known he was dangerous.

Too bad she'd ignored that on New Year's Eve.

"You can start on Sunday," she went on. "I'll tell the others. Actually, you should come to our meeting that afternoon. They'll want to give you their food preferences."

"Great!" Jack grinned like a schoolboy given a new video game. "Since I won't know what to shop for that night, how should I plan dinner?"

"You can order pizza and a salad." Recalling Lucky's requirements, she added, "Be sure there's a vegetarian one. Pineapple and mushrooms are fine."

"Done."

It was on the tip of her tongue to repeat that she wasn't agreeing to let him raise the baby. But he already knew that. "See you."

Jack waited until she drove off. Watching over her. Ah, that sense of safety.

She'd better not get used to it, Anya told herself sternly. When she thwarted him again in two weeks, he might never forgive her.

THE WOMAN CONFOUNDED him. Anya seemed as stubbornly independent as ever, so Jack had no idea why she'd said yes to letting him cook.

As he took the stairs down to the doctors' parking section on the ground level, he reflected that he'd put himself in a position to be pushed around by her housemates. Let them bring it on. It would be good training because from what he'd heard, toddlers could out-demand and out-harass anybody.

Already, menus flashed through Jack's mind. The vegetarian dishes posed an interesting challenge. It was also an opportunity to provide healthy meals for his little girl.

His daughter. The garage lights blurred beneath a sheen of moisture. Jack could have sworn he saw rainbows from the corners of his eyes.

Sunday couldn't arrive soon enough.

Chapter Twelve

Monday night's menu:

Green salad with tomatoes, apples and cheddar cheese
Lentils and bulgur wheat with walnuts
and chopped apricots
Fresh-baked pita bread
Hummus
Apple pie

Jack had Mondays off after working an overnight shift, so he spent much of the afternoon planning and shopping for the week's meals. He arrived at the house around 4:30 p.m., letting himself inside with a key that Karen had loaned him for his tenure as household chef.

After posting the menu, he cast an appreciative glance through the window at the flower-filled yard and the wetlands beyond. Yesterday had marked the start of Daylight Savings Time, bringing lingering daylight to the mid-March afternoon. The sunshine set the grays and greens aglow and picked out brilliant spots of red and yellow wildflowers. Just beyond the fence, a large raccoon paused to stare back at him, bold and unafraid.

Now, down to work. Hungry people would soon be arriving.

Yesterday, after serving pizza and interviewing the residents about their food preferences, Jack had explored the kitchen, inventorying the spices and cooking gear. Today, he assembled bowls, pots, utensils and ingredients on the counter.

Pleased at being in control of his environment, Jack set to work. He'd considered making a splash tonight by fixing salmon—until he calculated the cost of buying enough for six people. Given the high cost of groceries, he had to be realistic, especially considering he might soon have to equip his apartment for child-rearing.

He'd hit on a less costly entrée involving lentils and a cracked whole-wheat grain. He'd bought the ingredients at the Little Persia Mart, along with fresh-baked pita bread and hummus redolent of garlic, olive oil and chickpeas.

Half an hour later, with preparations well under way, he heard a car pull into the driveway. The first to enter his new domain was Karen, who'd changed her hair from strawberry blond to black with a silver streak in front. She was wearing a black top with silver threads and a long charcoal skirt that suited her new color scheme.

"Find everything okay?" she asked.

Jack gave her a thumb's up. "Perfect."

She retrieved a fruit drink from the refrigerator. "The kitchen's a bit squirrelly. I never liked having to angle around to get into the pantry, but I couldn't change the entire floor plan."

"Doesn't bother me. The new appliances put our apartment to shame." Jack particularly admired the range, with two high-intensity burners, a pair of medium burners and a simmer at the back. "Who sets the table?"

"I will tonight," she said. "We'll eat in the dining room while you're here. That other table's too small."

"Good idea." Jack resumed chopping an onion.

Standing by the fridge, Karen read the menu. "How do you fix the lentil dish?"

Jack indicated the recipe he'd set up in a plastic holder. "It's all right there. I'm doubling it."

"You might want to triple it," she said. "We're big eaters."

Jack performed a fast calculation. "I should have enough ingredients."

"That's a good sign for the future. Parents have to be flexible." She lifted her drink can in salute.

"Indeed they do."

While she carried china and tableware into the dining room, Jack put the wrapped pita in the oven to warm. Next he began frying the onions, and as they cooked he washed the romaine lettuce, drying it in a salad spinner. A few minutes later, Lucky wandered in to observe, having changed from his nurse's uniform into a muscle T-shirt and weather-defying shorts.

Either the guy overheated easily or he was emphasizing his masculinity in the face of this male intruder into his domain. However, Jack detected no hostility as Lucky watched him dice.

"Where'd you learn to cook like that?" his companion asked.

"High school." Thank goodness boys no longer drew sneers for taking cooking classes, at least in California.

"I appreciate the vegetarian menu." Lucky coughed, as if it hurt to thank Jack for anything.

Quit projecting onto the guy. You two could be allies here. "My pleasure."

From the den came the musical sound of Anya's voice. Even without being able to distinguish the words, Jack could instantly peg her mood: a little tired but upbeat. And fairly energetic, considering her condition and that she'd worked all day.

He'd been glad to find her in his operating room on Friday, but that had been three days ago and he hadn't caught even a glimpse of her since. Jack kept his face averted, not wanting Lucky to see how eager he was for the sight of her.

He needn't have worried. Muttering something about a snack, Lucky darted into the pantry.

The women were moving this way. "You should tell your sister where to get off," Zora was commenting.

"You'd think she'd notice I haven't agreed to her plan," Anya grumbled.

"Your cousins seem to already assume you have." Zora stopped at the entrance to the kitchen. "Oh! Jack. I forgot you'd be here."

Anya, shorter and rounder, steered her friend aside so she could enter. "Smells fantastic."

"Menu's on the fridge." Jack chopped apples into bite-size squares.

The friends took side-by-side positions as they read the menu. "Why do you put apples in the salad?" Zora asked.

"Because tomatoes have no flavor this time of year, although I toss in a few for the lycopene," Jack said.

"What's that?" Zora asked.

"It's a nutrient in red fruits and vegetables," Anya told her.

Jack nodded. "Helps prevent DNA damage, cancer and heart disease."

"All that?" Zora responded. "Aren't you afraid they'll put doctors out of business?"

"Not quite yet," he said.

Anya drifted to peer over his shoulder. The smell of disinfectant that clung to scrub nurses faded beneath her appealing blend of femininity and flowers. "Enough talk about diseases. It bothers my stomach."

"Me, too." Zora headed for the pantry. "A few raisins won't spoil our dinner, right?"

"Brace for impact," Jack murmured to Anya.

"What?" When she turned toward him, their faces were so close that he brushed a kiss over her lips. She blinked in surprise.

"Sorry." But he wasn't.

Zora's squawk must have echoed through the entire house. "You rat! How dare you hide in here and spy on us."

"Hey! Cool it." Lucky dodged out. Seizing a broom from inside the pantry, Zora swept at his heels as if shooing vermin.

"What were you doing in the pantry?" Anya demanded.

"Eavesdropping," Zora declared as she stuck the broom back in the closet.

"Organizing the supplies for Jack." Lucky folded his arms, a position that made his muscles bulge.

"Is that right, Jack?" Anya asked.

He chopped the last of the dried apricots into a bowl. "Leave me out of it."

Facing Lucky, the women planted hands on hips, mirroring each other's body language. "No one's buying it," Zora said. "You're a snoop."

"Believe whatever you want. I have better things to do." The male nurse fled with what dignity he could muster.

Jack tried not to be self-conscious about performing for an audience as he continued cooking. He liked having Anya there but wasn't so keen about Zora's presence until she said, "I sure admire what you're doing."

"Don't encourage him." Anya softened her words with a smile. "But this *is* a treat."

"For me, too." Jack handed her the salad bowl and gave Zora a serving plate piled with pita. "Mind putting these on the table?"

"Sure."

Zora left, but Anya hung back. "Why would this be a treat for you? Or were you just being polite?"

Stirring the nuts and apricots into the lentil dish, Jack gave her a serious answer. "I grew up without a family. This is fun."

"And I grew up with too much family." She sighed. "Too bad we couldn't have averaged it out."

"I hope your experience hasn't poisoned you forever." Jack didn't mean to lecture her. Still, this seemed like a chance to reach out. "Just because your sister tries to push you around…"

The doorbell rang. "Wonder who that is," Anya said, scooting out.

Avoidance. Well, what had he expected?

AWARE THAT ZORA was wrestling with the issue of how, when and what to tell others—including her ex-husband—about her pregnancy, Anya empathized with her friend. And understood Zora's envy of Jack's support.

So far he'd done well, choosing a menu that even Lucky approved of. And as Jack worked smoothly in the kitchen, his blue-checked apron emphasized his strong build and easy comfort with his own body.

Definitely comfortable in his body. Ambling into the living room to find out who'd rung the bell, Anya still felt a thrill of electricity, remembering the tenderness of Jack's stolen kiss. But despite her hunger for more, the intimate contact didn't augur well for his promise to leave her out of the child-rearing process.

Or for her ability to stand her ground.

Karen reached the door first, admitting Rod. He'd trimmed his graying hair and foregone the usual hat. "Thanks for inviting me," he told his hostess and gave Anya a friendly nod.

Anya wasn't sure where she stood at the moment with Rod's mercurial personality. Because he was a guest in the house and presumably on his best behavior around Karen, Anya supposed they'd get along well enough.

Jack peered out of the dining room, a bottle of salad dressing in one hand and a container of hummus in the other. "You invited him? No wonder you suggested I triple the recipe."

"It didn't seem fair to leave your uncle home alone," Karen replied cheerfully.

"Yes, I might get into all sorts of trouble." Rod gave her shoulders a squeeze that almost amounted to a hug.

Jack rolled his eyes. "Like an overgrown kid."

"That's right," said his uncle. "I'm here at my most infantile to test your parenting skills."

"Enjoy it while you can," Jack answered. "You'll have to grow up fast once—if—junior comes to live with us."

"Junior?" Anya asked.

"Junior-ette." In the dining room, Jack waited until the

others were settled before taking the empty chair across from Anya.

"No footsy under the table," Rod warned.

"You're in a good mood," Jack said to his uncle as he passed the butter to Karen.

"I just found out the girls are coming back next week for spring vacation." Rod explained that he'd received an email from Tiffany. "Apparently they've been so cooperative since visiting their grandmother that their parents agreed to let them do it again."

"That's wonderful news," Karen said.

"Okay if I bring them to dinner next weekend?" Rod asked. "Especially since Jack's cooking."

"And paying for it," Lucky put in.

Heads bobbed agreement. "We can add a card table for extra places," Karen said.

"Invite their grandmother, too. I'm prepared to be flexible," Jack said.

I'm not agreeing to anything, no matter how flexible you are. But as the words echoed in Anya's mind, she was glad she hadn't spoken them aloud because she'd have blushed. Jack *was* flexible in all sorts of ways that didn't bear dwelling on.

"You don't think this is a little too easy?" asked Melissa, who'd been quiet until now. "I mean, allowing the girls to return so soon when their parents have been completely rigid until now?"

Rod's smile faded. "You may be right."

"I hope their folks aren't suspicious." Karen plucked half a pita from the napkin-wrapped stack.

"They could create a lot of trouble if they are," Rod said ruefully.

Speculation flowed as to what Portia and Vince might be planning. "We'll have to be careful," Jack said. "If they learn that Helen's in league with you, that'll be the end of it."

"And Vince won't be satisfied with a discreet win," Rod said. "He's a heavy-handed bully."

Anya imagined jack-booted security troops raiding the house and yanking the girls from the dinner table. She'd been watching too many of Lucky's macho TV programs.

"We might need a backup plan for the girls' activities," Karen said.

"If Vince realizes I'm involved, I doubt we'd be able to fool him." Rod passed the salad to Melissa. "Although I appreciate the input, this discussion is making me grouchy. Let's change the subject."

The table fell quiet. Melissa clicked her tongue, which drew everyone's attention. "If you guys don't mind, I could use an objective opinion about something. Especially with Jack here."

"What's Jack got to do with it?" Anya asked.

"It's his profession." Melissa traced a slim finger over her misty water glass. "I'm facing a major decision. I have to give my answer soon and if I make the wrong choice, it will affect the rest of my life."

That aroused Anya's curiosity. Maybe Jack's presence *was* a good thing for her housemates, beyond his cooking talents.

"I'll help if I can," he said.

Melissa's hands fluttered gracefully. "I've been considering having a baby on my own because...well, never mind the background. But to deliberately bring a child into the world without a father, that troubles me. Now an opportunity has come up at work."

"Not mentioning any identities," Karen reminded her.

"Of course not." Like doctors and nurses, they respected patient confidentiality.

"Go on," Jack urged.

A woman in the fertility program had delivered healthy triplets after undergoing in vitro fertilization, Melissa explained. The patient and her husband had frozen three more embryos but decided they couldn't handle more children. Also, after a difficult pregnancy, the mother's health might be compromised if she tried again.

"They're wonderful people, and their babies are darling,"

she said. "I'd mentioned that I was considering artificial insemination. The mom asked… Well, she offered to let me have their embryos—on the condition that I use all of them. She's eager to have this resolved. If I don't implant them soon, she might choose someone else."

"Three embryos?" Zora crossed her arms as if shielding her abdomen. "Seriously?"

"You should discuss this with your doctor," Jack told Melissa.

"I have. Dr. Sargent says if I choose to go ahead, he's fine with it." Melissa pulled back her long, honey-blond hair and re-clipped it with her barrette. "I wish this weren't so sudden, but I have to give them an answer. Also, I'll need to start taking medications right away to go through the procedure this cycle."

That *was* soon. "It isn't right for them to pressure you," Anya said.

"But it's a miraculous offer. Still, having triplets could be overwhelming in a lot of ways." Melissa regarded Jack as if he possessed magical insight. "How likely is it that they'd all take?"

"Frozen embryo transfers at Safe Harbor have about a fifty percent success rate," he said. "I'm sure Zack Sargent went over that with you."

"Yes, but he tends to be gung ho about the egg donor program," she replied frankly. "I want an objective opinion."

All eyes fixed on Jack.

Anya wondered if he could be truly objective, considering his desire to raise junior-ette.

"It's unlikely that all three embryos will implant," he said thoughtfully. "However, since you can't discount the possibility, you'd better be prepared. You should consider your physical condition, your motivation and your support system, and whether they're able to handle three children at once."

"Support system is fine," Karen announced.

"I'm grateful for my friends, and I'm in good physical

shape." Melissa swallowed. "As for raising three little guys, well, I'd be lucky if that happened."

"They might be born early," Jack warned. "What if there are complications?"

"If she obsesses about everything that can go wrong, she'll never have kids," Lucky countered.

"That doesn't mean she shouldn't consider all the risks," Zora argued. "I remember when one of the nurses provided eggs for a surrogate. She went through a grueling regimen, with all kinds of hormones. There were some serious dangers, too."

"A frozen embryo transfer is much less stressful than an egg donation," Jack responded. "It takes less medication to prepare the uterine lining than to stimulate the ovaries." He glanced quickly at Anya. "I'm not sure this is the best topic for dinner-table conversation, though."

"That's okay. I'm finished eating," she said.

"There," Lucky announced triumphantly. "As I said, there's no reason to obsess about dangers."

"What about the risk of having triplets?" Zora returned Lucky's frown and doubled it. "*Somebody* has to remind her of the down side."

"And *somebody* has done that plenty," he snapped.

Rod waggled his eyebrows. "Shall we have fisticuffs for our postprandial entertainment? I'll referee."

Karen chuckled.

"Thanks for your input, Jack," Melissa said. "And you too, Zora. You're right. It's important to consider all sides."

"Speaking of sides, what's for dessert?" Rod rounded his eyes at his nephew.

"That was probably the most tortured segue I've ever heard," Jack answered. "In case you guys hadn't guessed, my uncle will bend a conversation like a pretzel to get to dessert."

"What *is* for dessert?" Lucky asked.

"Yes, Jack, what's for dessert?" Karen teased.

"If you guys can't read a menu, you don't deserve any apple pie." Jack pushed his chair back.

"I'll clear!" That was Lucky.

"I'll serve!" Karen added.

"Where's the pie?" Rod, of course.

Grinning at the surge of responses, Jack said, "In the fridge," and nearly got trampled by the herd stampeding past him into the kitchen.

Anya followed more slowly with a couple of serving dishes. Jack's debut as household chef had been a triumph. Too much of a triumph, in her opinion.

She hadn't considered that this test might bring him closer to her housemates. Already they were looking to him for advice, accepting him as an arbiter of sorts. Although she couldn't help being proud of him, what would it be like if he was raising their baby?

She'd have a hard enough time staying away from Jack and the child on her own. Now her friends were becoming his friends, too.

She'd left Colorado to preserve her freedom. Come September and the baby's delivery, would she have to leave Safe Harbor, too?

Chapter Thirteen

Jack's surgeries ran longer than expected on Friday morning. Because he saw patients in the afternoon, he decided to skip lunch rather than postpone appointments. "Also, that would make me late for fixing dinner," he remarked as he washed up, speaking as much to himself as to his uncle.

"Unacceptable, since we might have guests," Rod responded, though his recent upbeat attitude was blunted by uncertainty. The girls were expected to arrive today, but Helen hadn't been sure when or whether they'd be flying, taking the train or traveling by car.

"I was planning on them joining us tomorrow night," Jack said.

"Why not both meals?"

That meant making larger dishes, with a possible extra supermarket run. Rod had eaten with the household all week, which had increased Jack's work, but ultimately he approved. He was glad to see his uncle's friendship with Karen blossoming. And Jack hadn't been entirely comfortable with abandoning his uncle at dinnertime for two weeks.

So far, the meals had gone smoothly, aside from Zora's dismay on Tuesday when he'd fixed asparagus, which she hated. There'd also been a touch of awkwardness last night when he preheated the oven for lasagna and discovered belatedly that it was filled with soiled plates and cups, now burning hot.

Flustered, Zora and Anya had admitted hiding their breakfast dishes in the oven because they'd been running late and hadn't had time to empty the dishwasher. "It's a house rule," Anya had informed him. "We can't leave stuff on the counter."

"We didn't think about you using the oven," Zora had added.

"You should have looked inside before you turned it on." Anya had crossed her arms. "Imagine what a toddler might have put in there."

Jack had agreed and resignedly used pot holders to empty the oven.

But now, as he removed his surgical gloves, he realized that he was far less concerned about kitchen mishaps than about Anya's stubbornness in holding him at arm's length. Although his primary goal in serving as cook was to prove his readiness to be a dad, he'd hoped the experience might draw them closer.

He could have sworn she also longed to be closer. Those sideways glances, the teasing tension between them and, more important, the moments when they simply talked. They'd discovered they shared a fondness for nature documentaries on TV, especially those featuring birds, although neither had ever owned a pet bird.

"I'd rather watch them in the wild," Anya had said. "I think there are birds nesting in Karen's bushes and maybe out in the estuary."

He'd loaned her his binoculars so she could sit on the patio, put up her feet and bird-watch. After dinner one night, they'd sat outside, taking turns observing the birds and occasionally looking up details on their phones. They'd agreed that a hummingbird might be nesting in one of the honeysuckle bushes, especially because when Jack approached for a closer look, it had dive-bombed him with a sharp noise that warned him to retreat. He did, to Anya's amusement.

Yet when he'd suggested they bird-watch again last night, she'd declined and made a vague reference to having plans with Zora—pulling back, just when he'd hoped the barriers between them were falling.

Jack brought himself up sharply. Anya was honest about her approach to emotional attachments: when things got tough, cut and run. Much as he longed for her to stay in his life, as a resource for the baby and for other, very personal reasons, he'd better remember that in the end, she'd leave. She might not even give him warning. She still hadn't informed her sister about skipping their grandmother's birthday party next month. Unless Ruth had picked up the signs—which surely she ought to—she was in for an unpleasant last-minute shift in arrangements.

So far, Anya was running true to form. Only a fool would assume she'd change.

"Since you're feeding me dinner, I suppose I could bring lunch to your office this afternoon," Rod commented as they sauntered out of the operating suite.

"Tuna melt," Jack said.

"Kind of late for the cafeteria to fix a hot sandwich."

"Cold tuna on rye will be fine."

"Done."

On the main floor, Jack let his uncle precede him out of the elevator but nearly ran into the slightly shorter man when he stopped suddenly. "Hey!"

Rod didn't answer. He'd gone rigid.

Near the entrance to the fertility support services suite, a cluster of familiar figures caught Jack's eye. Hospital administrator Mark Rayburn, M.D., distinguished by his thick, black hair and the build of a former high school football player, dominated the group. Karen stood out, too, with her black-and-white coiffure. But it was their companions who'd surely riveted Rod's attention.

Vince Adams lacked Mark's height, but he stood out anyway. Maybe it was his aggressive stance—feet planted apart, head up and nostrils slightly flared—or the pin-striped dark suit that looked as if it had cost thousands of dollars.

Beside him, lean and fashionable in a hot-pink designer dress and jacket, Portia stood poised in her high heels. She must be about thirty-eight now, Jack figured, but already her unlined forehead and cheeks hinted at Botox injections. The bright red hair that Tiff had inherited had been tinted auburn and woven with strands of gold and honey-brown.

He'd seen photos of the pair in a magazine, portrayed as a beautiful power couple. To Jack, they seemed hard, with an underlying cruelty that flickered like hellfire through the cracks in their veneer. But that was because he'd witnessed how they'd manipulated the legal system.

Rod had no gift for disguising his emotions. Even from behind, his taut body language told Jack he was glowering.

"Hang in there," he murmured to his uncle.

Judging by her uneasy expression, Portia had spotted them. So had Karen, although she betrayed only a flicker of recognition.

When Vince turned, triumph distorted his features. He not only loved winning, but he also enjoyed grinding his opponent's face into the dirt. Obviously, he and his wife had become suspicious about the girls' behavior, which accounted for their visit to Safe Harbor. But why were they at the hospital?

The administrator didn't miss the tense, silent interchange. A furrow between the eyebrows was all the sign he gave, however, that it concerned him.

"If it isn't Dr. Vintner." Vince just couldn't let the moment pass, could he? "Good to see you again." His sneering tone converted the pleasantry into an insult.

"The pleasure's all yours," Rod growled.

"I didn't realize you were acquainted with members of my staff, Mr. Adams," Mark said.

"Rod is my ex-husband." Portia blinked as if startled. "Jack? I had no idea you were back in Safe Harbor."

"Hello, Aunt Portia." Jack strained for civility. "I've been here for two years now."

"Jack's a fine surgeon," Mark said. "The head of our fertility program, Dr. Owen Tartikoff, brought him on board."

"Does Jack work with Dr. Rattigan?" Vince addressed his question to the administrator.

Cole Rattigan, Lucky's boss, was a world-renowned specialist in male fertility. Did Vince, who reputedly was unable to father children, plan to consult him?

"I'm an ob-gyn," Jack said.

"I take it that means no." Vince kept his eyes on the administrator. "Now, what about those cutting-edge labs you mentioned?"

"They're on the next floor down," Mark said. "Karen, thanks for reviewing our egg donor program."

"Glad to do it. Nice meeting you, Mr. and Mrs. Adams." Karen shook their hands, then tossed off a quick, "Doctors," with a nod to Jack and Rod, before vanishing into her suite.

Since Rod remained frozen between the visitors and the elevators, Jack touched his arm to interrupt his fixation. "You owe me a sandwich."

Rod was vibrating with unspoken rage. But after a moment, he took a few steps to the side, no doubt in deference to the administrator.

As the trio passed, Mark kept up a running narration to the visitors. "Our original plan called for acquiring the dental building across the plaza. When it fell into protracted bankruptcy proceedings, we had to improvise. That's why our fertility offices are scattered across several floors. We installed the laboratories in our basement."

"Doesn't a basement mean problems with dampness and mold?" Vince swaggered by as if Rod weren't there. Portia spared a thoughtful glance for Jack.

"We've installed advanced HEPA filtration systems." The administrator pressed the down button. "The temperatures and sterility are strictly regulated. I'll let Alec Denny, our director of laboratories, provide the details."

To Jack's relief, the elevator arrived, and he was able to lead his uncle away at last. "That was a shock," he said once the others were out of hearing range.

Rod moved stiffly. "They're here to spy on me."

"Surely they wouldn't waste Dr. Rayburn's time to do that," Jack said.

"Oh, but they love to gloat." Unhappily his uncle added, "This means no more time with my daughters."

"Not for a while," Jack agreed.

Rod rolled his shoulders, fighting the tension. "Don't you have patients waiting?"

"Yes, actually. See you later. Tuna on rye." As he headed for the adjacent office building, Jack was glad they'd be having dinner with Karen. She might have insights to share.

As for Tiff and Amber, he hated missing a chance to see them. But they were aware now that Rod and Jack loved them. Vince and Portia couldn't keep them apart forever.

"THEY'VE RENTED A beach house a few miles from here, on the Balboa Peninsula," Karen said that night over a serving of Jack's peanut butter pasta. "Portia seemed genuinely worried about how much her mother misses her granddaughters."

"Worried or guilty?" Rod asked dourly.

Even with seven of them around the table, Anya was keenly aware of the girls' absence. She'd been looking forward to seeing them tonight or tomorrow, or both. Having grown up in a family of nine, sometimes she missed the joyous babble, the give-and-take of a group where interactions crisscrossed like global airline traffic lines on a grid.

"It does reduce the risk that Tiff will run away again," Jack ventured, although the situation had clearly put a damper on his mood, too.

"Why were they at the hospital?" Anya asked. "Dr. Rayburn doesn't give tours to the general public."

"They were dropping hints about some type of endowment," Karen said.

"It's a ruse to spy on me," Rod replied angrily.

"Maybe Vince just wants to move to the head of the line for a consult with Cole Rattigan," Jack said. "I understand he books up months in advance."

"Oh, he tries to work in any patient who's in urgent need." Lucky plucked a second dinner roll from a basket. "Of course, if they *had* come to the office, I couldn't mention it."

"Is that a no-they-didn't or are you obfuscating?" Zora asked.

"Is he doing what?" In contrast to the generally downbeat mood, Melissa sounded amused. Her spirits had lifted since she'd begun receiving injections of estrogen and progesterone in preparation for receiving the embryos.

"Confusing the issue," Zora translated.

"No one's confused about anything except your weird word choice," Lucky batted back.

"I thought you two had stopped picking on each other. Just spare the rest of us, okay?" Karen promptly returned to the subject of the day. "When Portia mentioned her daughters, I suggested they might enjoy volunteering at the hospital. I said our program encourages an interest in science."

"How'd that go over?" Jack asked.

"She seemed interested."

"And Vince?"

"Not so much."

"It'll never happen." Agitated, Rod glared across the table at Anya. "I don't understand why people fail to appreciate parenthood when it falls in their lap."

"Excuse me?" Jack asked.

Anya was grateful for the sharp response. Her pregnancy was none of his uncle's business.

"You heard me." For whatever reason, Rod continued to target his anger at her. "Why are you forcing my nephew to prove himself over and over? Just sign that waiver you considered such a minor detail when the shoe was on the other foot."

"Butt out," Anya said, summing up her position.

Around the table, the others regarded Rod with varying degrees of disapproval. Lucky's face tightened, Melissa stopped smiling, Zora frowned and even Karen looked distressed.

"You're a fine one to talk," Jack put in. "When I proposed bringing the baby to live with us, you brought up every obstacle in the book."

"I had to be sure you meant it," retorted his uncle. "Obviously, you did. And to keep your own mother ignorant of it—"

"What are you talking about?" Storm clouds darkened Jack's eyes.

"You hadn't told Mamie you're going to be a father."

"My absentee mom who didn't even stick around to raise me?" he snapped. "Why should I?"

"She's older now, and she has regrets."

"Where is this coming from?" Jack regarded his uncle sternly. "I thought you and your sister communicated by exchanging Christmas cards."

"I gave her a call to catch up on things," Rod said. "You should talk to her more often yourself."

Although pleased to no longer be the object of Rod's tirade, Anya resented his criticism of Jack. Honestly, just because the man was upset didn't give him the right to scattershot his anger at everyone else.

"Wait a minute." Jack's jaw pushed forward belligerently. "You called to catch up, or to tell her Anya's pregnant? That takes one hell of a nerve!"

"After what happened today..." Rod seemed, for the first time, to notice the negative reactions from the others. Stubbornly, he persisted. "It struck me that Mamie might never have another chance to be a grandmother. She deserves to be in the loop."

"No," Jack said. "She doesn't."

"Well, too late." His uncle swallowed. "We hadn't been in touch for a while, so I called her."

Fury radiated from Jack. "This is Anya's and my concern. Not yours, and not my mother's."

"It is now." Rod cleared his throat. "She was deciding whether to attend a conference in LA next week and this tipped the scale."

Next week? That was when they'd scheduled the ultrasound, Anya recalled. Just what they needed, another form of pressure at a key moment. How typical of families—even from far away, they had a gift for meddling.

"Call her back and tell her she's not welcome," Jack snapped.

"You call her," Rod said.

"I want her as far from Anya and me as possible."

To the best of Anya's knowledge, Jack had never openly rejected his mother before. "Are you sure?" she asked him. "I mean, she's your mom, so of course I'll leave it up to you."

He gave her a nod of acknowledgment, then resumed glaring at his uncle. "Why can't you grasp the fact that my mother doesn't give a damn?"

"If she's so indifferent, what's the big deal if she stops by?" Rod asked with an attempt at his usual flippancy.

"The big deal is that I should have the right to break the news to her when and if I want to." Jack's hand tightened around his fork. "If we choose to put this baby up for adoption, there's no reason for her to know. Ever."

"You're wrong." Rod straightened, regrouping. "She does care, more than you think."

A flicker of uncertainty pierced Jack's fury. "She said that?"

"I heard it in her voice."

Noting the conflict in Jack's expression, Anya wished she were sitting close enough to touch his arm and offer silent comfort. *Stay out of it, you idiot,* she warned herself.

"I'll talk to her," Jack said tightly.

"And tell her not to come?" his uncle queried.

"And tell her whatever I damn please." Jack stood up. "There's ice cream in the freezer."

"On my way." Lucky hurried out, escaping the tension.

"I'll help." Melissa rose gracefully, and the others began clearing the table.

"Anya?" Jack swung toward her. "A moment alone?"

"Sure." She'd hated saying no to him about the bird-watching last night. They'd had fun, peering into the twilight, listening to the chirps and trying to identify the various species. And tonight, he'd defended her to his uncle. As if they were in this together. Which, until the baby's birth, she supposed they were.

Conscious of the others watching—despite their attempts

to pretend otherwise—she kept her gaze straight ahead and her pace moderate as they climbed the stairs. Once on the second floor, they hurried to her room. The sunset cast a scarlet glow across the bed and bookcase. Anya switched on the lamp. "Shoot."

Jack paced the floor.

Funny how a man's presence changed everything, emphasizing the smallness of the room and filling the air with subtle allure that reminded Anya that she'd tossed her comforter over invitingly rumpled sheets.

Stop, now. That's how you got into this mess.

He halted. "I apologize for my uncle's behavior."

She waved away the apology. "Not your fault."

"Would you mind…" He broke off.

To her, the glitter in his eyes spoke of old wounds reopened—and old hopes springing to life. "Meeting your mom?" Anya guessed.

"Or even…" Jack hesitated again, uncharacteristically. Then he said, "If she does care, it shouldn't be in an abstract sense. I need to be sure."

She hazarded a guess. "You want to invite her to the ultrasound. That's quite a switch." Moments before, he'd been prepared to boot her all the way back to whatever third world country she was currently aiding.

"It hit me all of a sudden, but I didn't want to mention it in front of my uncle," Jack explained. "What do you think?"

Having his mother present might be like tossing a lighted match onto dried-out California underbrush during fire season. Yet it meant a lot to Jack, and thus far, he'd been willing to meet Anya halfway.

But if his mother *did* take a stand against her, what then? Though Mamie wasn't likely to volunteer to help raise her granddaughter, considering she'd ducked out on her own son. And she'd have to possess incredible chutzpah to pressure another woman to take on the duties she herself had shirked.

And so far, Jack had respected Anya's feelings. It was time to trust him.

With the sense of taking a dive off a cliff, Anya said, "Okay."

He waited, as if expecting more. Then he noted, "I'm not even sure she'll be able to come. I suppose it depends on her conference schedule."

It would be inconvenient but not impossible to change the sonogram appointment. Anya saw no need to bring that up yet, though. "Whatever."

Jack ran his hands over her shoulders, massaging them lightly. "Will I ever figure you out?"

"I hope not." In her view, keeping him off-balance promoted equal power in the relationship. But right now, she was content to relax and enjoy the magic sensations his fingers inspired. "You could do more of that."

"Happy to comply, ma'am," he responded with a heart-stopping smile.

Anya leaned closer. His chest materialized beneath her cheek. "Mmm."

Strong arms closed around her, and she nestled there. Would it really be so bad if, together, they…?

Stop right there. She'd already taken a step in his direction, figuratively speaking, by agreeing to allow his mother to come to the ultrasound. That meant, she conceded, that if Mamie unexpectedly offered her son the nurturing he'd been denied all these years, Anya could hardly refuse to give him—them—the baby.

That might mean having to leave Safe Harbor afterward for her own emotional safety. Freedom could be a lonely place, but for now, they'd reached a welcome accord.

All the same, she ducked away before their embrace could lead to more.

Chapter Fourteen

On Saturday, Jack reported that Mamie had cheerfully agreed to attend next Thursday's ultrasound, scheduled for 7:30 p.m. at Dr. Cavill-Hunter's office. "She seemed upbeat about the whole situation," Jack said as he set out the ingredients for his planned dinner of angel-hair pasta with wine and onions.

"She isn't upset that Rod broke the news about the baby, rather than you?" Anya asked.

She felt a little guilty that Jack had spent more than he intended on these large meals, and was glad he'd decided to fix a low-cost entrée tonight. His explanation that the alcohol in the wine would evaporate during cooking hadn't been necessary, but she appreciated it.

"I'm not sure it's sunk in that she's about to become a grandmother." He placed the cutting board on the stove top to chop onions, turning on the fan to draw off eye-burning fumes.

"Every woman reacts differently, I guess." Anya was slicing tomatoes on a second cutting board. She'd volunteered to assist, having discovered that conversations with Jack flowed more naturally when they worked side by side. Perhaps due to their shared experiences in the O.R., they moved easily around each other without colliding.

"What about *your* mother?" Jack scraped the onions into a large pot and set to dicing garlic cloves. "You've hardly mentioned her."

With a start, Anya admitted she hadn't thought about how

her mother might react to the baby. Molly Meeks's name suited her retiring personality. Even before arthritis had sidelined her, she'd been almost a background player in the household, relying first on Ruth to help raise her second and third children and then on Anya to supervise the triplets.

"Mom's always been overshadowed by my grandma—my father's mother," she said. "Not that Grandma was underfoot. She lived around the corner from us and values her independence. But on important issues, her views tended to prevail."

"She's the one who's turning eighty next month?"

"That's her." Anya hoped he'd refrain from inquiring about the gathering. It *was* awkward that she hadn't responded yet. But Ruth had stopped tallying childcare requests on social media, and although that didn't amount to an acknowledgment that Anya might not show up, it implied her sister might be facing reality.

Or preparing another line of attack. Anya sighed.

"If you're tired, you should sit down." Jack moved his cutting board to the counter. "I can finish the salad."

"No, I just…" *Don't want to discuss my family issues.* "You're being wonderful," she said.

He flashed a grin. "I am, aren't I?"

The meal turned out to be another of his triumphs, though she couldn't get the conversation about their mothers out of her head. She had enough issues from her own family. Was she prepared to take on his issues, too?

The next few days passed quickly. Mamie planned to arrive in Los Angeles on Wednesday for her conference. On Thursday, Rod was going to collect her from her hotel at 4:00 p.m. and bring her to the house so she could enjoy dinner with everyone and meet Anya prior to the sonogram.

But on Thursday morning, everything changed. A disgruntled Jack caught Anya in the hallway of the hospital.

"Can we reschedule the ultrasound?" It turned out his mom had to attend a press conference early that evening for her Haitian charity, he explained. "She apologized profusely and swears she can come Friday afternoon."

"I'm not sure. It was hard to make arrangements for a weekday evening, let alone a Friday." Because of Dr. Cavill-Hunter's overnight shifts in labor and delivery, her office hours didn't start until 6:00 p.m.

"Mamie can't attend in the evening. Her flight's at 7:30 p.m., and she has to be at the airport an hour and a half early." As usual, Jack referred to his mother by her first name.

It struck Anya that Mamie would be missing tonight's dinner, too, on which Jack had spent a small fortune. He'd bought steaks and was planning on making twice-baked potatoes stuffed with cheese. But that was less important than the sonogram.

"I don't suppose my doctor *has* to be there," Anya conceded. "And it will be easier to find a tech to work during the day."

"Adrienne can review the results with us later." His gaze locked onto Anya's.

"Let me see what I can set up. I'm just sorry she'll miss your delicious cooking." Anya hoped he didn't think she was criticizing his mother.

Jack shrugged. "Mamie has a tendency to play the drama queen. But it sounds like this is an important press conference. There are major potential donors in the L.A. area."

"It's a worthy cause," Anya agreed, although she only vaguely recalled the nature of the project—something about providing security for Haitian women living in tent encampments. "We'll figure out the ultrasound."

That proved more difficult than expected. Dr. Tartikoff had scheduled a complex surgery for early Friday afternoon and was relying on Jack to assist. The sometimes crusty head of the fertility program, on learning of the circumstances, promised to free Jack by 3:30 p.m., but that was the best he could do.

Locating an ultrasound tech presented further problems. Zora had back-to-back assignments and another tech was out with the flu. It would be unfair to bump a patient who'd had her session planned weeks in advance.

"I'm sorry," Zora told Anya over lunch. "I'm disappointed I'm going to miss out on meeting the famous Mamie Ryder, too." Rod had been regaling the dinner table all week with tales of his sister's colorful exploits around the world.

"I'll fill you in," Anya responded distractedly. Her main concern was that the ultrasound might not take place this week at all. She was trying not to dwell on the implications of meeting Jack's mother.

"I'll do it myself," Jack said a short time later when she informed him she couldn't find a tech. She'd spotted him in the busy corridor just outside the cafeteria. "Performing sonograms was part of my training."

"Aren't you a little rusty?" she asked.

He steered her out of the path of a gurney being pushed by a volunteer. "You mean like performing an operation with a rusty knife?"

"Ouch!"

Jack laughed. "I assure you, I'm competent. And it isn't an invasive procedure, so I can't very well cause harm."

Anya thought of a plus. "Also, you get to show off for your mother."

"She *is* proud of my accomplishments," he assured her. "Mamie's seen me operate, via remote camera. She found it fascinating."

It was good to hear him speaking well of his mother. In fact, this past week, he'd spoken up during Rod's tales, adding a few flattering details about Mamie. Squelching an uneasy sense that he and his mother might soon join forces against her, Anya said, "I'll line up an examining room, then."

"Thanks." Jack traced a finger across her cheek.

She stepped back, surprised at the tender gesture given in full public view. "Have you forgotten how bad the gossips are around here?"

"You mean they'll be shocked that two people having a baby together show signs of affection?" he teased.

She chuckled. "You never know."

On Friday, despite Anya's efforts to train her mind away

from the upcoming procedure, she became increasingly nervous as 3:30 p.m. approached. She'd lined up a room and made sure ultrasound equipment would be available. And, she reminded herself, she already knew the baby's gender. So what was the big deal?

Yet she dropped her purse twice in the nurses' locker room and arrived at Dr. Cavill-Hunter's office on the second floor of the medical building before recalling that the sonogram was to take place on the third floor where Jack shared quarters with Dr. Tartikoff.

It was 3:25 p.m. Afraid she might be keeping him and his mother waiting, Anya took the stairs up a floor rather than wait for the elevator. As she climbed, she noticed how tightly her jeans were fitting, a reminder she'd soon have to buy maternity clothes. By twelve weeks, some women were already ballooning. Anya had made a point of eating moderately, hoping to delay displaying her condition to the world as long as possible.

She wouldn't be able to hide it much longer, though. Not that many people weren't already aware of her situation anyway.

Anya put her shoulder to the heavy third-floor door. She'd barely wedged it open and was shimmying through when the phone rang in her pocket.

Another change of plans? She plucked it out.

Ruth.

Oh, great timing. Irritably, Anya sent the call to voice mail, but she was so nervous she must've tapped the wrong spot. "Anya?" came her sister's voice. "Hello?"

If she cut off the call now, Ruth would take offense. And with good reason.

Anya put the phone to her ear. "I'm here. Listen, this is a bad time."

"I'd hoped you'd be off work by now."

She *was* off work, but Anya couldn't explain to her sister what she was really doing. "Uh, I am. But there's a meeting."

"You haven't responded about the birthday party." Barely

pausing for breath, Ruth pressed on, "Everyone's counting on you. Grandma would be heartbroken if you aren't here. You're her favorite grandchild."

"Don't be ridiculous." Including cousins, the third-generation count reached well into the double digits.

"It's obvious to everyone but you." Ruth must have prepared to go on this offensive before she placed the call. "You'll be arriving a few days early, as we agreed, right?"

"We didn't agree." Tensely, Anya wondered if her voice carried into the nearby offices. "I'm not in a place where I can talk."

"Are you coming or not?"

She nearly responded in the negative. But why should she let Ruth's bossiness prevent her from honoring her grandmother? She'd learned over the past few weeks that her duck-and-run philosophy could cheat her out of some very happy moments. Instead, she decided to address the real problem. "I'm not running a day care center. People can watch their own children."

"Selfish as always!" Her sister's ragged voice rose to a shrill note. She sounded tired and resentful—and was aiming it all at Anya. "Everyone's pitching in, although most of the work falls on me, as usual."

"You live there," Anya pointed out. "Besides—"

"It isn't my fault you chose to move to California," Ruth went on. "I've got four kids and I'm carrying another."

"Somebody else can take up the slack." Although Ruth might be the oldest of the cousins, that shouldn't obligate her to run every family gathering.

"That's what I'm trying to do," her sister snapped. "I'm delegating. And your job is supervising the children."

"I appreciate how hard you're working." Guiltily, Anya conceded that she hadn't given her sister enough credit for bringing everyone together. "It isn't fair for everyone to assume you'll organize the whole party. But parents can make their own babysitting arrangements. I wouldn't expect someone else to take care of my child, if I had one."

"But you don't. You're too busy living it up, being single and hanging out at the beach." Now, where had Ruth picked up that idea? "You're letting everyone down—as always."

Anya badly wanted out of this conversation. Not to mention that her watch was edging past 3:30 p.m. "We each make our own choices."

"If that's how you feel, just stay home!" The call went dead.

Ruth had hung up on her? Despite the temptation to call back, Anya turned off her phone. Discussion tabled until whenever. But she was glad she'd stood up for herself.

She let herself into the waiting room. Several women looked up from their magazines. At the receptionist station, she spotted nurse Ned Norwalk.

"Come on in." He indicated the interior door.

A patient frowned in her direction. Because Anya had changed out of her uniform, the woman might have assumed she was jumping the line to see the doctor.

Must be my day to tick people off.

Anya hurried to the designated room. Inside, she found Jack alone with the portable ultrasound equipment plugged in and ready for action.

His white coat was much more flattering than operating scrubs, and no ugly cap covered his thick dark hair. Half his patients probably had crushes on him, Anya reflected. Well, so had she, until...

Actually, she still did. But that was irrelevant.

"I'd have been here sooner, but my sister called at the worst possible moment." She kicked off her shoes.

"I can't wait to hear all about it." Jack raised an eyebrow. "Would you like me to leave the room while you change?"

That seemed silly, Anya thought as she picked up the hospital gown set out for her. "Just turn your back."

"As my lady wishes."

After he swung to face the door, she shed her clothes and put on the gown. "Where's your mom?"

"Rod called. They'll be here any minute."

That raised another potential problem. "About your uncle…"

Jack squared his shoulders. "You'd rather he wasn't here."

"Right."

"I don't like the way he treats you either. You don't want him here, so he won't be."

Anya tied the gown in front, a fruitless task because it gaped open. Who had designed these things, a Peeping Tom?

"Ready." She sat on the edge of the examining table.

Jack came alongside her. From this position, he towered over her, yet the gentleness of his expression soothed her. Stretching out, Anya quivered at the realization that he was about to touch her bare abdomen and run his hands over her.

As a doctor. But also as a father.

"We should start. My mother has a tight timetable." He picked up the scanning paddle, which reminded Anya of a computer mouse. "I'm out of practice, so it may take me a while to find the right angle."

She leaned back, her head slightly elevated by the table. "You can take pictures, too, right?"

"Yes! Don't let me forget. First baby pictures." Gently, Jack spread gel on her stomach. "It's a little chilly. Sorry."

Anya scarcely noticed. She was too keenly aware of his large hand stroking the gel across her abdomen. "No problem."

"At this point, the tech would normally explain that the paddle emits very high frequency sound waves, above the range of human hearing," he said. "That's where we get the word *sound* in ultrasound."

"And they bounce off structures inside me to produce an image," she finished. Sonography was used in many types of medical diagnosis, as Anya was well aware.

"Structures," he repeated as he laid the paddle on her tummy. "Otherwise known as the baby." His intake of breath belied his clinical tone.

On the monitor, gray tones shifted and seethed. For all Anya could tell, the darker shapes might be her kidneys or her bladder—oops, better not think about that, with the device pressing down right there.

Then she saw, unmistakably, a tiny backbone visible through the fetus's nearly translucent skin. The paddle moved, and into view came a beating heart, the rhythm faster than an adult's. As Jack adjusted the paddle, she discerned the shape of a curled baby, from its head to its rump, arms and legs moving.

"She's wiggling," she said, astonished even though she should have expected this. "A lot. I can't feel her yet."

"That's because she's only about two inches long. She has plenty of room for gymnastics." On the equipment, Jack flipped a switch and the rushing, thumping sound of a heartbeat engulfed the room.

A glow filled Anya, a miraculous sense of the person inside her—those fingers and toes already formed. Tiny eyes stared about almost as if the baby could see her parents.

Jack drew in a ragged breath. "This is unbelievable. I've watched a lot of ultrasounds and delivered a lot of babies. But this is different. It's our daughter."

Pulling her gaze from the screen, Anya noticed tears misting his eyes. He became blurry until she blinked and cleared her own tears.

She'd been fighting this connection for months, and now it nearly overwhelmed her. When the baby twitched, Anya could have sworn she made out a tiny nose shaped like her own.

She'd never understood how women could swear that once they held their baby, they almost immediately forgot the anguish of childbearing. Now, though, she teetered on the edge of forgetting the pain, not of childbearing but of child-rearing.

Endless piles of diapers, uncounted bottles to warm, cries in the night driving sleep to oblivion as each baby woke up her sisters. But Anya wasn't carrying triplets as her mother had. This was a single small girl.

Jack swallowed. "Look at her. She's really there, Anya. Our daughter."

Your daughter. She meant to say that aloud, but the words caught in her throat.

She's my daughter, too.

The door flew open. Startled, Anya realized she'd forgotten they were expecting company.

With a swish of fabric, a flood of exotic perfume and a flash of color, a dark-haired woman swept into the room. Tall and slim, she had spiky short hair and sharp eyes. Brilliant blocks of red, yellow and green marked her long halter dress.

As Jack switched off the Doppler sound of the baby's heartbeat, Anya stared at the apparition who'd just joined them.

"I'm here! We can start now." Her gleaming smile encompassed them both in the greeting.

Mamie Ryder had arrived.

Chapter Fifteen

Jack's first response, to his astonishment, was irritation. Did his mother have to arrive *now?*

This was his and Anya's private moment, their first meeting with their daughter. He'd seen Anya's resistance melting and her heart opening. Couldn't Mamie have given them a few more minutes?

Grudgingly, he bit down on his reaction. "Mamie," he greeted her—even when he was small, she'd preferred he use her name because "Mommy" made her feel old. "I'd give you a hug, but…" He lifted the paddle.

"Don't let me interrupt," she sang out. "Sorry I'm late. We hit a ridiculous amount of traffic."

"Not that much," Rod observed, entering behind her, his fedora slightly askew as if he'd run from the parking garage. "We were late leaving the hotel."

"All that packing." Mamie smiled at Anya. "This must be the new mommy. Hi. I'm Mamie."

"Nice to meet you." True to form, Anya wasted no words.

When her attention flicked to Rod, Jack recalled his promise. He zeroed in on his uncle. "Thanks for driving and for waiting outside."

Rod's mouth opened and promptly shut. "It *is* a bit crowded in here. I'll be out there playing with my phone."

That had been easy. Perhaps chauffeuring Mamie had proved trying. Jack spared no sympathy for his uncle, considering that it had been Rod's idea to invite her.

All the same, he appreciated that his mother had made the trip to Southern California.

Despite being in her early fifties, she struck him as ageless. Only twenty-one when he was born, she'd been a youthful mom, full of energy and vitality. In absentia, Mamie might inspire disappointment or even resentment, but in person, she was a force of nature.

Jack indicated the screen. "There she is. Our little girl."

Setting down her shopping bag, Mamie advanced toward the monitor. "My goodness." She frowned. "Are you sure it's a girl?"

"Yes," he said.

"Then what's that?" She indicated something poking from between the baby's legs.

"It's the umbilical cord." He moved the paddle to show a better angle.

"Oh. I see!" She searched for another comment. "Have you picked a name?"

"No." Jack doubted that Junior-ette qualified.

"My mother's name was Lenore," Mamie reminded him. "It's beautiful, isn't it?"

"It is." Jack became aware of Anya taking in this scene with a puzzled expression. He, too, was wondering when his mother would show the sense of wonder he and Anya had felt when they first glimpsed their child.

She will. Give her time.

"What was your pregnancy like?" Anya asked. "With Jack, I mean."

"In what respect?"

Anya rephrased the question. "Was it complicated? Or did it go smoothly?"

Mamie blinked. "I'm afraid I've forgotten. Honestly, my late husband was much more excited than I was."

Jolted, Jack stood there numbly. Did his mother have any idea what she'd just revealed?

"Well, you did a good job." Anya deserved credit for filling the pause before it could lengthen uncomfortably.

"Oh, I'm very proud of my son." Mamie's smile lacked warmth, as if she were reciting a line she'd rehearsed.

To Jack, this encounter was both disconcerting and disconnected. His mother had traveled thousands of miles for this, yet her fidgety body language implied an eagerness to leave.

Achingly, he realized he'd hoped for much more—that, as a mature adult, he could finally perceive the deep well of love that he'd missed when he was younger. At some level, he'd believed his mother's drive and dedication had torn her away from him but that the delight of meeting her granddaughter would reveal how much she cared.

He should have known better. Anger flared at himself for being gullible.

Mamie cleared her throat. "Do you have a nanny lined up?"

Anya gave a start. "No, we aren't...not yet."

"Don't wait till the last minute. I hear good nannies are hard to find," his mother advised.

"Thanks for the tip." Was Anya being ironic? Jack couldn't tell. And he had to rely on her, of all people, to keep the conversational ball rolling while he collected his thoughts. To his gratitude, she did. "That's a gorgeous dress."

Mamie whirled, showing off the striking design. "It's from Haiti, of course. So are the sandals." She lifted her feet to reveal strappy shoes that, to Jack, appeared to have soles shaped from recycled tires. "I only buy clothes made by the poor. They're so desperate! You should see the conditions they live under. As a mother, your heart would break for their children."

"I'm sure it would," Anya agreed.

"That reminds me. I brought a gift for the baby." From her shopping bag she pulled a large, angular metal construction. It was a lizard with a blue head and tail, orange legs and a green and yellow pattern on its body. "I'd have wrapped it, but they'd never have let it through airport security."

Anya waved her hand. "Just more paper to put in the recycle bin."

"Exactly!" Mamie beamed. "It's made out of old oil drums. Isn't it gorgeous? Look at the artistry. It's a gecko, by the way."

"Very cheerful," Anya said. "It'll be stunning on the wall."

That was diplomatic of her, considering that she planned to give up the baby. He'd relayed that to his mother when he'd phoned to discuss her visit, but apparently the information hadn't sunk in. Or she'd chosen to ignore it. The conversation had been a little strained, as if she were trying to say the right things but wasn't sure what those were. Jack had tried to be encouraging, despite his qualms.

"I suppose it is a bit large to put in the crib." Mamie held the gecko at arm's length, studying it. "You might hang it overhead, though, to stimulate Lenore's imagination."

With those sharp edges and possibly toxic paints? Clearly his mother hadn't wrapped her head around the idea of a baby. But she'd meant well.

"Jack, how about some screen shots of, uh, Lenore?" Anya prompted. "I'll bet your mother would like to take one with her."

"Sure."

"I'll show them off to my friends in Haiti." Returning the sculpture to the bag, Mamie rubbed her hands together. "They're thrilled that I'm going to be a grandmother."

As Jack adjusted the paddle and clicked to save a picture, he processed the fact that Mamie had spread the word about her grandchild despite his warning that they were considering putting her up for adoption. If Mamie were a doting grandma, it might be understandable, but he had the troubling sense that the baby appealed to her primarily as a way to show off to her friends.

Don't be judgmental. But he was still trying to absorb the statement that she hadn't been thrilled about her own pregnancy, about having him.

As he worked, Anya asked about the press conference, and Mamie waxed eloquent. "We must attract more businesses to revitalize the economy. Did you know Haiti is the poorest country in the Western Hemisphere? Unemployment is sixty to eighty percent. Just a few years ago, the island was devastated by an earthquake. Two years later, half a million people were still living in tents."

She cited shocking statistics about diseases and further damage from a hurricane. Passion blazed from Mamie's face.

Jack felt guilty. The work she was doing mattered to a lot of people. Still, she was the only mother he'd ever have. And today she'd reopened a wound that ran soul-deep.

With a knock, Rod returned to tell them that it was time to leave for the airport. Jack was sure that news came as a relief to everyone.

When Rod and Mamie were gone, the room suddenly felt peaceful. "Huh," Anya said.

After switching off the machine, Jack wiped the gel from her stomach. "My mother's an original, isn't she?"

"Are you okay?" She watched him sympathetically.

He nearly answered with an automatic yes, but that wasn't true. "I felt like we were actors in a stage play," he said as he helped Anya sit up. "Everything about that scene with my mother rang false. What did I miss? Am I that out of touch?"

Outside in the hallway, voices murmured as Ned escorted a patient past. "We should go somewhere else," Anya said.

"Good idea." Jack's phone hummed in his pocket. "Excuse me." Plucking it out, he read an unfamiliar number. Cautiously, he answered. "Dr. Ryder."

"Jack? Are you still at the hospital?" It was a man's voice.

"Right next door," he said.

"It's Zack Sargent. Thank goodness I caught you."

Jack was glad to deal with a professional matter. "What's up?"

"I'm scheduled to perform an embryo transplant but I must have caught my daughter's stomach flu because I just threw up." Zack *did* sound shaky. "I can't expose the patient to this. The embryos are already thawed. Owen thought you might still be on the premises."

"Yes. I'd be happy to step in." A potential conflict occurred to Jack. "Who's the patient?"

"It's Melissa Everhart," Zack told him. "I know you're acquainted with her personally but I've cleared it with her."

"In that case, how quickly do you need me there?" Given that the embryos were thawed, it was important to proceed at once, but Jack hoped he could spend a few minutes with Anya first, to clarify his feelings about Mamie.

"She's prepped now."

After getting the details about where to report, Jack signed off.

"Emergency?" asked Anya, who'd dressed while he was talking.

Although Melissa would no doubt fill her in later, that was the patient's choice. So Jack merely said, "I'm afraid so. But I'd like to meet you later." Another problem occurred to him. "And I still have to shop for dinner. I suppose I could throw together some kind of pasta dish."

"I could do the shopping," Anya said. "What's on the menu?"

"I was going to spring for salmon if my mother decided to delay her flight." What an optimistic idiot he'd been to imagine her doing such a thing. "I have a favorite recipe I got from a medical school colleague."

"Tell me what to buy." Anya raised a finger. "Wait. There's no reason for you to cook for my housemates tonight. We could eat at your place."

"Great idea." And that would make the salmon more affordable, too. "Save the bill and I'll pay you back. No arguments." From memory, Jack listed the ingredients for the meal and gave her a key from his ring. "I don't want you standing outside with the groceries."

"I'll be alone in your apartment?" She grinned mischievously. "Could I leave a rubber spider in Rod's bed?"

"How will you know which room's his?"

Her eyebrows shot up. "Honestly. You guys do smell different."

"Too much information." He assumed she was kidding about the spider anyway.

"I'll put the equipment away." She indicated the rolling cart beneath the sonograph machine, which Ned Norwalk had fetched earlier from a hall closet.

"Thanks. See you soon."

Heading out, Jack fixed his mind on the procedure ahead, reviewing the necessary steps. No surgery was required; for the patient, an embryo transfer felt much like a Pap smear.

The procedure involved the use of ultrasound to aid his manipulation of the catheter loaded with the embryos. The angle of the catheter was vital, both for the patient's safety and for proper placement.

Before he knew it, he was climbing the stairs to the second floor. For now, everything that had happened—seeing his daughter, encountering his mother, striving to understand his mixed emotions—could remain safely tucked away.

HOLDING THE GROCERY sack in one arm, Anya let herself into Jack's apartment. From outside, she lifted Mamie's gift bag and set it beneath a small table, atop which she placed the key.

Despite having lived around the corner from Jack for a year, she'd never ventured into his apartment until now. The living room was about the same size as the one she and Zora had shared, although the kitchen and hallway layouts were flipped. The place smelled of lemon oil and cleanser—a cleaning service must have visited recently—and the furniture included a cherrywood entertainment center and a tan curved sofa. Because Anya had expected a pair of bachelors on tight budgets to buy minimalist gear, she wondered if Rod's ex-wife had left these behind.

She was laying out her purchases on the kitchen counter when she heard the front door swing open. Instantly she recognized Jack's footsteps.

"Hi." His mood seemed upbeat as he regarded her. Performing the procedure—something to do with fertilization, she gathered—must have invigorated him. "Find everything okay?"

"I hope I got the right kind of apricot preserves." Anya indicated the jar. "And I bought the refrigerated horseradish. I think it's stronger than the other kind."

"Sounds perfect." He whipped a pair of aprons from a drawer, brushing past her with a rush of lime scent mixed with disinfectant. "You mind fixing the salad?"

"My specialty."

The kitchen was organized with surgical precision, with none of the messy jumbles that Anya recalled from the few other bachelor pads she'd visited over the years. As they cooked side by side, they kept the conversation light, instinctively delaying the emotional topics that thrummed beneath the surface.

Jack reported that the procedure had gone smoothly without providing details. And Anya explained that she'd texted Karen, who'd assured her the household could assemble dinner from the leftovers cramming the fridge.

"Cooking for everybody was a big job. You were astonishing," she told Jack as she sliced tomatoes.

"I've enjoyed it."

Now that she'd raised the topic, Anya braced for him to mention the reason for his cooking. She could hardly refuse him custody of the baby after all this. That meant she'd have to leave Safe Harbor, and him, and her friends, unless she planned to be intimately involved in raising her child. At the prospect, the light seemed to drain from the room. What a bleak prospect: losing this family of friends and especially Jack. How was she going to bear that? Thinking about a future without him was much too painful.

"Did you buy a plastic spider?"

"What?" The question jerked Anya back to the moment.

"For Rod's bed."

Grateful for the interruption, she arrayed the tomatoes around the salad bowl. "On further reflection, it struck me as childish."

"We're talking about my uncle here," Jack teased. "I have my own score to settle with that rogue. Although maybe driving my mom is punishment enough."

"The Friday night traffic coming back from LAX must be awful." She hoped Rod wouldn't arrive until after their meal.

"He called to say he'll eat dinner in L.A. to miss the worst of it." Jack gazed down at the baking dish. "I'm supposed to marinate the fish in lime juice for a couple of hours. But it should taste fantastic anyway. Too bad I don't have Myrna's number so I can ask her."

"Myrna?"

"Fellow med student." With a half smile, he added, "I assure you, she's happily married and not at all interested in me."

"Doesn't matter. If this salmon is as good as you say, I can forgive you anything."

And it was. The fish melted in Anya's mouth. With crusty French bread and salad, the meal proved memorable. Jack served it on his best china, a flowered set that he confirmed had once belonged to his aunt.

Anya nearly blurted that they had to give up the baby because she couldn't bear to move away from him. Only she kept picturing Junior-ette as she'd appeared on the sonograph screen, tumbling happily in the utter safety of...

Of me. Her mom.

"I could use your help." Jack set down his fork, and Anya realized that she wasn't the only one in anguish.

Yanked from her reverie, she took a deep breath. "You want to talk about it now?"

"You heard what my mother said." A muscle worked in Jack's jaw. "She never wanted me."

"She didn't say that, exactly."

"She might as well have." He scowled. "My whole childhood, I blamed myself for her absence. I was too much trouble, too hard to take care of. Now I find out I never had a chance."

"She does care about you, on some level," Anya noted. "Why else did she come today?"

"Because Rod shamed her into it." Bitterness darkened his words. "When I was a kid, she used to blow into town with an armload of presents, charming everyone. I adored her and always thought someday we'd be close. Now I know we never will."

"What she said today hurt you." Overwhelming as Anya's family could be, she'd never had reason to doubt their love.

"I'm not just hurt, I'm angry." His hands clenched into fists. "I've been a damn fool for clinging to her all these years when she barely makes a show of doing the right thing. Her only reaction to the ultrasound was to wonder if the baby was a boy after all. And that sculpture she brought—how could any sane person consider putting it in a crib?"

From her seat around the corner of the table, Anya cupped one of his fists with her hand. "I think she was genuinely trying to behave the way she should. But her instincts were all wrong."

"What do you mean?"

She wasn't sure how she understood this, but it was the only way her impressions of Mamie made sense. "Some people are tone deaf or color blind. And others have a hard time sensing emotions and gauging reactions. It's like she had to rehearse, and she kept watching us for clues about how she should act."

"She had to fake being a grandmother?" Jack's forehead furrowed.

"Something like that," Anya said. "I'm not excusing her because it's unfair that you had to grow up the way you did. I'm guessing your grandparents weren't real champs in the hugs and kisses department either."

"You're right about that." His wrist turned and his hand clasped hers. "How could she *not* experience how miraculous it was to see the baby?"

"How can some people bliss out on a symphony that others find boring?" Anya mused. "There are women who just don't have the maternal instinct, no matter how hard they try to fit into others' expectations."

He went very still. "Are you talking about yourself and our baby?"

Tell the truth, Anya. "No." Tears filled her eyes. "No, she is the most wonderful thing I've ever seen."

Warmth and tenderness blazed as he lifted her hand and kissed it. "For me, too."

Today they'd shared the most intimate connection of Anya's life, even more than when they'd conceived the baby. And she longed to be closer still.

When Jack pulled her up into a hug, she tossed her napkin on the table and tilted her face for a kiss. A long, loving kiss that blossomed through her entire body.

This time, as they made their way to his bedroom, she didn't pretend it was a momentary indulgence or anything less than the chance to claim Jack as she'd been yearning to do all along.

And never mind the consequences.

Chapter Sixteen

To Jack, Anya had always been beautiful. Tonight, in the room that too often echoed with solitude, she was radiant.

Touching her aroused him at every level. She held their baby inside this exquisite, velvety body; in her parted lips and questioning gaze he read an openness he'd never sensed in her before. And she understood him, understood his life, had just solved a fundamental mystery and identified an issue he hadn't even grasped until today.

Treasuring her sweet natural scent, he eased off her shirt and jeans. No need for words; she never seemed to have much use for them, and for once, neither did he. Brushing her hair back from her heart-shaped face, he trailed kisses across her full mouth and ran his thumbs down her swelling breasts.

Her eager groan hardened him. When she pulled down his jeans, Jack aided her eagerly. Then he collected her onto his lap, sitting on the edge of the bed, drawing her hips down against his hardness and entering her slowly.

As they merged, he gasped from the intensity. The self-protective instincts he'd honed over a lifetime dissolved. Anya of the silent watchfulness, Anya of distances, Anya of sudden, unpredictable moods—he loved her. Wildly, despite the risk, despite the way she'd always retreated when he needed her. Now they were one.

Jack shifted his hips, and Anya eased up and down along his shaft, her dark hair screening them with a private cloud.

What a joy to run his palms down her back and trace the swell of her derriere.

Ecstasy seized him. After a brief, vain struggle to resist, he let the thrill take him. He luxuriated in Anya's moaning as they veered fast, faster, into a zone of brilliant light. Colors exploded; heat flooded him.

After an eon of pleasure, Jack wrapped his arms around Anya. "Let's stay here forever."

She laughed softly and rested her cheek against his neck. "Okay."

"Or we could wait until we catch a second wind."

"Okay."

A chuckle welled up in him. "You're agreeable tonight."

Her palm caressed his cheek, rough with a day's growth of beard. "Don't take this personally, but you're the sexiest man I've ever met."

"Why can't I take it personally?"

"It might go to your head," she whispered in his ear and rubbed her soft core against him.

"And that's a problem?" He could scarcely breathe as she reawakened his senses.

"The other nurses already fall at your feet."

"Who cares about them?" he answered, struggling to concentrate on what he was saying. But it was a lost cause because the rest of him had become supercharged.

"That was fast," Anya murmured.

"Let's not waste it." He lifted her until she slid onto him again. Then Jack rolled Anya onto the sheets. When her legs wrapped around him, he lost himself in her. The sensation of belonging was so intense, it filled him again and again, just as his body filled hers.

His climax came like the roll of a heated ocean, wave after wave beneath a fiery, liquid sky. No horizon, no limits, only a glorious shared blaze.

In an aftermath like a summer sunset, Jack held Anya among the tangled sheets. "I love you." He let the words linger for only a second before he said, "Did I mention that I love you?"

"Twice."

"As many times as we made love," he teased.

She nuzzled him without speaking. She hadn't responded that she loved him, too, but then, Anya wasn't the type to blurt something like that out on impulse.

While she was thinking it over, Jack decided to go for broke. "Marry me," he said.

GROWING UP, Anya had instinctively censored her own wishes and interests, her mind echoing with her father's imagined disapproval. So her dream—and increasingly urgent need—had become to truly be herself, independent and free of intrusive criticism and judgment.

Now, her love for Jack nearly smothered that need. Oh, how she yearned to shout "Yes!" and transform into the bride doll atop the wedding cake. To lie beside him every night, to share the precious moments as their baby grew, to talk earnestly and to sit silently, always and forever.

A fine fantasy. Reality had a nasty way of intruding, though.

And now she had to choose: take what her heart wanted or insist on what her soul demanded. How could she give Jack up, especially now that he'd trusted her with his future? After the emotional desertion Jack had suffered from his mother, after the betrayal he'd seen devastate his uncle, he was still willing to reach out to her.

"Anya?" Jack propped himself on one elbow. Half covered by a sheet, the man was spectacular. Rather than the bulked-up build of a jock, he had a solid, well-muscled strength coupled with the delicate skills of a surgeon.

She had to stop thinking such things. Or did she?

"I love you, too." Anya took a shaky breath.

A relieved smile curved his mouth. "Was that so difficult?"

"Huh."

"I guess that's a yes." His forefinger tapped the tip of her nose. "Now say yes to the other part."

Marry me. "I can't," she said miserably.

His muscles stiffened. "Can't or won't?"

"Marriage is too big a step." Did they have to go that far, involving the rest of the world in their private business? Maybe they could meet in the middle. "I have an alternate proposal."

Skepticism warred with hope in his expression. "Shoot."

"Let's live together." That wasn't the same, Anya knew, but she forged on. "Plenty of people do." And if they weren't married, he'd have no right to assume he owned her. Not that Jack acted bossy now, but marriage changed people. A nurse she'd worked with in Denver had been deliriously happy after her honeymoon, only to be stunned at how demanding her bridegroom soon became about her cooking, her spending habits and her occasional girls' nights out.

"Live together for how long?" Jack asked warily.

She hadn't considered that. "To raise the baby."

"Twenty years?" His tone was dubious.

"That sounds about right."

"What if we decide to have a second child?"

Anya clapped her hands against the sides of her head. "Honestly, Jack!"

"It wasn't a joke. You're refusing to commit to me or to a family," he accused.

"I refuse to be boxed into a role," she countered. "Taken for granted. Assigned to childcare for the duration."

Sitting up against the headboard, Jack blew out a frustrated breath, then folded his arms. Was he angry? She couldn't tell.

"I *am* willing to make a commitment." Anya sat up, too. "Only not the formal, public kind. I love you, Jack. I'll never love anybody else." She was growing teary again, darn it. "But you're a powerful guy, the lord of the operating room. You might get full of yourself. Don't argue. You'll start taking for granted that you're my boss at home, too. And I can't bear that."

He studied her. "Marriage scares you."

"You could say that." She bit her lip before adding, "Does it have to be all or nothing?"

"You know my family history."

Yes, she did. And he knew hers. "Marriage is no guarantee of permanence."

"Hmm." The cryptic response was maddening. *Like the cryptic responses I usually make.*

"I'll communicate better, I promise," she volunteered.

He still didn't answer. Anya leaned back. He'd allowed her to think things over, and she had to do the same.

A BEAUTIFUL ANYA strolling down the aisle in a white dress, the moment when he slid the ring onto her finger, the celebration with their friends and family—all recorded to enjoy when they were old. Such things mattered. Most of all, Jack craved the vow to always be there for each other. How could he accept anything less?

Glancing at her sweet little face—knowing how stubborn she could be, but also how funny and warm—his heart squeezed. He loved her. She loved him, too. Anya had said so straight out, and she never babbled easy words.

It all boiled down to trust, Jack reflected. And whether this was a risk worth taking.

Would she stick with him? If they faced serious medical issues or a financial crisis, would the absence of marriage vows make a difference? He suspected it might. But he understood, too, what a wedding represented to Anya.

They each had to trust the other. In the meantime, they both had to give a little, too. "Okay," he said.

Her eyes widened. "Seriously?"

"On one condition."

Now *her* arms folded, making them a matched set. "What's that?"

"Relationships hit rough patches—it's inevitable," Jack pointed out. "I have to be sure you won't run for the hills when that happens."

"I promise," she said.

"Prove it."

She looked startled. "How?"

"Face up to your family." As her jaw dropped, he added, "I'll go with you, if you want."

She averted her gaze. "It's next weekend."

"So?" He'd clear his schedule. If any of his patients couldn't wait, Zack Sargent owed him a favor, and he suspected Owen Tartikoff would fill in, too, when he heard the reason.

"They'll all be there—my parents, my siblings, my cousins," Anya said. "We should wait for a better occasion."

"Not good enough." He hated to push her. If she balked, they'd be back to square one. But their confused instincts—his to mistrust, hers to duck tough issues—were the greatest enemy to their future. "You're stronger than you think, Anya, but you have to believe that, or every time we argue, I'll wonder if I'm going to come home to an empty house."

"I wouldn't do that!"

"Are you sure?"

She swallowed. "Jack…"

He touched her hair, wondering what he'd do if she refused. "Hmm?"

She appeared to be thinking hard. "I'm not ready to answer you."

"As you mentioned, the gathering's next weekend, and I'll have to cancel appointments," he reminded her.

"Give me twenty-four hours," she said.

They were both getting a lot of practice at compromising, Jack mused. "Done."

Her smile flashed, lighting up the room. Then she snuggled closer, and he was grateful for this truce, however long it lasted.

ANYA HAD LEFT by the time Rod came home. Jack refrained from mentioning her visit, although his uncle couldn't miss the smell of his cooking and probably picked up other clues. The man was like a bloodhound.

Jack had no tolerance for his uncle's prodding. His nerves were strung taut because his future was being decided inside Anya's unpredictable brain.

Rod stuck a chunk of French bread into the toaster oven. "I've missed having leftovers."

"I thought you ate dinner." Jack loitered in the kitchen doorway.

"I grabbed a quick burger." His uncle finger combed his hair.

"At the airport?"

"Nearby," Rod explained. "Mamie didn't want me to park, so I dropped her and her luggage at the curb. I presume she got off okay."

"I'm sure she's fine. She's a seasoned traveler." Jack never worried about his mother.

Rod laced his fingers on the table. "I owe you an apology."

"For inviting her?"

He gave an embarrassed nod. "I figured this would be a watershed moment for my sister. Instead, she kept chattering about how great you looked, how nice Anya is and the marvels of modern technology. The woman saw her first grandchild in action and she didn't have a word to say about it. Oh, except for asking what I thought about naming her Lenore."

Jack chuckled. "What did you say?"

"I said that's your and Anya's decision." Rod regarded him with a puzzled frown. "You don't seem upset."

"About what?" Mamie was the last thing on Jack's mind.

"She owes you something," his uncle said. "An apology for dumping you on our parents like a pet poodle. Now that it's her turn to be a grandmother, she ought to act like one."

"And you even missed the best part," Jack replied. "She told Anya she scarcely remembers being pregnant with me, that my father was much more excited about it than she was."

Rod smacked his forehead. "Jack, I'm sorry."

"Since you're the only relative I can rely on, I forgive you."

A groan greeted this response. "You couldn't rely on me this time. I let you down. I overestimated my sister."

Jack shrugged. "Just because a person becomes a biological parent doesn't mean she has nurturing instincts." He recalled Anya's insight. "Just as some people are tone deaf or color blind, others can't handle intimacy."

The toaster bell rang. Rod plucked out the hot bread. "That's borderline profound. Is this Anya's influence?"

"Yes."

"I underestimated your girlfriend. On average, I came out even." His uncle spread butter thickly. "Mind fetching that jar of preserves you hide in the lettuce bin?"

"I didn't think you ever opened the lettuce bin."

"Only when I'm searching for where you hide the preserves," Rod said.

Yielding to the inevitable, Jack went to oblige.

When Anya got home, she found her housemates in the den, sharing a bottle of sparkling apple juice. If they noticed her tangled hair—she'd misplaced the brush she usually kept in her purse—they had the tact not to comment.

"Big day!" Melissa announced. "I don't suppose Jack said anything to you about it."

Said anything about what? So much had happened that Anya couldn't sort through it all. "Jack doesn't discuss his patients with me, if that's what you mean."

"Melissa was implanted," Karen said. "With three embryos."

"Congratulations." Anya remembered the earlier dinner-table discussion. "Isn't Zack Sargent your doctor?"

"Stricken with a sudden illness." Lucky angled back the recliner, which he was hogging, as usual. "Stomach flu, I hear."

Was there any gossip too minor to escape his radar? Anya wondered.

"I'm on pins and needles!" Ordinarily the calmest member of the household, Melissa fidgeted on the sofa. "I have to wait another week before I can take a pregnancy test."

"I'm thinking positive. We'll have a house full of babies." Karen grinned at the prospect.

Not if I move in with Jack. Anya hadn't considered how that would affect her housemates or Rod. She certainly didn't intend to share a small apartment with *him*. Well, she'd deal with those issues later.

"It's very unlikely the embryos will all attach," Melissa reminded Karen.

"I'm sure at least one will," her friend said. "And there'll be two infants, anyway."

"I thought Anya was giving hers up," Lucky said.

"I didn't mean…" Karen halted guiltily. She must have found out about Zora, and hadn't meant to let it slip.

"Who else is pregnant?" Lucky demanded, and immediately answered his own question. "There's only two possibilities, and if it were you, you'd be crowing from the rooftop."

Sitting at the table apart from the others, Zora stared moodily into her glass of juice. "Just shut up about it."

"Who's the dad?" He broke off as the other women glared at him. "Yeah, I know, none of my business. Oh, please tell me it wasn't break-up sex."

Melissa steered the conversation away from Zora. "I'd be due in December," she said. "Anya, you mentioned September, and, Zora—"

"November," Zora muttered.

"If it's a multiple birth, mine are likely to come early," Melissa said. "In any event, it would be nice to set up a nursery. Lucky, you might have to move out." She chuckled.

"First positive thing I've heard all day." Zora barely cracked a smile, though. Something must have upset her, beyond the revelation about her pregnancy.

"I think I'll go upstairs." Anya didn't have to fake a yawn. "Zora, you look tired, too."

Her friend mirrored her yawn. "Yeah, I'll go up, too."

On the second floor, Anya said, "My room."

But Zora turned away. "I need to sleep."

"It's way too early." Anya caught her arm. "Come on. Don't keep whatever it is bottled up inside."

A sigh. "I suppose not."

In Anya's room, they settled on the window seat. Through the glass, she noted the darkening sky over the estuary, with stars appearing between the deep-blue-on-blue clouds. During her two months in this house, she'd grown to love this view.

"Did you tell Andrew about the baby?" Anya prodded.

"No." Zora stared blearily at her hands. "I never got the chance. He…" She broke off.

"What did he do?"

"He got married in Las Vegas last weekend," she choked out. "Betsy told me today. She waited till the end of the day because she knew how upset I'd be."

"Did you mention that she's going to be a grandmother?" Anya asked.

Zora shook her head.

"You *are* going to tell him about the baby, right?" Before her friend could answer, Anya added, "It's not like Betsy won't notice you're pregnant."

"Her first loyalty is to her son, not me," Zora said miserably. "Oh, I don't want to talk about this anymore. What about *your* day?" Gray eyes bored into hers. "What happened at the ultrasound? Did you meet Jack's mother? And what were you doing for the past few hours?"

"It's complicated."

"Start anywhere."

Anya sketched the day's events. In retrospect, Mamie had been rather funny, except for her unhappy effect on Jack. As for the salmon dinner, she hoped he'd fix it again for her, soon. And the rest…she was still figuring that out. "If we move in together, his cooking will be a big plus." Along with a lot of other things.

"You guys are together." Zora swallowed. "I should be glad for you. I *am* glad for you."

"I'll still be here for you." Anya clasped her friend's hands. "And I haven't agreed to go to Colorado. Seriously, this whole business is kind of crazy. I'm not a mom. Just because my body betrayed me…"

"Are you out of your mind?" Zora's thin face became more animated than it had been all evening. "You must be the stupidest person I ever met."

Anya dropped her hands and scooted back a few inches, which was all the space she had. "Thanks a lot."

"Shut up and listen." Zora drew herself up. Even sitting down, she was taller than Zora. "That man's in love with you. And you adore him, although the idea scares you half to death."

"All the way to death." Quickly Anya corrected, "It isn't love that scares me. It's marriage."

"It's relationships, with or without a license," her friend insisted. "If I had a guy like Jack begging to marry me, I'd jump at the chance."

"There are strings attached," Anya said. "If I go to Colorado, it'll be like Christmas all over again. My whole family trying to reorganize my life, laying guilt trips on me."

"And if you don't go?" Zora pressed.

Anya's gaze fell on the end table, where an empty space reminded her of the African violet that had once lived there. "I can't keep a plant alive.… I'm afraid I'll be like his mother, with all the wrong instincts." Now that she'd opened up, more truths spilled out. "Sometimes I hated my little sisters. I'd never have harmed them, but the weight of the responsibility was horrible. Every day, diapers and more diapers. Waking up all night, hearing their cries, and never being sure what was wrong or if I could help—I just wanted to run as far and as fast as I could."

"What your parents did was unfair." Zora seemed to have gained strength as she listened. "You shouldn't have had to shoulder so much of their responsibilities. But, Anya, you're only having one baby, not three. Plus most mothers get cranky with their kids once in a while. And you'll have Jack to help."

"I wish he wasn't insisting I go to my grandmother's birthday party. They plan to stick me with supervising the kids without even asking me if that's okay." She'd hardly have a free minute to spend with her grandma or anyone else.

"Jack's right. You have to stop seeing yourself as this helpless teenager backed against a wall by your big bossy family," came the response.

"If I refuse, it'll be a nonstop battle."

"You're an adult and you're having a baby—just stand up to them," Zora reproved. "Besides, you'll have Jack on your side. Do you have any idea how lucky you are? If Andrew were a tenth the man that Jack is, I'd be in heaven."

Tears sparkled against Zora's cheeks. She'd spoken from the heart. Most people would agree with her, too, including Jack.

But Zora and Jack had missed the point. *And so have I.*

With that realization, Anya suddenly knew what she had to do.

Chapter Seventeen

Having once attended a medical conference in Denver, Jack wasn't daunted by its large airport, and he easily navigated the hour-long drive to Anya's hometown using the computer system in their rental car. But as they left the main route and bumped along a narrow road on the final leg of their journey, he was keenly aware that they were traveling not only into a different landscape but also into the past. *Her* past.

For him, this high grassland with its mountainous backdrop brought no memories, merely a faint headache due to the altitude, over a mile above sea level. He turned on the car's heater against the cold, crisp late afternoon air—another change from Southern California. Having been warned that April might bring almost anything, he was grateful that the forecast contained no snowstorms.

What did all this signify to Anya? It was impossible to discern from her stone-wall expression.

A week ago, she'd informed him of her decision. "I need to find out exactly what I want from my life," Anya had told him. "Do I want my family involved? Do I want to be a mother? I love you, but people who love each other can't always live together. What I realized is that the person I most need to confront is myself."

She'd sent a message to her sister to say they'd be arriving today, Saturday. Since then, Anya hadn't mentioned her family.

Although Jack found her announcement unsettling, he

knew it was important that she face her issues and reach a conclusion. Once she resolved this, there should be no more question of her disappearing when things got tough.

By tomorrow night, he'd have his answer. He hoped it would be one that made them both happy.

"You're giving her too much power," Rod had argued when he heard about their bargain.

Jack had disagreed. "I'm keeping our daughter, regardless of whether Anya chooses to stay in the picture. But I love her, and we can't build a future unless she's ready to commit whole-heartedly. Don't forget that it was me who insisted on this trip."

"You may regret it," his uncle had muttered over their take-out fried chicken dinner. Since Jack had finished his cooking stint, he'd indulged in fast food most evenings. But while he enjoyed the freedom from a rigid schedule, he missed the give-and-take around the dinner table. Mostly, he missed Anya.

"She's taking the bull by the horns," he'd told Rod. "Considering her usual operating method, this is an improvement."

"Remains to be seen," Rod had said, but he'd kept his peace after that.

Anya's hometown, when they reached it, had an Old West design, including the weathered wooden facade of the tack and feed store Anya pointed out, which her parents owned. "If you want any cowboy boots or a hat, you can buy that there," she said.

"I wonder how Rod would look in a Stetson."

"Weird."

"In other words, his normal self," Jack joked.

"He should stick with fedoras," she mused. "They've grown on me."

Past the commercial district, the car rolled onto a road bordered by homes set far back on lots large enough to accommodate horse corrals. Following Anya's directions, Jack turned left at the next intersection.

He felt a quiver of unease. They'd brought sleeping bags,

since the only motel in the area was fully booked. Anya had explained that guests would camp out where they could, mostly in her parents' and grandmother's houses. It was the "mostly" that bothered him. Sleeping in a chicken coop or barn wasn't his idea of fun.

It's only for one night, so no complaints. He'd hate to come across as a spoiled city boy.

Another turn, and he spotted the address on the mailbox. A sprawling ranch house was half-hidden behind a cluster of RVs parked along a wide driveway. "Looks like most of the gang's here already."

Anya gripped the armrest. "They're probably out back, barbecuing."

Rolling down a window, he inhaled the delicious scent of grilling. "Hope there's enough for us."

"I should have brought a dish. I don't know why I didn't think of it." Anxiety laced her words.

"How exactly would you have carried a casserole through airport security?" He piloted the compact car between the larger vehicles. "Surely they don't expect that."

"I have no idea what they expect," Anya admitted. "I haven't been reading their texts or any other messages."

Jack had believed the point of this exercise was to break her habit of avoidance. She obviously saw that in relative terms. Or rather, in terms that excluded her relatives. "I'll bet they loved that."

"I guess we'll find out."

He parked close to the house on a patch of gravel. "You did mention you were bringing me, right?"

"I said me and a guest."

"That's it?" Jack groaned aloud. "Anya!"

She cupped her hand over his on the car seat. "I'm sorry. I'm already stressing out. If I'd had to argue with Ruth ten times a day, I'd be a wreck."

He had to admit, he understood the logic of her approach. Nevertheless, "This is a good way to drive other people crazy."

"I won't do that to you." She tightened her grip on his hand. "I promise, Jack. The difference is that you listen to me, and they don't."

"Glad to hear there's a difference."

She loosened her grip. "Might as well get this over with. Leave the suitcases."

"You think we might be heading back to Denver tonight?"

"It's a possibility," she told him, and got out of the car.

APPREHENSION FILLED ANYA. For heaven's sake, this was only her family, yet the arguments from last Christmas rang in her memory. She was letting everyone down, her father had said. She ought to grow up and stop playing truant, Ruth had snapped. Even Grandma hadn't showed her usual enthusiasm for Anya's nursing career.

"I counted on you to be around in my old age," she'd said, and turned to hug one of her great grandchildren before Anya could reply.

Her younger sisters had been so busy texting their friends and sharing inside jokes about college that Anya hadn't really had a conversation with any of them. In retrospect, she supposed they'd been deliberately ducking the quarrels. *Following my example.*

She squared her shoulders and rang the bell. That felt odd, since she'd grown up in this house, but in many respects, she was a stranger.

As was the little girl who opened the door. About four, she had an open, freckled face. "Hi," she announced. "Which one are you?"

Behind her trailed other youngsters, including a familiar two-year-old with dark blond hair. "Kiki," Anya said. "Remember me?"

"Aunt Anya!" The tot raced into Anya's arms as she and Jack entered the hall.

"I'm Belle," said the girl who'd opened the door, and Anya finally placed her as the daughter of her older brother Benjie. Or possibly Bart. Since they were identical twins who'd each had two children, it was hard to keep track of which was which.

The floor creaked beneath an onrush of feet, and Anya looked up to see a swarm of people. Ruth stood out, appearing reserved but relieved, too. The triplets were giggling—honestly, at twenty-one, the girls should be past that—and there were Bart and Benjie and a host of cousins and husbands and wives. They parted before Anya's father, his leathered face a study in mixed emotions.

"I was afraid we'd chased you away for good," he said, then halted as he took in her maternity top. "What's this? Or perhaps I should say, who's this?" His gaze moved to the man at her side.

"Dad, this is Jack Ryder." Anya let the circumstances speak for themselves.

Her father thrust out his hand. "Hello. I'm Raymond Meeks, Anya's dad."

"It's an honor to meet you, sir." Jack shook his hand firmly.

In the introductions that followed, Anya sensed the unasked questions—about her pregnancy, her relationship to Jack, her decision to attend. She let them go unanswered, for now. Mostly, she appreciated the outpouring of welcome.

"Everybody's been on my case since they found out I didn't get your consent about the child care," Ruth admitted as they made their way through the house to the large rear deck, where heat lamps had been turned on to take the edge off the chill. "I guess it was a heavy load to dump on one person."

"How did you decide to handle it?" Anya ventured, her defenses ready to spring up if Ruth took that as an opening.

"We hired a couple of teenagers," her sister said. "They're playing games in the den." Fixing her gaze on Kiki, she commanded, "Off you go."

After a last dazzling smile at her aunt Anya, the toddler obeyed. "What a doll." Although she'd have liked to cuddle her niece longer, Anya was pleased about the sitters. She also sympathized with her sister's advanced state of pregnancy.

"Organizing all this must have been hard for you, especially now. I forgot—when are you due?"

"Next month," Ruth said. "And you?"

"September."

"Are you and Jack…"

Anya didn't hear the rest of the question, because she'd just spotted her mother sitting by the food-laden table. Sitting in a regular chair, from which Molly arose with only a trace of stiffness. "Mom! When did this happen?"

Her mother beamed. "Oh, I still use the wheelchair sometimes, but my new medication is working wonders. Goodness, look at you!"

Another round of hugs followed. Anya was full of questions, which Molly answered gladly. The doctor had started her on a new type of drug called biologics, combined with an older drug. The results had exceeded expectations.

Since Jack was handling the large crowd smoothly, shaking hands and introducing himself, Anya turned her attention to the older woman waiting quietly at the side of the deck. Grandma Rachel's stern expression reawakened Anya's doubts.

You came here to face up to your family. Don't chicken out.

She stooped to embrace her grandmother. "Happy birthday."

When they separated, tears sparkled on Grandma's lashes. "I was afraid you'd stay in California."

"I nearly did," Anya admitted. "I posted my pictures in the family album, though." In lieu of gifts, her grandmother had requested that everyone upload favorite pictures on a website for all to enjoy. One of the cousins had volunteered to incorporate them into a scrapbook later.

"We laid quite a guilt trip on you at Christmas." With a nod at Jack, currently surrounded by Anya's brothers and cousins, Grandma asked, "Who's your young man?"

Anya took a seat beside her. "Jack."

"That's it? He only has a first name?"

"Dr. Jack Ryder," she said.

"A doctor. That's nice." Grandma tapped Anya's left hand. "No ring?"

"He asked," she replied. "I'm deciding."

Catching their glances, Jack approached. "This must be the birthday girl." When he flashed his killer smile, Grandma beamed.

Anya introduced them, and they shook hands, Jack careful not to squeeze the old woman's frail bones. "You're quite the catch," her grandmother said, to Anya's embarrassment.

"So is your granddaughter," he answered.

Grandma slanted an admiring gaze at him. "You're a smart young man."

"And a lucky one."

Inside Anya, anxieties melted. While she didn't entirely trust this sense of emotional safety around her relatives, it was lovely for however long it lasted.

Ruth's husband, Bryce, called out that he'd grilled the last of the hamburgers, and everyone gathered for a blessing over the food. Once Anya's dad finished giving thanks, they lined up to fill their plates. The children and their sitters went first, then retreated to the den. The adults filed into the dining room, where a series of tables covered with cloths extended into the living room.

Anya was wedged between Jack and her younger sister Sarah. She listened with interest as Jack chatted with Bryce about the feed store, where her brother-in-law was assistant manager and the heir apparent when their father retired in a few years. Then Anya turned to Sarah, eager to learn more about the girls' upcoming graduation.

All three triplets were earning RN degrees at the University of Colorado. Until now, Anya had figured that was Grandma's influence.

But Sarah said, "We went into nursing to be like you. It's so exciting that you're a scrub nurse. Do you and Jack operate together?"

"He operates. I assist." In response to more questions,

Anya filled in the blanks. "He earned his M.D. and did his residency in obstetrics at Vanderbilt."

"How'd he end up in Safe Harbor?"

"It's my hometown," Jack said from her other side.

Anya couldn't resist bragging a little. "He was selected for a surgical fellowship by the head of our fertility program, Dr. Owen Tartikoff."

"Wow!" Sarah ruffled her short hair, a few shades lighter than Anya's. Her coloring was darker than that of the other two triplets, who were identical. Sarah, born at the same time but conceived from a different egg, was their fraternal sister. "That's impressive."

"Some people think so," Jack responded lightly. "But Anya keeps me humble."

"She's amazing, isn't she?" Sarah said. "She's my role model."

Across the table, Ruth dropped her fork with a clatter. *Oh, here it comes.* Anya set down a forkful of potato salad.

Blithely, Sandi—another of the triplets—asked, "Why did you move so far away, Anya? There's a world-class hospital in Denver."

"So she could have fun, fun, fun in California." Ruth's statement dripped with resentment.

"Hon…" The endearment from Bryce carried a warning note. Bryce was a good man, although his long hours left her sister with much of the hard work raising their four—soon to be five—children, as well as tending their vegetable garden, chickens and dairy goat.

"I'd like to have fun, fun, fun in California," Sarah said wistfully.

"Sounds good to me," said the third triplet, Andi.

Since Ruth appeared about to ignite, Anya hurried to correct their impression. "That's not why I left. I did it so I could be myself."

From the head of the table, her father joined the conversation. "You could be yourself right here just fine."

"Seriously?" After years of trying to be diplomatic, Anya

had had enough. "I could hardly hear myself think. Everyone had expectations of me. Sometimes they fit, like when Grandma encouraged me to become a nurse. Other times, they were simply slots for me to fill."

"We all have obligations," Ruth snapped. "You ran out on yours."

Around them, the conversation dimmed. Under the table, Jack's hand cradled hers. Having him on her side allowed her to catch her breath and weigh her response.

In the past, she'd have retreated into angry silence, or snapped that it wasn't her fault Ruth had chosen to marry at nineteen, drop out of college and bear one child after another. Instead, she replied calmly, "I met my obligations and then some."

"You have to be kidding!" Ruth flared.

Their mother spoke up then with more force than she'd mustered in years. "Anya spent her high school and college years looking after me and the triplets. They should have been my responsibility, but I could barely take care of myself. She worked incredibly hard."

Ruth cleared her throat. "I don't remember it that way."

"You were married and out of the house by then, so you didn't see it."

"I was right here," Anya's father joined in. "It didn't seem to me she had it so tough."

Molly turned to her husband. "Ray, you were working from dawn to dusk at the store. So you may not have noticed that she took over the grocery shopping, the cleaning, even scheduling my doctor visits, all while attending college and commuting an hour each way."

"The younger girls pitched in," he said stubbornly.

"Yes, the triplets helped with meals, but they didn't take over many of the other chores until after Anya left. We also hired a cleaning service and our two wonderful daughters-in-law volunteered to drive me to appointments. Anya used to do all of that herself."

Anya blinked back tears. If she hadn't been afraid of shaking the table and everyone's dinners, she'd have run around to embrace her mom. "I knew that you needed me, Mom. But once the girls were old enough to handle things, I was ready to leave."

Her father cleared his throat. "I guess I was a little hard on you."

Anya wasn't going to let him off so easily. "A little? All you noticed were my screwups."

"I wasn't that bad, was I?"

"You were always picking on her," Benjie said. "Honestly, Dad, I even told you a few times to lay off."

He had? No one had mentioned that to Anya.

"I'd forgotten that," their father admitted.

"It was like Anya couldn't do anything right," Bart chimed in. "You were always comparing her to how Ruth used to do things."

That was true, but she hadn't been aware that her brothers had noticed it, too.

"Well, Ruth did a great job," said their father, his forehead wrinkling.

"And moved out the minute I got the chance," Ruth admitted, adding, "Luckily, I fell in love with the right man. Didn't I, Bryce?"

"You did. And other than that, I'm staying out of this conversation," said her husband.

Raymond Meeks's shoulders sagged. "Girls, I'm sorry. Maybe I've been too hard. And, Anya, I was on your case at Christmas because your mom was having trouble adjusting to her new medication, and on some level I blamed you."

"Well, I didn't," Molly said. "Anya, you deserve to lead your own life. I'm proud of you."

"So am I." Her father regarded Anya. "I've been worried about your mom, and a little guilty for being gone a lot. Maybe that's why I magnified every mistake you made. Thank you for everything you've done."

"That goes double for me," her mother said.

A murmur of appreciation ran around the table. A rush

of joy filled Anya. In spite of their missteps and misunder-standings, her family loved her.

"We've missed you." Sarah touched her shoulder. "You gave us the best advice about classes and professors."

"And our boyfriends," noted Sandi.

"Those were *my* boyfriends you kept stealing," teased Andi.

"That's because I'm cuter," said her identical sister.

Everyone chuckled, including Ruth. Anya was glad she hadn't lashed out or withdrawn, as she would have before Jack. If she had, this discussion might not have happened.

"Besides, if she hadn't moved to California, she'd never have met me," Jack commented. "And we wouldn't be having our daughter."

That changed the subject quite effectively, as Jack no doubt intended. From along the table, questions flew: "You know what sex it is already?" "What will you name her?"

The answer came instinctively to Anya. "Rachel." She heard the murmur of approval and saw the sparkle of pleasure on her grandmother's face. Afraid she might have presumed too much, she amended that to, "Rachel Lenore," and glanced at Jack for confirmation.

"Isn't that a beautiful name?" he said. "It's for both our grandmothers."

"The best present you could have given me." Grandma smiled. "And your sister's naming her new boy after your grandfather, Harold."

Ruth took a breath. "I suppose it's all worked out for the best."

"Too bad you had to give up your life in high school for us," Sarah noted, while the other triplets nodded.

Anya waved away the apology. "I only have one regret."

Everyone waited.

"If I'd been able to join the botany club, I might not have killed the African violet Jack gave me."

Amid a ripple of laughter, a child scampered in to ask about dessert.

"I almost forgot about the birthday cake!" Benjie's wife leaped to her feet. "I'll light the candles."

"I'll dish out the ice cream," volunteered Bart's wife. "Who wants vanilla and who wants chocolate?"

Others hurried to clear the table, insisting that the older generation and the pregnant women relax. "That feels odd," Ruth admitted, while Sarah carted off her plate.

"I'm glad you hired the sitters," Anya told her.

"Me, too." Ruth's mouth twisted in irony. "Honestly, I wasn't thinking straight. There's no way you could have supervised all those little ones and spent time with the rest of us."

"We're used to believing Anya is a superwoman," her mother said.

"Or just my annoying younger sister." Ruth cringed. "Which I hadn't realized I was doing, until now."

The rest of the family returned, along with all but the youngest children. Someone dimmed the lights, allowing the candles—two large ones spelling out 8-0—to shimmer atop the sheet cake.

As Anya surveyed the beloved group and joined them in singing the birthday song, joy swelled inside her. How lucky she was to be part of this family, and most of all to share this moment with Jack. Yes, she knew she could stand on her own now, but she also realized they were stronger together.

And a lot happier.

THEY SLEPT THAT night on Grandma's foldout couch, with a single sleeping bag spread out beneath them and the other serving as a cover. Exhausted from the long day, plus a touch of jet lag and the effect of altitude, Anya expected to fall asleep instantly.

Instead, her brain replayed her experiences at dinner. Her younger sisters' admiration...Molly's unexpected rise to her defense, showing Anya's father and Ruth how limited their perspective had been...Jack's steady presence, bolstering her confidence. The world had shifted. She could be herself now, wherever she was.

In the dimness of Grandma's living room, she inhaled the scent of lemon oil from the antique armoire. Against the wall, moonlight showed dark rectangles that she remembered were old family photographs of her great grandparents and great-aunts and uncles, of the town in the horse-and-buggy days, of people and places long gone yet still living in their descendants.

Her hand drifted to her abdomen. Rachel Lenore would come here for holidays, discovering her cousins and her roots. What a marvelous sense of connection she would have, just like Anya had.

Beside her, Jack stirred. "Do you still want to live with me?" he murmured.

It seemed an odd question. "Of course."

He heaved a sigh, then rolled away from her.

Had she said something wrong? Puzzled, Anya tried to figure it out. But before she could, sleep stole over her.

Chapter Eighteen

On Sunday, Anya bubbled with high spirits. Although Jack had the nagging suspicion he'd outsmarted himself, he enjoyed seeing her happy and reconciled with her family.

In the morning, children tumbled underfoot until the sitters came, and the noise level rose further as more relatives arrived, including newcomers who hadn't been able to attend last night. Jack took charge of the row of waffle-making equipment, producing piles of deliciously browned waffles while the triplets stirred batches of mix. People ate in shifts, scattered around the house. It was a big jovial party, and by midday, when he and Anya left for the airport, he could identify almost all the adults and quite a few of the tots.

What a great experience—and what a pleasure to relax in the quiet car as they drove to Denver. Anya seemed to share his enjoyment, both with her family and without them. All his life, Jack had longed to be part of a group like this, and the Meekses had exceeded his expectations. Yet he also understood, at the gut level, why Anya craved distance, as well.

He'd insisted on her confronting them, and she'd done so. Now he had to keep his word, even though the prospect of raising their daughter when he and Anya weren't married troubled him. It was too easy for people to throw away a relationship under the pressure of an illness or injury, a financial setback, problems with a child or a temporary divergence in their interests. Despite the high percentage of marriages that broke up, at least the steps leading to a divorce forced the couple to face the seriousness of what they were doing and encouraged them to seek counseling.

Jack yearned for the commitment. Old-fashioned though it might be, he longed to have Anya as his wife and to be introduced as her husband. Their rings would tell the world that they belonged to each other.

But although Anya had resolved some of her issues, she apparently hadn't changed her mind.

The next few days in California, they barely had a chance to talk, let alone decide where or when to move in together. At the hospital, Anya cast Jack the occasional quizzical glance, as if trying to gauge his thoughts. He couldn't reassure her while his mood remained restive.

The following Saturday, her housemates invited him and Rod for dinner. "It's our turn to cook for you," Karen told Jack when she stopped by his table in the cafeteria.

"Need any help?" He missed being the master chef, although not every day.

"We'll be fine. Maybe Rod can pitch in," she said.

"Uh-oh." His uncle's culinary catastrophes were notorious. "I hope you'll put him in charge of arranging pickles and olives on a relish tray."

"That bad, huh?" She grinned.

"Worse."

"Guess I'll pass on suggesting he help cook."

On Saturday, Jack assisted with an overflow in Labor and Delivery, performing two emergency Caesarian sections. Afterward, he had to wait for Rod to pick him up, since his uncle's car was once again on the fritz. They arrived at Karen's house a few minutes past six.

The days were already lengthening, and he spotted flocks of birds circling. He wondered whether they were in the midst of a northward migration or if they'd be nesting here.

"Is it me, or has the smell improved?" his uncle asked as they strolled along the driveway.

Jack inhaled. "I can say with confidence that your smell hasn't improved."

"It should have. I borrowed *your* deodorant."

"Now I know what to buy you for Christmas."

When they reached the porch, Melissa swung open the door, abandoning her usual reserve. "I'm pregnant!"

"Congratulations." Jack shook her hand. "This is terrific news." He was glad he'd been able to contribute to this joyful result.

"*That's* how you congratulate her?" Rod gave the woman a hug. "That's the proper response."

"As one of her physicians, I prefer to behave like a professional."

"Since when did you start sending out your shirts to be stuffed?" his uncle retorted.

Jack ignored the gibe.

"I can't wait to find out how many babies I'm carrying." Melissa ushered them inside. "Three more weeks and we can do an ultrasound, right?"

"Correct," Jack said. A sonogram was usually performed five weeks after an embryo transfer, both to determine how many had implanted and to ensure the pregnancy was progressing normally. Of course, she was Zack Sargent's patient, so Sargent would be supervising her care from now on, rather than Jack.

Inside, Karen was setting out roast chicken, potatoes, steamed vegetables and a small brownish loaf that she explained was a vegetarian turkey substitute called tofurkey. Anya appeared with a bowl of salad.

Hurrying to her side, Jack said in a low voice, "Sorry I couldn't come early. I was hoping to talk privately."

She blinked. "Oh. About that...." She frowned at Lucky, who hovered nearby. Jack could almost have sworn the man's ears were quivering. "Later, okay?"

Reluctantly, Jack nodded.

As they took seats at the table, he noticed that Zora didn't seem to share the general high spirits. Anya had mentioned during the trip that her friend was pregnant by her exhusband, who'd just remarried. What a jerk.

From a sideboard, Karen fetched wineglasses. "Let's toast our houseful of pregnancies."

Lucky appeared from the kitchen with a bottle of grape juice. "Good thing I have my quarters downstairs," he said as he poured. "Gives me a break from the supercharged estrogen level."

"I doubt you're in any danger from our hormones," Melissa said. "Is he, Jack?"

"Cole Rattigan is the expert about male hormone levels," he said. "But I doubt it."

They raised their glasses of juice. "May all the pregnancies in this household be safe and healthy," Karen said. "May the babies grow up secure and loved."

"Hear, hear!" Rod glugged down his juice in a single show-off gulp. He promptly choked, spluttering and coughing while Karen pounded him on the back.

"Serves you right," Lucky said.

"That's mean." Zora frowned at him.

"Was it?" The male nurse shrugged. "Sorry, Rod."

Jack's uncle started to answer, wheezed painfully and sipped water. He recovered well enough, though, to take second helpings of the food.

The discussion moved from Melissa's big news to the latest recommendations for maternal nutrition, and then to the name Anya and Jack had chosen for their daughter. Everyone agreed that honoring both grandmothers was inspired.

"Speaking of daughters." Rod cleared his throat. "Tiffany emailed me today—they'll be spending part of the summer here."

"Are they staying with their grandmother?" Karen asked.

He grimaced. "No such luck. Their mother will be riding herd on them at the beach cottage. Vince plans to visit when his schedule allows."

"Which means they'll be under lock and key." Jack ached for his uncle. Despite Rod's breezy manner, the situation must be torture. "Karen, any chance the girls will volunteer at the hospital as you suggested?"

"That would be fun." Anya sparkled with enthusiasm. "They're such cuties."

"I don't know." Their hostess set down her fork. "I've heard—though this is very preliminary—that Mr. and Mrs. Adams might be interested in sponsoring male fertility research. Naturally, the hospital would love that."

"Which means the Adamses will be spending a lot of time here," Jack observed.

"And I'd be persona non grata if I screw it up." His uncle scowled.

"Dr. Rattigan must be thrilled." Lucky dug into his tofurkey, which nobody else was eating. "It could be a good thing for me, too. If the program expands, there might be a new administrative position."

"Perfect timing for you," Melissa said. "You could stay at Safe Harbor *and* use your new masters degree."

"This is all speculation," Karen said sternly. "I want the girls to volunteer at the hospital, too, but Rod's right. We can't risk antagonizing a major donor."

Being rich shouldn't give Vince the freedom to strut around the hospital like a peacock, taunting the man he'd ripped off. However, Jack understood the realities. "We'll figure something out."

"The girls enjoyed helping out at the animal shelter," Anya reminded them.

Rod sat up straighter. "That's a good idea. I'll run it by Helen."

One way or another, Jack reflected, having the girls nearby would open up possibilities. Also, a major expansion of the men's fertility program might lead to the hospital acquiring the empty dental building, bringing additional space for a range of uses. *Including offices for newer doctors like me.* Obnoxious as they might find Vince Adams, his potential involvement with Safe Harbor Medical wasn't entirely a bad thing.

Dinner ended with a pecan pie from the Cake Castle bakery. Jack was considering how he might steer Anya away from the others when she said, "Excuse me. Jack and I have a few things to discuss. See you guys later."

Startled, he accompanied her upstairs. "Thanks. I was wondering how to handle that diplomatically."

"Oh, was I diplomatic?"

Jack chuckled. Then, at the risk of tripping on the steps—or of being observed from below—he circled her waist with his arm. "I missed you the past couple of days."

"Me, too." Mischievously, Anya kissed his cheek, then pulled him toward her bedroom. "I have something to show you."

He tried to keep his mind off the fact that they hadn't made love since before the trip to Denver. "I'm sure I'll like it, whatever it is."

"You will." She underscored her reply by closing the door behind them.

Alone, finally, Jack caught her and planted a kiss firmly on her mouth. Mmm. Pecan pie and Anya. His favorites.

She melted into him. Jack forgot everything but her, and the bed, and her softness. Anya apparently did, too, until they bumped the table as they crossed the room. "Oh!" She wriggled free. "Seriously, we need to talk."

"How about we talk later?" He was breathing hard.

She sighed. "With all those people downstairs straining to hear?"

"Ignore them."

"Including Rod? He already doesn't like me," Anya said.

"He's coming around."

"Does he know we're planning to live together?" she asked.

Jack had to admit that he hadn't told his uncle yet. "I figured I'd wait until we have more definite arrangements."

"We could rent a new apartment." She grinned. "Or keep yours and kick your uncle out."

"I can't do that!" However, neither could he expect Anya to share a place with Rod. And once the baby arrived, they'd need both bedrooms. "Unless he has a better place to move. Like here."

"That would solve two problems," Anya said.

"What's the other one?"

"Karen needs the rent."

Enough about his uncle. They had more important topics to discuss. "What did you want to show me?"

Anya smiled. "This." From a small table, she lifted an African violet. "I named her Paula the Second."

That was it? "A plant?"

She turned the purple-flowered plant lovingly in her hands. "It's a leap of faith, to prove to myself that I can nurture something without killing it."

"You can do a lot more than that." Jack gave up trying to avoid pressuring her. "Damn it, Anya, I love you. You're going to be a wonderful mother. I want us to spend our lives together."

To his annoyance, she merely handed him the pot. "Take a closer look."

He spared a quick glance at the deep green fuzzy leaves. "It's very pretty. One of these days we'll be able to buy our own home with a greenhouse window. You can grow all the African violets your heart desires."

"They're non-toxic," she said cheerfully. "Safe to have around children."

"Wonderful." Why had he fallen for the one woman in the world who could drive him to the edge of madness? "We can plant an entire vegetable garden. Anya…"

"Look harder."

Gritting his teeth, Jack stared at the violet again. From the soil jutted a shiny piece of paper, which he'd assumed held care directions.

Plucking it free and gently blowing a few crumbs of soil into the pot, he unrolled it and studied the glossy pictures of jewelry. "Rings." His throat clamped shut.

"We can pick them out together," Anya said. "That is, assuming your proposal still stands."

"Yes." He swallowed, and took a deep breath. "You enjoy keeping me on edge, don't you?"

"Not deliberately." She reached for him. "I've been in awe of you since the day we met."

Setting the plant on the table, Jack drew her into his arms. "You could have fooled me."

The face that lifted to his was open and vulnerable. "If I'd let on, I'd have been just another of those nurses who follow you around like puppy dogs."

Jack didn't know whether to laugh or growl. Instead, he tightened his hold on her. "You planned the whole thing?"

"Just the opposite," Anya admitted. "I kept you at bay for my own safety."

"And now?"

"I love you too much," she said raggedly.

"Really?" He could hardly believe it.

"You overwhelmed my good judgment." She buried her face in his chest. "Promise not to take advantage."

Grinning, Jack moved back a step, pulling her with him. "I plan to take advantage every chance I get."

"Don't push your luck."

"Let's see how it goes," he said, and lowered her onto the bed.

As THEY LAY contentedly side by side, Anya's head was still spinning. Marrying Jack and trusting him meant no more guarding her emotions. They'd be sharing their home, their hearts and their baby. Or babies. Always and forever.

It wasn't as if she had a choice. Last Sunday as he'd fixed waffles for her family, he'd been the calm center of a swirl of people. Watching him, she'd tumbled off a cliff—or finally recognized that she'd been in free fall for a long time.

He was Anya's other half. A very different, masculine other half—they wouldn't always see eye to eye. There'd be disagreements and difficult choices. Sometimes they might hurt each other without meaning to. But he wasn't sitting in judgment on her, and she was strong enough to set him straight if he ever tried.

They belonged together. All week at the hospital, she'd barely restrained herself from shouting to the world that he was hers.

Burrowing into him, inhaling his wonderful scent, Anya released the last of her self-protective fear. She didn't need it anymore.

Love had taken its place.

* * * * *

REQUEST YOUR FREE BOOKS!
2 FREE NOVELS PLUS 2 FREE GIFTS!

HARLEQUIN

American ★ Romance®

LOVE, HOME & HAPPINESS

YES! Please send me 2 FREE Harlequin® American Romance® novels and my 2 FREE gifts (gifts are worth about $10). After receiving them, if I don't wish to receive any more books, I can return the shipping statement marked "cancel." If I don't cancel, I will receive 4 brand-new novels every month and be billed just $4.74 per book in the U.S. or $5.24 per book in Canada. That's a savings of at least 14% off the cover price! It's quite a bargain! Shipping and handling is just 50¢ per book in the U.S. and 75¢ per book in Canada.* I understand that accepting the 2 free books and gifts places me under no obligation to buy anything. I can always return a shipment and cancel at any time. Even if I never buy another book, the two free books and gifts are mine to keep forever.

154/354 HDN F4YN

Name	(PLEASE PRINT)

Address	Apt. #

City	State/Prov.	Zip/Postal Code

Signature (if under 18, a parent or guardian must sign)

Mail to the Harlequin® Reader Service:
IN U.S.A.: P.O. Box 1867, Buffalo, NY 14240-1867
IN CANADA: P.O. Box 609, Fort Erie, Ontario L2A 5X3

Want to try two free books from another line?
Call 1-800-873-8635 or visit www.ReaderService.com.

* Terms and prices subject to change without notice. Prices do not include applicable taxes. Sales tax applicable in N.Y. Canadian residents will be charged applicable taxes. Offer not valid in Quebec. This offer is limited to one order per household. Not valid for current subscribers to Harlequin American Romance books. All orders subject to credit approval. Credit or debit balances in a customer's account(s) may be offset by any other outstanding balance owed by or to the customer. Please allow 4 to 6 weeks for delivery. Offer available while quantities last.

Your Privacy—The Harlequin® Reader Service is committed to protecting your privacy. Our Privacy Policy is available online at www.ReaderService.com or upon request from the Harlequin Reader Service.

We make a portion of our mailing list available to reputable third parties that offer products we believe may interest you. If you prefer that we not exchange your name with third parties, or if you wish to clarify or modify your communication preferences, please visit us at www.ReaderService.com/consumerchoice or write to us at Harlequin Reader Service Preference Service, P.O. Box 9062, Buffalo, NY 14269. Include your complete name and address.

HARI3R

Looking for more exciting all-American romances like the one you just read? Read on for an excerpt from THE TEXAN'S BABY, *the first book in a new series,* **TEXAS RODEO BARONS,** *by New York Times bestselling author Donna Alward.*

Lizzie Baron pressed the buzzer.

There was a click and then a voice. "Hello?"

"Uh…hi. I'm looking for Christopher Miller?"

"That's me."

"It's…uh…" She scrambled to think of what she'd said to him that night. "It's Elizabeth."

There was a pause.

"From the bar in Fort Worth."

The words came out strained.

"Come on up."

She could do this. She paused as she got off the elevator.

A door opened and Christopher stepped into the hall. Her feet halted and she stared at him, her practiced words flying out of her head.

He was staring at her, too. "It really is you," he said. "What the hell are you doing here?"

For weeks, Chris had been wondering if he should try to find out who she was. They'd met at a honky-tonk after a less-than-stellar rodeo performance on his part. He'd figured he'd nurse his wounds with a beer and head back to the motel where he was staying.

And then he'd seen her. He'd ordered another beer, looked over at her and she'd smiled, and all his brain cells turned to mush.

When he'd woken the next morning, the bed had been empty. That had been nearly two months ago.

"Elizabeth." He stepped aside so she could enter his apartment.

"Call me Lizzie. Everybody does."

"You didn't say your name was Lizzie the night we met."

"I was trying to be mysterious."

"It worked." He put his hands in his pockets. "How did you find me?"

"Rodeo's a small world."

"You're saying that you got my address from rodeo records?" The blush was back. "Yes."

"Why would you do that?"

"Because I need to talk to you."

Quiet settled through the condo. Whatever she wanted to tell him, she was nervous. Afraid.

And then it hit him upside the head. "Look, do I need to be tested for an STD or something? Is that why you're here?"

"What the hell would give you that idea?"

"Hey, you're the one who disappeared and only gave me your first name. Now you show up weeks later, looking completely different, and say you need to talk to me. If it's not an STD, what the hell…"

His mouth dropped open.

"No," he whispered. "No, it isn't possible. We used condoms."

She looked up, misery etched in every feature. "I assure you it is possible. I'm pregnant, and the baby's yours."

Look for THE TEXAN'S BABY
by Donna Alward in June 2014
wherever books and ebooks are sold.

American Romance®

He's just the hired help…

What kind of a cockeyed Pollyanna is Colin Cade working for?
Her porch is rotting, her "guest cabin" is cheerless, and her land
and livestock have only a geriatric cowboy to care for them. Yet
Hannah Shaw is positive she can turn her ranch into a successful B and B—and that Colin's the man to make it happen.

But Colin can't stick around. He lives with the loss of his family
by avoiding the memories, and the way he feels around
Hannah and her young son is like a knife to the heart. Trouble
is, he's better at ignoring his own pain than someone else's, and
bright, cheerful Hannah has a heart as haunted as his own. She
deserves to be happy—but maybe not with him….

Look for
Her Cowboy Hero
from *The Colorado Cades* miniseries

by TANYA MICHAELS

from Harlequin® American Romance®
Available June 2014
wherever books and ebooks are sold

Also available from *The Colorado Cades* miniseries
by Tanya Michaels:

Her Secret, His Baby
Second Chance Christmas

American Romance®

To save a SEAL…

Libby Dewitt, pregnant and alone, brings out the hero in navy SEAL Heath Stone. Despite her own troubles, her heart aches at all Heath has been through. To save this SEAL, Libby is ready to fight—for love! But can Libby help him overcome his tragic past and love again?

Look for
The SEAL's Baby
from the *Operation: Family* series
by LAURA MARIE ALTOM
in June 2014 from
Harlequin® American Romance®.
Available wherever books and ebooks are sold.

**Also available from the *Operation: Family* series
by Laura Marie Altom:**

A SEAL's Secret Baby
The SEAL's Stolen Child
The SEAL's Valentine
A Navy SEAL's Surprise Baby
The SEAL's Christmas Twins

American Romance®

One Night With A Cowboy

There's no room in day-care owner Lana Carpenter's life for casual flings. After all, her dream of adopting a baby is closer to becoming a reality than ever. So why is she still mooning over the sexy cowboy who made her forget everything but the strong, sure feel of his arms around her?

It wasn't supposed to be more than one unforgettable night between consenting strangers. But when Sly Pettit spots Lana's photo in the local paper, he grabs at the chance to see her again. The guarded rancher is falling hard for Lana, but it can only end in heartbreak…unless Sly can trust her with the secrets that keep him from believing that, just maybe, they could have a future together.

Look for
A Ranchers Honor,
the first title in the new *Prosperity, Montana* miniseries

by ANN ROTH,

available June 2014 from
Harlequin® American Romance®.
Wherever books and ebooks are sold.